Hunted in Calusa Cove

The Aegis Network: The Everglades Division
Book 1

Jen Talty

I want to thank Kris Norris for holding my hand through the writing of this novel. I would not have gotten through it without her support.

Chapter One

The Everglades didn't keep secrets—just swallowed them whole. And if it didn't like the taste, it let it get tangled in the reeds—waiting there until something more unsettling unleashed it into the murky water, where it could prey on the innocent.

Bradford "Buddy" Ballard knew that better than most. But today wasn't about the things hidden in the Glades. It was about new beginnings, a change of pace, and a career that wouldn't haunt his every move.

And it had nothing to do with a certain female he'd been dreaming about for years—absolutely nothing.

At least that's what he told himself.

The flat-bottom skiff under his boots hummed across the channel as fat bugs whizzed past his head. The air was thick, the kind of thickness that turned every breath into a chore. This was the part of the Everglades he'd forgotten about. The part he'd chosen to ignore. The part that wasn't so magical—because almost everything else about this spot was the only place he felt like he could carve out a home.

He stared at his cell sitting on the mount on the console and tried not to think too hard about why he wanted to hear from *her* so badly. She knew he'd come back to town. They'd texted a couple of times about it. He'd even shot her one when he'd left Jacksonville, and he'd gotten a *great, see you when you get here.*

But not a peep since, and that shouldn't bother him. Not to mention, he couldn't have reached out to Fallon. Actually, he should've, but he worried things might end up out of the friend zone, and he wasn't sure he could handle that.

He pushed those thoughts aside and focused on the task at hand.

Sterling Fox, a fellow Aegis Network Operative, stood at the bow, binoculars up, steady as a gun turret. They'd been mapping approach routes for an eco-outfitter who wanted an honest security assessment and not the brochure version of "safe." Buddy preferred jobs like this—practical, quiet, a clean problem to solve—no crime scene tape. No blood. No bodies to be taken out in bags.

The radio clipped to his shoulder crackled. Static hissed, then a voice, clear with strain. "FWC Officer Reeves requesting immediate backup in Sector 7. Body found, possibly alive. Repeat—alive."

Buddy's pulse increased the second Fallon Reeve's voice tickled his ears. It was just the sound of an old friend. A crackly noise through the airwaves. It wasn't something that should give him sweaty palms. And that wasn't why Buddy reached for the tiller. "We're changing course." Or at least not the only reason.

Sterling lowered the binoculars and looked back over his shoulder. "We're not paid for that," Sterling said without heat. He'd been working with Buddy for the last couple of months up north. That wasn't a long time, but long enough to know that Buddy wasn't the kind of man to steer away from trouble when trouble came calling.

"Then we're volunteering." Buddy pushed the throttle and the skiff jumped, the bow skimming over brown-green water. Mangroves shouldered in on both sides, narrowing the channel to a seam. The smell of rot slipped under the cypress, a hard, sweet note that didn't belong.

The mangroves didn't care what anyone thought of them. Tangled roots arched out of shallow water—sometimes no deeper than a man's knee, more or less—like gnarled fingers reaching for something they'd never quite hold, creating a maze that could swallow a boat if a person weren't careful. They filtered salt, trapped sediment, and made nurseries for things with teeth—all while standing in water that would kill most trees in a season.

Buddy had learned early that mangroves were the Everglades' first line of defense, the kind of barrier that didn't just protect the coastline but reminded humans that nature here played by different rules. Red, black, white—three species doing the same job in their own stubborn way, turning the shoreline into something that was half land, half water, and entirely unforgiving if people didn't respect it.

Sterling braced against the forward rail and checked the handheld GPS. "You remember you're not FBI anymore. That we're not expected to be there. Actually, we won't be welcome."

"Believe me," Buddy said. "I remember."

The radio popped again—shorter transmission, clipped directions, the cool cadence of someone trained to keep panic out of her words. Sector seven. Coordinates. Airlift en route. Then a male voice he recognized as Dawson Ridge acknowledged.

Buddy's knuckles whitened around the tiller. He listened with the trained ear of an FBI agent. The old habit of building a scene from sound and static was muscle memory he hadn't been able to strip out, even when he turned his badge in and walked away.

"Two boats ahead," Sterling said. "On the right bank. I've got movement—three figures at the waterline."

Buddy throttled down just enough to cut wake. The Everglades ate evidence and spit out alibis. You didn't churn a scene like this. He eased the skiff behind a fringe of mangroves, close but not crowding, and scanned.

Fallon was exactly where she said she'd be—knee-deep in black water at the edge of the roots, uniform soaked to the ribs, hands red with swamp muck and effort.

For a brief second, Buddy held his breath. Her long auburn hair dangled in a braid, which floated on the water. Her skin—slightly paler for most Floridians—

glowed under the sun as it tried to peek out from between the clouds. She carried herself with more confidence than most had in their pinky. Not only was she beautiful, but she was also strong, intelligent, and way out of his league for a million and one reasons.

He pushed those thoughts right out of his mind and focused on the scene in front of him.

Two men flanked her in the water, one tall and rangy with a snake-wrangler's easy balance—Trent Mallor— and another broader through the shoulders, face shadowed by a hat and a week of rough stubble. Cullen Monroe.

Buddy had met Cullen a few times. A former Marine and Silas' nephew. Silas was the heart of Calusa Cove. If someone wanted to know anything about the history or the current gossip, Silas was the guy to see. He was a little gruff and totally misunderstood. However, he was the kind of man who'd give up his shirt to a stranger. And take in a nephew struggling with PTSD when he had nowhere else to turn.

Between Trent, Cullen, and Fallon, small and limp as a rag, was a young girl.

Damn. He'd seen this scene one too many times. "Hold here." He scanned the vegetation, looking for signs of boats, huts, people... anything. He found absolutely nothing.

"Fallon," Buddy called, voice low so it didn't bounce off the trees. "It's Buddy. We heard your call. We're here to help."

Fallon didn't look back. "You're welcome to watch,

but stay off my scene," she said, perfectly calm, like she had breath to spare when she didn't. "Actually, if you want to help, float near the open water, signal medivac, and don't touch anything that bleeds." Her tone carried the crisp edge of authority Buddy had always respected.

"Copy that." Buddy leaned over and took the bag with flares off the skiff's floor.

"Chopper's coming from over there," Sterling said, already moving to the bow, pointing north. "I can hear it, but I can't see it."

"Keep looking for it." Buddy handed him the flares. The helicopter thump was still distant, a heartbeat through wet air, but coming fast. "I'll keep an eye on the water. Too many things in this muck that will come out of nowhere and take you under." Buddy looked back through the green. Fallon had the girl halfway free of the mangrove roots, legs dead weight, head lolling. Fallon was a professional. More than good at her job, something Buddy had witnessed firsthand when they'd crossed paths four years ago while he worked the Ring Finger case.

He also had to admit—he'd been interested. But she was too young. It wasn't so much the age gap, just her age. Although she was an old soul, he found himself in this weird space between attraction and friendship.

For four years, he chose the latter.

Mostly because he lived an hour away for the first two years, and then because his job shifted within the FBI, not only changed his location, but it literally changed his life. However, he'd maintained friendships over the years with people in Calusa Cove, including one with Fallon, though theirs was mainly through texts and phone calls and sometimes danced on the side of flirtatious.

That was an understatement. But it was a necessary lie he told himself because the truth tugged at places in his heart he'd long ago buried.

Trent bore the brunt of the victim's weight without complaint. Cullen moved like a man who knew failure and wasn't about to repeat it. Fallon's jaw was set, her eyes all focus. She spoke to the girl in a tone that made room for surviving.

"Almost there. Keep breathing. That's your only job," Fallon said in a voice that rolled across the air like honeysuckle.

The rot stink thickened—predator breath, old meat—and for a tight second, the water outside the roots went flat as glass.

"Gator," Buddy said loud enough for them to hear, but not so loud it would freak the gator out.

"Already handled," Trent called back, easy like he was discussing beer. "I hurt his feelings, now he's just watching because he can."

Buddy didn't smile, and he certainly didn't find Trent's off-handed remark amusing. He kept his focus on that gator, and the path between him, the girl, and Fallon.

The hum of the chopper grew as it appeared and banked along with the twists and turns of the main channel.

Sterling sent a flare into the air.

The chopper came in low, noise hitting hard, then the rush of displaced air.

Buddy stepped onto the bow and windmilled an arm twice—here, here—and the pilot adjusted, hovering the disc of metal and rotors as close as they could. The wash picked up a mist of swamp water that salted Buddy's lips and turned everyone into slow-motion ghosts.

Fallon and the men heaved the girl onto the airboat's deck while the helicopter's medic team lowered a basket. Trent, Cullen, and Fallon secured the young woman in the basket. Buddy's chest clenched. That girl couldn't have been older than fourteen. Sixteen tops. He shoved the thought where it belonged—behind a locked door he refused to open in daylight.

This wasn't his case. It wasn't pulling a paycheck. It wasn't his problem.

Fallon, Trent, and Cullen steadied the basket as the medic team pulled it into the chopper. Once secured inside, the helicopter banked right and took off toward the hospital.

Fallon looked toward the skiff. "Thanks for signaling them."

"Anytime," Buddy replied.

"It's good to see you. Good to have you back in Calusa Cove," she said, a smile breaking slightly. "Heard you rented Hayes and Chloe's old place. Have you moved in yet? You know, I live right behind it. White house. Blue shutters."

"Moved in last night, if you could call it that and yeah, I heard from Chloe that you were living there."

A police boat nosed in. Dawson stood at the helm with Chloe standing beside him, hand on the rail, hair snarled by rotor wash. Their body language screamed all business. Tape would go up where tape never made sense, and someone would try to account for what the water wanted to hide.

Buddy didn't miss this—most of it anyway.

Sterling tapped Buddy's elbow. "We done?"

"Almost." Buddy stepped across to Fallon's airboat, careful of his boots and where they landed. "You good?" He held her gaze. Same crisp blue eyes. Same determined gaze. Same freaking everything. She was not only beautiful but also intelligent, driven, and outspoken. He liked that. Maybe a little too much. But he also knew a bit about her history and in part, that might've been why he was drawn to her. "That couldn't have been easy."

She wrung swamp water from the end of her braid with a quick twist and pointed with her chin toward the mangroves. "I don't believe she was in there long. If she'd been floating, the gators would've had her, and honestly, it looked to me like someone hung her shirt on the groves purposely. Like they wanted her out here to die, but wanted someone to see her, which is strange all by itself. Not many people come back here. Wouldn't have found her had Trent and Cullen not been illegally fishing."

Buddy chewed on that thought for a moment. "What did you see on her? Notice any markings? Brusing?" He couldn't stop his brain from going through the motions if he tried, especially when it involved dead bodies.

Fallon's mouth flattened. "Wrist grooves. Fresh. Zip

ties, wide. Ankles too. One sneaker. Mud on it that isn't from here—grain is finer, lighter color. There was a smell...not swamp. Cleaner or fuel, maybe."

Buddy glanced at Sterling, who'd taken out his phone and was tapping on the screen—taking notes, no doubt, he was good that way. "Okay."

Dawson cut his engine and drifted in, his gaze tracking everything at once. He might be a small-town police chief, but he had big-city instincts. "Nobody moves until I say so," he called. "We're going to do this right. Fallon, you holding the line?"

"Copy," Fallon said. She lifted her voice without raising it. "Trent, Cullen—I'm going to need you to stay put for a little while longer."

Trent lifted both palms and smiled like a man who expected the lecture and might bring donuts later to make it square. Cullen didn't smile at all. His eyes were on the water, dark and far away.

Chloe hopped down to Fallon's deck and touched her shoulder. "You okay?"

"Yeah." Fallon's gaze slid back to Buddy and held it, like she needed... something, but he didn't know what.

"Hey Buddy," Chloe said. "I'm gonna need you to stay outside my chain unless requested."

"Understood." He meant it.

He also meant to be useful.

Dawson tossed a roll of tape to Chloe. "Box off the root line. Fallon, walk me through your approach and extraction, then start your report. Trent, Cullen, I'm gonna want to hear what you have to say now and then, statements at the station. Don't make me chase you."

"Yes, sir." Trent using the word "sir" was new. But Dawson had earned the respect of all of Calusa Cove within the first few months he'd rolled into town, so it wasn't all that surprising.

Cullen nodded once.

"Sterling," Buddy said, keeping his voice low. "Grab three wide shots of the canopy gaps and the waterline. From our boat only. Nothing on her deck. No angles that step on their chain."

Sterling raised his phone once, twice, three times— deliberate, respectful—and pocketed it. "Done."

Buddy looked at the water where the girl had been, noticing how long it took the surface to settle at the edge of the roots. A faint, opalescent sheen winked there, almost invisible under shade.

"See that?" he murmured.

"Fuel," Sterling said. "Or cleaner. Trace."

"From where she came, not from here," Buddy said. The current pushed left. The sheen drifted right, lazy, as if it had seeped from still water to moving water. "Fallon." He pointed to the spot Sterling had noted.

"Already got it." She turned her attention back to Dawson.

Fallon gave Dawson her sequence. She didn't dramatize, didn't soften, just laid it out in succinct lines that made Buddy's admiration click into place. When she finished, she finally let out a breath that sounded like it hurt to hold.

Dawson flicked his gaze to Buddy. "You two done helping?"

"For now," Buddy said. "We'll get out of your way."

"I'll need statements. I'll call when I'm headed back to the station." Dawson pointed a finger at Buddy's chest. It wasn't unfriendly. They'd done the jurisdiction dance once or twice and always worked well together. But that was when Buddy carried a badge. He didn't have that added layer anymore. And honestly, he was damn glad about that. "And don't backseat the case from your couch."

Buddy did his best to put on an innocent face. It probably didn't convince anyone.

They pushed off. Sterling took the tiller without being asked, and the skiff drifted back into the open water. Buddy stood with a hand on the rail and watched until he could no longer see her.

They ran the skiff slowly until the channels widened and the air thinned. Buddy's phone buzzed with a text from an unknown local number. He opened it.

Fallon.

His heart did a little jump in his chest.

Thanks for the help. Would love to grab a cup of coffee or have a drink to catch up. It's been a while.

Buddy stared at the screen for a beat, then tucked the phone away without answering. Not because he didn't have words. But he didn't think texting her back in the middle of a crime scene was appropriate.

Then again, his thoughts weren't all that appropriate anyway.

He sighed. She was too young and not his type. Of course, neither of those things were really true. She might be ten-ish years younger, but they were both adults. And she was exactly the kind of woman he liked—in every way.

Which made her fucking dangerous.

"Let's get back to work," Buddy said.

Sterling nodded and fed the engine. The skiff lifted and slid forward, leaving the rot-stink and the secrets to ferment behind them. Ahead, the channel widened to a bright scar of sun and Buddy reminded himself that his days searching for answers regarding murder, death, and missing girls were long over. That's not what he was paid to worry about, and he needed to focus on other things.

Not this case.

And certainly not Fallon Reeves.

Chapter Two

Massey's Pub smelled like fried shrimp, old wood, and the citrus cleaner Juniper swore by, even though it made Fallon's eyes sting. Locals packed the bar like always. Their sunburns fading into stories. A baseball game murmured on the TV with the sound turned low. Someone had left their flip-flops under a high-top and forgotten them, which felt exactly right for Calusa Cove.

Fallon took her usual table by the front window and ordered a blackened grouper sandwich and a rum runner with a floater. She wasn't driving. She lived down the street, across from Harvey's Cabins, and her yard butted right up against Buddy's rental.

She checked her cell—still no reply from Buddy.

She put her phone face down.

It was ridiculous to be annoyed. She'd texted him a thank-you—and, okay, a not-so-subtle "coffee or drink sometime"—from the swamp because she'd been riding adrenaline and gratitude and maybe the memory of a man with a kind heart and a generous wallet when it came to her annual fundraiser. He didn't owe her anything. It wasn't an invitation for a date—just casual friends who occasionally texted the not-so-casual sexual innuendos to one another. But lines existed for a reason.

She tucked the phone under her napkin as if that might stop her from looking again.

Sipping her drink, she glanced around the bar at all the usuals. Not much ever changed in Calusa Cove. The town had its fair share of drama, but the people and the nightly routine generally stayed the same.

For years, she'd thought about moving away. When she'd decided to become a Fish and Wildlife Officer, she figured she'd move north. Go anywhere but the place Tessa had disappeared. However, she could never bring herself to leave. It was as if she had to torture herself with the memory. Remind herself that it could've been— should've been—her.

When the Ring Finger Killer had finally been caught —right in their own backyard—she'd thought maybe the mystery behind what happened to her best friend had been solved. Only, of all the trophies Dewey had kept, Tessa's finger wasn't among them.

And none of his victims had ever been that young, not even when he'd first started.

The air in her lungs flew out like a wild raven when Buddy stepped into the main dining area with a woman. She was petite, with shoulder-length hair, dark eyes that missed nothing. Black jeans. Black tee. No badge, no gun in sight. She moved like someone who could disappear without leaving a ripple.

The woman laughed at something Buddy said, easy and warm, and Fallon's stomach did a tiny, stupid drop.

Well. That explained the lack of response.

She took two gulps of her beverage, letting the rum burn as it went down, and reminded herself that Buddy's romantic choices were none of her business, and that, regardless, she wasn't looking for Mr. Right. She never was. She lived her life by one rule, and that was to live in the moment.

Juniper—the new owner, since Paul's wife finally sold and moved out of town—beelined for them with menus. Buddy scanned the room like it was habit, and his gaze caught on Fallon before she could pretend she hadn't been watching the door. He hesitated, said something to the woman beside him, then crossed the room.

"Hey Fallon," he said with that kind, warm smile that had this weird effect on her that she didn't want to acknowledge. "How are you holding up?"

"I'm fine," she returned the smile, because she could fake it like the best of them. "Massey's on a Wednesday. Bold move."

"The grouper's always good," he said. "Sterling heard the ribs were good, so now he won't even try the catch of the day, but that may be CIA talking."

"Sterling's CIA? That explains the clean-cut look."

"It should explain more than that," he said. "And this is Dovelynn Quinn." He angled a hand toward the woman approaching. "Goes by Dove. Ex-Army, sniper."

Dove slid into the third chair without waiting to be asked, flashed a grin that could talk its way past most locked doors, and said, "You saved a life today." She lifted two fingers to Juniper and asked for two beers and one basket of fries. Juniper nodded like they'd known each other for years.

Despite herself, Fallon found herself smiling. "I had help."

"From where I stood, you ran the show," Buddy corrected.

"Is that your way of not saying you'd know how to follow orders if it was you out there in the gator-infested water with me?" Fallon teased, trying to act like this was a normal conversation with an old friend. Because in a way, it was.

Dove laughed. "I'd like to see Buddy take an order from anyone."

"Just remember, I'm lead in this satellite office," Buddy said. "You answer to me."

Juniper delivered beers and fries for them and Fallon's sandwich. Buddy didn't touch his glass. Dove did, lifting it in a little salute. "To not dying in the swamp," she said.

"I'll drink to that." Fallon lifted her glass.

They ate and talked around the edges of the day. Dove told a quick story about a drone that got chased by an osprey, and Buddy asked the kind of neutral questions that showed he cared without delving too deeply into her past in front of present company. She appreciated that. Not that she'd care. Everyone knew because she ran the annual Tessa Project. However, Fallon often got emotional or intense about it, making others uncomfortable.

He also didn't mention her text. She didn't either.

When his phone buzzed, he checked it and stood. "Need to confirm tomorrow's vendor drop," he said. "Don't buy the whole bar a round—on me."

"I make no promises," Dove said.

He threaded through the crowd toward the back hall and was gone.

Dove watched him go and shook her head. "He's got a tell when he's pretending not to worry."

"Oh?" Fallon stabbed a fry. "What's that?"

"His shoulders go very Marine—like. Stiff, you know? But he was never a Marine," Dove said. "It's his 'I'm fine, we're fine, everything's fine' posture. Only, he's coiled too tight to be fine."

"Do you know what's bothering him?"

"I'm not exactly sure," Dove said. "It could be the girl you found earlier. It could be the fact the case he worked today dropped us before the job was even done, and right now, our load is light. Buddy hates being idle. Drove Timothy, our boss in the Jacksonville office, nuts."

Fallon hadn't seen Buddy in two years, since the opening of the Crab Shack. And before that, only when he'd been in town working a case. But they had some text chats, a bunch of late-night phone calls, though that didn't mean she knew him well. However, she could tell he wasn't the kind of man who took to relaxing easily.

"How long have you two been—" she glanced toward the direction he'd gone in "—an item?"

Dove choked on her beer and laughed so hard she had to set the glass down. "Me? With Buddy?" She wiped her mouth, eyes bright with wicked amusement. "He and I work together. He's technically my boss, and he's... well... not my type."

"That felt like a very diplomatic pause."

"It was me deciding whether to say, 'he's too earnest' or 'he commits to furniture.'"

"Furniture?"

"He had this chair in the Jacksonville office, and he had to bring it with him. He couldn't buy a new one. It had to be that one, and rumor has it, he brought it from the FBI," Dove said. "That's a man who wants a harbor. I'm a storm. Also, I like 'em rougher around the edges." She glanced around the restaurant, "Like—oh, hello."

Trent Mallor walked in, hat in hand, hair damp from a shower or the river. Either way, he looked like he'd been carved out of sun and bad decisions. He clocked the room, saw Fallon, and tipped his head with a grin that had gotten him out of at least three minor infractions in the last five years.

Dove's smile turned feral. "That right there is more my style," she said. "Who is he, and is he single?"

"Name is Trent, and be my guest," Fallon said, contemplating warning Dove. Trent wasn't the worst person—actually, he was just misunderstood. And while he was a decent man, at the end of the day, he wasn't going to ever settle down. Like ever. Then again, Dove seemed like the kind of woman who could handle herself. Besides, watching Trent try to wriggle away from a woman who could read his tells from sixty yards might improve her evening.

Dove stood, smoothed her tee like she was about to give a TED Talk on heartbreak, and slid toward the entrance. She intercepted Trent cleanly with a "Hey, you look like trouble," and he laughed, which was the wrong move because Dove's eyes lit like a cat spotting a laser pointer.

Fallon took a bite of the sandwich and pretended she wasn't watching.

Buddy returned a minute later, rolling his sleeves like the air had gotten warmer.

"Everything okay?" she asked.

"Yeah. That was Sterling," Buddy said. "He thinks we need another whiteboard. I told him no one needs another whiteboard."

"I like a good whiteboard," Fallon said. "It's great for visualizing."

"I prefer lists," he said. "At least you can fold a list and put it in your pocket."

They fell into a silence that wasn't uncomfortable, exactly. She knew him well enough that when he chose his words carefully, or chose not to say anything at all, it was all about letting her—whoever—decide what they talked about, or didn't talk about. It was his way of being... respectful. Also annoying.

"I texted you." Jesus, she wished she hadn't said anything. If she'd left it alone, it wouldn't matter. It would've just died a quick, easy death. Not this painful death that now required a conversation.

He met her eyes. Didn't flinch. Didn't blink. Didn't even crack a freaking smile. "I saw it. I haven't had the chance to respond. I had a few work things to deal with. I was going to answer when I got here, but then I saw you."

"You don't have to explain. I understand." And boy did she. Had she not brought it up, he wouldn't have gone into the laundry list of excuses, ending with the final blow to her ego—the lie—because no way had he actually planned to respond.

"For the record, I'd love to get together sometime and... catch up."

"Cool," she managed, then took a big bite of her sandwich to avoid smiling like an idiot. But once the food was in her mouth, she needed to cover her lips because all she could do was grin from ear to ear.

"Oh, shit," Buddy mumbled.

She lifted her napkin, turned in the direction Buddy was staring and noticed Trent, whose mouth had fallen open.

"I don't know which one of them needs to be warned off the other," Buddy murmured. "But my money's on Dove. I bet she'll eat him alive."

"And he'll enjoy every second of it," Fallon said.

"I thought you and Trent were close." Buddy's phone buzzed again. He glanced down, and something in his face shifted—from easy to intent. He didn't stand. He didn't grab for control. He was just... focused. "Sorry," he said. "Do you mind?"

"Go ahead," Fallon said.

He read, thumbed a quick reply, and set the phone face down. "Sterling again. He really wants that stupid whiteboard."

"I'm shocked you're fighting him on it. Dawson and Chloe use them all the time."

Buddy chuckled. "I can barely read my own handwriting. I'll use a corkboard with printed lists before I get another flipping whiteboard."

Fallon's phone vibrated under the napkin.

Buddy arched a brow.

She slid it free and saw Chloe's name.

Chloe: *Stable. Brief consciousness. One word. "Blue." Could be nothing. Could be everything. Don't chase it tonight. I promise to keep you posted."*

"That was Chloe. The girl we found earlier had a brief moment of consciousness." Fallon lifted her gaze. She knew Buddy would want to know, even though this wasn't his case. Besides, he might have some insight. "She said one word. Any idea what Blue means?" she asked.

Buddy held his beer halfway between the table and his mouth. His lips parted and he stared at her for a long moment. His right eye twitched. He cleared his throat and set the glass on the table. "Do Chloe and Dawson believe this is a human trafficking case?"

"They haven't said. Is that what you think? Why did you jump to that conclusion on a word? I get she's young. Looks like she hasn't eaten in days. She's obviously been detained. But it could've been kidnapping—not trafficking."

"Agreed," Buddy said. "She could be a runaway. Could be undocumented, which is why they still don't have a positive ID. Could be any number of things. I didn't mean to speculate. It's just that I have some experience in this area."

"And something made you go from blue to human trafficking. Why?"

"It's not necessarily the word. It's the entire situation." He shifted. "But, we shouldn't jump to conclusions this early. I know better. Whoever was present when she woke briefly could've misunderstood. It could be the first color she saw when she opened her eyes. The last color she saw before she fell—or was dumped—into the water. It could be a name of someone, or something. It's really too early to go down this rabbit hole."

She stared at him for a long moment, looking for more of those tells that Dove mentioned. His shoulders were high. His jaw tight. His right eye twitched, and he rambled faster than she was used to. He was holding something back.

But before she could comment on that, Dove reappeared beside them with a basket of fries she hadn't paid for and a look that said she'd been shot down. "Your friend is a menace," she said. "I made a joke, and he didn't like it. Next thing I know, we're no longer talking about hooking up. As a matter of fact, he told me to take a hike."

"I wouldn't call him my friend," Fallon said automatically, because labels mattered in small towns, then heard herself and grimaced. "He's more like an overprotective big brother."

Buddy choked on his beer and stared at her like she'd said something criminal. Granted, she'd dated Trent a long time ago, so calling him family sounded strange to some. But, that's what she considered him these days. "Depending on what you teased him about will guide his reaction. He can be a sensitive soul."

"I doubt that," Dove said. "I mentioned something about how weird the whole Python Challenge is down here, and how I couldn't understand why anyone would do it. I mean, aren't snakes a part of the ecosystem in the Everglades?"

Fallon smacked her palm to her forehead. "Don't ever say that again out loud. Not unless you want to get shot."

"I don't understand." Dove blinked a few times, looking thoroughly confused.

"Pythons aren't native to Florida," Buddy explained. "They've invaded the Everglades and are destroying everything in their path, including alligators. Trent over there owns an Alligator Farm. He's also a snake wrangler, and not just pythons. He's a nature lover. A snake and gator lover, even if he does the odd poaching thing, he does them for all the right reasons, if that makes sense. And, he loves the Glades more than most."

"Trent and I agree on making sure the Everglades remain the swampy marshland we've always called home," Fallon said.

"Copy that," Dove said, amused, and slid into her

chair. "Next time I see Trent, I'll be sure to be slightly more informed and pretend to like reptiles, even if they're disgusting creatures."

"Good thing for you, he's all about second, third, and fourth chances when it comes to women." Fallon raised her drink." He doesn't discriminate when it comes to breasts."

"Are you speaking from experience?" Dove asked. "Because that might be weird considering how you described him."

Buddy coughed and pounded his chest.

"I might be." Fallon laughed. "However, I'm one of the few females that scare the crap out of him."

"I'd suggest staying away from Trent." Buddy rested his hand on the back of Fallon's chair, and his thumb brushed her shoulder. "He's not a bad guy. He's grown on me over the years. But I wouldn't introduce him to my sister."

"You don't have a sister." Dove laughed. "But enough of that conversation. Sterling wants to know if we can borrow your brain in the near future, Fallon. We're running a water grid for a client, and he's obsessed with not annoying FWC. Which is adorable and new."

"I can't tomorrow, but I can the next day."

Buddy lifted a hand. "We can always ping your boss, Keaton, since that's your day off."

She jerked her head and swallowed the lump in her throat. How the hell did he know she wasn't on the schedule in two days? "If you'd rather talk to Keaton, that's fine," Fallon said. "But it's not a problem. All I have that day is catching up on sleep and paperwork."

"Sleep is optional," Buddy said.

"Sleep is never optional," Fallon said. "But I've got time after eleven, if that works."

"Sounds good." Dove nodded.

Juniper dropped off the check. Fallon slid her card into the tray before Buddy could reach for his wallet, because she'd never known him not to insist on paying. "Don't," she said. "If I let you buy my dinner, someone's mother will plan our wedding before the ice melts."

"There's no ice in South Florida, and my mother passed a long time ago." Buddy flicked her card off the bill and slapped a wad of cash on the table. "I insist."

"Thanks for dinner, boss." Dove leaned back. "I'm gonna stay for one more drink and maybe that second chance."

"Don't stay out too late. Trent's not worth the trouble," Buddy said. "Seriously."

"You sound like he might have hurt your feelings." Dove snorted.

Buddy didn't bother answering. He just shook his head.

They stood in that awkward, not-unpleasant space where a night could end or tilt. Outside, the last light went copper over the water. Someone opened the door, and the Everglades sighed warm, salty air into the bar, a reminder that the wild waited just past the parking lot.

Fallon flung her small backpack-purse over her shoulder. "Stay out of trouble."

"That's no fun," he said. "So, how about that coffee? Not tomorrow, but the next day?"

"I could do that," she said as a smile tugged at her lips. Her pulse twitched. It had been six months since she'd been on a date. Seven since she'd been with a man.

She quickly reminded herself that this wasn't a date and that Buddy was just some guy who used to be law enforcement who was probably just greasing palms for his current job with the Aegis network.

Even though he'd made some interesting comments regarding her breasts once in a text message and then tried to backpedal.

"Wonderful. Why don't you come over to my place around nine?"

"What about work?"

He shrugged. "Just wrapped up a case, and Dove and Sterling are working on other things that don't require me to babysit them. So, I can spare a morning." He leaned a little closer. Maybe too close. "That's the nice thing about this job. When I'm working certain kinds of cases, I'm always on. But when I'm not, I'm free as a bird."

"That would make me crazy," she said. "See you in two days." She stepped into the warm dark, the hum of crickets rising. Away from Buddy. Away from the feelings and sensations he stirred. They weren't real. He was just looking for connections. He probably had meetings with Keaton, Fletcher, the head of Parks and Rec, and all the deputies on Dawson's payroll. It was how things worked.

She crossed the street, and her mind drifted back to

the earlier events—the girl who had kept breathing long enough to be found. Somewhere, "blue" meant something, and Fallon planned on finding out what.

Chapter Three

The county hospital understood late hours the way the military understood silence—temporary. The fluorescent lights caused the kind of fatigue no one talked about. Someone coughed, the sound quickly swallowed by the hum of vents and the soft shuffle of rubber soles.

Buddy flashed his visitor sticker at the security desk, signed his name on the clipboard that no one would read, and took the stairs—two flights, but enough to burn off the static in his chest. He'd never liked elevators at night. Too much reflection, not enough escape.

He found the right corridor when the antiseptic sharpened, cutting clean through the old coffee. Every hospital smelled the same after midnight—like something trying too hard to be pure—but the ICU always tried the hardest.

He passed an empty vending alcove, a nurse's laugh echoing from somewhere unseen. The hospital had that hollow feel every building did after dark—the kind that made you whisper without knowing why.

The tension in his shoulders crept up his neck and rolled down his back. He'd spent the day in meetings that he couldn't get out of and a road trip an hour away to discuss a case that Sterling might be assigned to, all while trying not to think about the Jane Doe found in the Everglades the day before who reminded him he could never save them all.

That phrase would haunt him for the rest of his life.

Deputy Jasper Newton, the newest recruit to Calusa Cove's police department, sat outside the last room, one boot braced against the wall, radio turned low. His hat was tilted over his eyes, but the man wasn't sleeping.

"Evening," Buddy said.

Jasper tipped his hat up with a finger, a grin twitching. "Welcome back."

"Thanks. It's good to be here."

"I was told you might wander in and play consultant."

"So, Dawson's expecting me," Buddy said with a small laugh.

Jasper shrugged. "Chief went downstairs to get caffeine before the cafeteria shuts down—Chloe's in with the girl. Over twenty-four hours since she was found, and we've got nothing. Chief is twitching."

"That doesn't surprise me about Dawson. He likes his town to be quiet." Buddy brushed the edge of the sticker on his chest with his thumb. "Is the girl conscious?"

"She's woken up a few times. Drifts in and out. Nothing substantial." Jasper nodded toward the door. "Chief told me you can go in."

"Appreciate it."

Buddy pushed the door open, stepping into the low hum of machines and recycled air.

Chloe stood near the window, arms crossed tight, gaze fixed on the girl in the bed. Jane Doe looked even younger under the sterile light. IV taped to her arm. A faint ring on her wrists where the restraint had been—he'd seen that mark before, too many times. It wasn't just the injury. It was the precision of it—clinical, practiced.

Her lips were dry and split. Her hair was a dark tangle against the pillow, still streaked with swamp water even after the nurses had done their best.

The monitor ticked out a steady rhythm that somehow made the silence louder.

Chloe didn't turn. "You just won me fifty bucks," she said.

He came to stand beside her, close enough to see his reflection in the window—two ghosts framed by the pulse of a heart monitor. "You were betting on me?"

"I was betting you wouldn't be able to help yourself," she said, and her mouth curved just enough to suggest she wasn't sorry about it. "I knew you'd give it a day, but then instinct would kick in and here you are."

He watched the slow rise and fall of the girl's chest. "Guess you know me better than I thought."

"I spent years watching you chase ghosts across this

state. You get that look, the one you have right now, and it's game over."

He glanced at her. "That so?"

"You're not here for a visit. You're here because you see a pattern, smell a puzzle, and a young girl is fighting for her life. You can't walk away from that."

He wanted to argue, but she wasn't wrong.

"Vitals are holding," Chloe said, switching to business. "She came around earlier. Scared. Thrashed hard enough to pull her IV. It wasn't purposeful, just instinct. They've had to sedate her a couple of times."

"Photos?"

"Taken. Clothing bagged. Chain of custody's clean." She gave him a sharp look. "Before you ask—which isn't your job anymore."

"No, it's not." Buddy folded his arms, eyes still on the girl. "You said she came around—did she say anything?"

"One word." Chloe rubbed the back of her neck. "Blue. Nurse isn't sure that's what she heard since the girl was so frantic. I'm not convinced, and neither are you, because you're here." She held up her hand before he could even open his mouth. "I know you were with Fallon when I texted her because I had lunch with her today, so don't deny it. She told me you reacted to the word. Told me you went right to human trafficking. Told me you then back-peddled."

"Okay. She mentioned the word, and yeah, I went there. And so have you and Dawson."

The door opened behind them, and Dawson's voice filled the small space before his body did. "Well damn, why couldn't you have come in last night so I would've won fifty bucks?"

Buddy turned. "I was busy."

Dawson held a to-go cup in one hand, a folder in the other, and the kind of exhaustion that comes from carrying a town on your shoulders. "You planning to make a habit of showing up at my crime scenes?"

"Wasn't planning on it."

"Good." Dawson's tone said he didn't believe him. "I'm not mad you're here, but this isn't a reunion tour. And I gotta say this shit, and you know it. So, let's get it out of the way, so we can do what we do best. You don't touch. You don't talk to nurses. You breathe near a piece of evidence, and I'll have you escorted out by Jasper."

Buddy lifted a hand. "Scout's honor."

"You were never a scout."

"True," Buddy said, "but I'm capable of behaving."

Chloe snorted softly, still watching the bed. "He's here because he has a theory on our victims' word choice."

"Oh, really." Dawson shifted his weight. He passed Chloe the folder. "Because we've got nothing. Lab has her clothing, but there was nothing identifiable. No ID, no wallet, no jewelry. Prints don't match anyone local or in-state."

"Nothing in the FBI missing persons database?" Buddy asked.

"We sent a picture over, but so far, no hits," Dawson said. "We've got her photo circulating, but unless she's got family checking in every few hours, it'll take time."

"Someone's missing her," Chloe murmured.

Buddy studied the girl's face. There was something about her jawline—stubborn, even in sleep. "She's young," he said. "Too young for no one to notice."

"Not always," Chloe said. Her voice softened, just a little. "Sometimes people disappear, and the world just keeps going."

Buddy couldn't argue that point. He'd seen it too many times.

"So, tell me your thoughts on what she said." Dawson inched closer to the window separating them from the private room and the hallway that led to the main corridor.

"Operation Blue Eden." Buddy hadn't said those words out loud in months. The name felt metallic on his tongue, like he'd bitten down on a bullet.

"What's that?" Dawson asked.

"The last big case I worked on with the FBI." Buddy kept his focus on the girl.

"It's a bit of a stretch to go from our vic saying blue to your case name," Dawson said. "But I don't believe in coincidences."

"I don't either. But it's more than just what we named the op." Buddy glanced between Dawson and Chloe. "Blue was also an internal code word used by the traffickers. It meant it was safe to move the victims."

"Okay," Chloe said softly. "But why would our vic use it? Because that doesn't make sense."

"I don't know." Buddy ran his fingers through his

hair. "It just struck me as an odd choice, and I wanted to mention it to you."

"Except you wrapped up that case," Chloe said. "Made seventeen arrests. Shut down a major pipeline."

"I did." Buddy nodded. "But we both know this shit is still going on." His throat tightened. "Anything else? Maybe if I know more, I can tell if there are any other similarities."

"Some sort of smudge on her wrist. Faded. Blue-gray," Chloe said. "Could be ink, could be grease. We won't know until the lab runs it."

That knocked the wind out of Buddy's lungs. "Can you send me a picture of that?"

"You know I can't do that." Dawson pulled out his cell and held up an image. "Why?"

It was too smudged to make sense of it.

"A couple of the girls we found were working sweat-shops in the Bayou. They had stamps on their wrists that indicated where they worked. They were temporary until they were sold—if they were sold. Some were older, and not the kind of girls that got the same high price on the market as younger ones." He swallowed the bile that bubbled in his throat.

"Any chance you've got unofficial copies of those ink stamps?" Chloe asked.

Buddy snorted. "I might be able to get you one, but as you said, I made those arrests. Unless someone reopened that pipeline, which isn't unheard of, those assholes are either dead or behind bars."

The nurse approached, holding a small envelope

sealed in red tape. "Chief Ridge? Detective Frasier-Bennett? I didn't want this misplaced."

Dawson took it. "What is it?"

"Debris from under her fingernails. Small, but I thought you'd want it noted before evidence transfer."

"Appreciate it," Chloe said.

The nurse's gaze flicked to Buddy. "Sorry, sir, but we need to keep the hallway clear for now."

"Understood," he said, stepping back.

Dawson nodded at Chloe. "Finish up here. I'll have Jasper keep watch 'til shift change."

When they stepped into the hall, the door closed softly behind them. The corridor smelled like tapioca and tired feet.

For a few beats, no one spoke, and Buddy did his best to categorize what he knew, what was simply jumping to conclusions, and what were ghosts he was trying to outrun.

"Alright," Dawson said finally. "I'm not saying you can't think. Just don't act on those thoughts without Chloe. You're a civilian, and most likely, this case will be taken out of my hands and handed over to state or even the Feds. Let us run it clean."

"Wouldn't dream of anything else," Buddy said.

"Yeah, you would," Dawson said. "But thanks for lying."

Chloe laughed under her breath, low and genuine. "He can't help it."

Dawson headed down the hall, muttering something about paperwork and shitty coffee.

When his footsteps faded, Chloe leaned against the wall, arms crossed again. "I know you still carry it," she said.

"Carry what?"

"That case in Georgia—the guilt."

He didn't look at her. "I'm trying not to."

She sighed. "Dawson's never going to say no to hearing your thoughts, and I'm not going to get in your face about it in front of him, but you didn't just leave the FBI because it was time. You quit because it got to be too much."

"And you didn't?"

"I was driven to find my sister's killer. Once that happened, everything in my world shifted. My priorities. My goals. And it wasn't just because of Hayes. It was because I had a singular focus. I wasn't burnt out. I didn't walk into the office one day, call my boss a fucking lazy bastard who kissed DC's ass, set my badge and gun on his desk, and waltzed out like years of service didn't mean anything."

"Why don't you tell me how you really feel about my departure," he said, his bitterness hitting his taste buds like vomit.

"I'm just saying you don't have enough time and space between what happened and where you want to go to not let this one hit you between the eyes," she said. "Go home. Get some sleep. Try not to chase ghosts tonight."

He wanted to argue that he didn't chase ghosts—that ghosts chased him. But the hallway lights buzzed overhead, and the thought felt too close to the truth to say out loud. His gaze drifted back to the glass, to the girl motionless under white sheets. "She said blue," he murmured. "What would you think if you were me?"

"The Chloe that was chasing her sister's killer would be going down the same rabbit hole you are." She inched closer, resting her hand on his forearm. "But the difference is that was one killer, and I had one purpose. My entire career was built on personal. You let one case *get* personal. There's a difference."

"Maybe." Only, he knew damn well, she was right. He rubbed the back of his neck. "You think she'll make it?"

"I've seen worse come back," Chloe said. "And I've seen better not. So flip a coin."

That landed heavy.

He nodded once, stepped back, and shoved his hands in his pockets. "Let me know if she wakes up again. And that's not me being obsessive. But I will admit the Georgia case changed me."

"I know, and I'll keep you posted."

When he stepped back into the stairwell, the air hit cooler, thinner. He leaned on the rail a second before starting down.

Below, the vending machine hummed beside the sound of his own thoughts. *Blue.*

He told himself it wasn't his case.

He told himself even if this was trafficking—it didn't involve him, and he should stay out of it.

He told himself he believed that.

He was good at lying to himself.

Outside, the humidity clung like breath. The parking lot was half-empty, the town beyond it asleep. Buddy paused under the yellow glow of a lamppost and looked back once. In the second-floor window, a pulse light blinked steadily. Blue, then gone. Blue, then gone. Like a heartbeat he couldn't stop hearing.

Then he turned toward the dark and started walking, knowing damn well he wasn't getting much sleep tonight.

Chapter Four

By eight-thirty, the town wore the heat like a damp shirt. The Everglades buzzed across the street—cicadas drilling, frogs croaking, alligators moaning that low, steady breath that said the swamp was ready for anything.

Fallon locked her front door, slid her phone into her back pocket, and paused when it buzzed. She glanced at the screen.

Unknown number. No preview.

That was never good, but it also never stopped her from looking at the unnecessary spam that seemed to come across her cell weekly. It didn't matter that she'd done a purge of her passwords. Somewhere, somehow, her data had been leaked, and she hadn't been able to stop the influx of spam that assaulted her phone and email.

She thumbed the screen, and the words hit like a palm to the sternum.

You can't save them all

No name. No punctuation. No call-back.

Training slid into place. She didn't reply. Didn't poke it. She took a clean screenshot, saved it, and let the message sit there until the sick little pulse in her neck eased a notch. She could send it to her boss, Keaton. Or to Dawson. Maybe Buddy first—since she was heading there anyway—to get a read before she lit up anyone's phone.

Because it was probably just spam.

She set off toward the Calusa Cove Café, one block down the sunbaked sidewalk, and looked forward to a bit of gossip with a few locals while getting her morning brew. Dawson's newest landscaper was out front of the Harvey's Cabins in his floppy hat, hose arcing across the gravel. A couple of tourists hauled coolers toward their trunks. The OPEN sign in the office window blinked along like it had all the time in the world.

No matter the heartache this town had tossed at her over the years—her missing friend, who was still technically missing, and the loss of her parents—she still loved this place.

The café door chimed as it opened, letting out a wave of coffee and sugar. Ceiling fans pushed heavy air in lazy circles. Regulars were posted up like fixtures—bait shop guys, two retirees who played dominoes with a vengeance, a pair of nurses on night shift, and Silas.

Who didn't love that crazy man?

"Hey there, Dynasty," Silas said. "My wife wants to know if you're coming to book club this month."

"Tell her I'll be there, and for the love of all that's holy, please stop calling me that."

Silas tipped his head back and laughed. "Not on your life. Besides, you kind of look like the actress who played the new Fallon on the newer version of that show."

"She has red hair, and mine is brown. Not to mention her personality is more like Trinity's. I don't even own a pair of heels." She glanced down at her flip-flops and wiggled her toes. Trinity would *never*. Yeah, her boss's wife wouldn't be caught dead in these. Glancing up at Silas, she added, "I can't believe you watch that crap."

"Started watching all sorts of different things since my brother's kid came to live here." Silas ran a hand over his white stubble. "Cullen, he doesn't want to watch anything military related. Crime shows affect him negatively, so it's high family drama and screaming women when he comes over. It's something different. Wife likes it and Cullen's lighter and he laughs more. Smiles more. And that's the point."

Cullen had grown up in Calusa Cove. He was closer to Trent's age than Fallon's, but she'd remembered Cullen from before he'd taken off for the Marines right after he turned eighteen. He'd been an outgoing and outspoken young man. He played a sport every season, he'd been popular, and no one would have ever describe him as shy.

But the man who'd returned a hero from the Marines was quite a different person. Quiet. Reserved. And a couple of years ago, he'd been afraid of his own shadow.

"I noticed he's been spending some time with Trent."

"Is there a problem with that, Dynasty?" Silas asked.

"Please. Quite the opposite."

"Good, because I've been encouraging it, which is funny because those two boys couldn't stand each other when they were kids. My brother and Trent's mom had to go down to the high school at least twice because of fights between those two. My brother and his wife didn't know what to do. Cullen was normally such a good kid."

"I'm a couple of years younger, but I can tell you that Trent was good at starting things and pushing people into finishing them."

"Trent's changed a lot since then. So has Cullen." Silas snagged his coffee from the counter, inched closer, and gave her a peck on the cheek. "Your dad would be so proud of the person you've become." Silas smiled and then disappeared out the door. God, she adored that man. He always said the perfect things at precisely the right moment.

"You look like you could use a coffee and a prayer," Heather said, already reaching for a cup.

"Close," Fallon said. "I need two. One black and one with oat milk. And whatever muffins didn't get murdered by sunrise."

"Blueberry and banana nut. That do?"

"I'll take one of each."

Heather tipped her chin toward the TV mounted in the corner. Last night's broadcast played on mute—Stacey Mohawk mid-smile, light brown hair shellacked into submission, the banner marching across the bottom:

Snake Wrangler Saves Young Woman in Everglades Rescue.

Fallon pressed her tongue to her molars. "Why won't any other station hire her?"

"I don't know. But she could stand in front of a thunderstorm and report sunshine," Heather said. "I didn't watch the news last night but heard all about the rescue from Silas. Did Stacey even mention your name?"

"As a concept," Fallon said. "Local FWC officer, assisting."

Heather snorted. "Trent gets the hero cut, and you get the weather. I don't get it. Stacey doesn't even like Trent. I think she called him a Cobra once."

"I'm not in it for the camera time."

Heather laughed. "She's in it for all of us."

The bell over the door jingled again.

"Speaking of trouble wrapped in handsome with an ego the size of Texas." Heather fanned herself. "Too bad I'm taken."

Trent sauntered in with that sexy swagger that everyone mistook for arrogance. He was anything but. Hat tipped back, jeans damp at the hem, grin fast and easy. He smelled like the river and aftershave and the kind of choices people explained to their mothers later. That kind of man used to appeal to Fallon, especially right after her parents had died. She'd only been twenty, and all she could think about was feeling the pain while trying to numb it at the same time.

"Well, look at what the river brought in," he said,

hopping onto the stool beside her. "You want me to sign your muffin?"

"Sign your own sugar rush," Fallon said, not looking at him.

He barked a laugh and jerked his chin at the TV. "I'd like to sign a snake and put it under Stacey's seat."

"Now, why would you want to do that?" she asked. "She made you look like a hero."

"Don't even get me started." He leaned in. "Stacey ambushed me last night at Massey's. Asked for an 'exclusive sit-down.' I told her the gator had more charisma and to go find him."

"You're going to end up on her enemies list."

"Already there." He grinned. "Pretty sure you are, too."

"Please. She can't spell my name."

He glanced at her, humor softening. "You good?"

"I'm about to be caffeinated," she said. "That's as good as it gets."

"Not what I'm talking about, and you know it." The creases in his forehead and around his eyes softened. Trent had a wild streak, no doubt. He'd raised hell as a teenager and got into the kind of trouble that had given him a reputation he hadn't been able to shed. But deep down, Trent was a wounded man with a big heart. She'd seen that side of him more than once.

"I'm hanging tough, just like always."

He smiled, soft and subtle. Not the flashy grin that was meant to melt girls' hearts and charm them out of their pants. "Did you get my list of donations for the silent auction? And I can work more volunteer hours if you need me to. Just ask."

"I will. And thanks."

Heather slid over a drink carrier and tucked a warm paper bag on top. "Two larges and two muffins. And tell Buddy I said hello."

Fallon reached for her wallet. "Who says I'm meeting Buddy?"

Heather made a face. "Only man I've ever known who gets a coffee with oat milk. And you take it black."

Trent tipped his hat at Fallon with his best you'll-miss-me-when-I'm-gone smile. "You and Buddy, eh? Why am I not surprised."

"We're in South Florida," Fallon said. "Not Canada." Focusing on anything other than his and Heather's observations.

"Semantics." His eyes sparked. "And mention to your friend Dove that it's rude not to respond to texts."

Fallon narrowed her stare. "You didn't actually give her another chance after the whole python thing?"

"Just do me a solid and ask her to give me a call," he said, pushing off the stool. Trent was a lot of things, but he didn't brag about his conquests. Actually, he was a private man when it came to his short-lived affairs. He might be a big flirt out in public, but once things got going, he was completely different. "See you at the fundraiser."

She rolled her eyes and took the tray.

Outside, the heat slapped her. The cabins shimmered in the morning light, hose water beading on the gravel like scattered beads. She crossed the street, coffees steady in the carrier, muffin bag hooked over her wrist, sweat already tickling down her spine.

Halfway down the block, a dark muscle car crept by. Tinted windows. Engine too loud. It rolled slow enough to be noticeable, slow enough to catalog targets without revealing an identity.

She didn't turn her head and instead, let her gaze slide, catching the angle of the plate as the sun hit it. She could only get a partial—7KD—and filed it the way her brain filed routes through mangroves or the way the sky went yellow-green before a storm was rolling two hours earlier than forecasted.

The car paused at the stop sign, as if it wanted to be seen. Then it eased on and—once she'd clocked it—accelerated just a hair too fast. She squinted, trying to read the rest of the plate, but between something possibly covering it and the glare of the sun, she couldn't see it well enough to catch the letters or numbers.

Tourists, she told herself. Contractors. Someone lost between breakfast and the highway.

Her shoulders stayed tight until she reached Buddy's steps.

He opened the back door before she could knock. Barefoot. Hair damp, combed, perfectly. T-shirt clinging in all the ways the heat would claim credit for if it could write copy.

"Morning," he said, voice steady, eyes already reading her.

She lifted the tray. "Payment for services rendered.

Black for me, one with oat milk for you because we don't need you complaining about your stomach. And muffins. I have no food, so this is breakfast."

"Works for me." He took the carrier, fingers brushing hers—warm. "Thanks for bringing this. Come in."

His place smelled like soap mixed with dust. Boxes lined one wall like they were waiting for orders. A corkboard leaned against the table, empty for now. The fan hummed overhead, pushing the same warm air in soft circles.

"You unpacking or just staging an intervention for your own clutter?" Fallon asked, setting the muffins down.

"Trying to see if staying feels like something I remember how to do." He handed her the coffee.

"Consider it a bribe." She pulled out a chair and sat. "I might need your brain."

"You do," he said, sitting next to her. He was so close she swore she could feel his pulse. "But go ahead and pretend you don't."

That pulled a smile she hadn't planned. It slipped away when she slid her hand into her back pocket.

She took out her phone, opened the text, and turned it so he could see. She didn't bother with a preamble.

His jaw drew tight. "I see you didn't reply."

"Of course not."

"Good." He held the phone in his hands while outside, a heron complained—harsh, indignant. "Can you forward it to me? And then you might want to send it on to Keaton and Dawson."

"Planned on it, but why do you want it?"

He ran his fingers through his hair and leaned back. He leaned forward, snagging his coffee and took a large gulp.

When he got like this, he was thinking about something profound. Thinking about something related to a case.

Only, he wasn't a fed anymore.

"What's going on?" she asked.

"That case I was working on—the one I closed right before I left the FBI—the guy I put behind bars taunted me with a line just like that." He turned and held her gaze. "It's not an uncommon phrase. I've seen other criminals, killers, drug dealers, you name it, use it. Hell, I've heard doctors say it. But this doesn't feel random. Nor does that girl you saved, and it's had me on high alert ever since."

Her heart rate sped up. She swallowed her breath, and it tasted like death. Her chest tightened, like someone had laced her into a corset and was tightening the threads to the point it was crushing her.

"What else happened that you're not telling me?"

"There was a car," she managed. "Dark muscle car. Dodge Charger, I think. Tints. Slow roll past the cabins. Partial plate—7, K, D. I couldn't get to my phone without being obvious or baptizing the street in coffee."

"Don't love that," he said gently. He pulled a legal pad from the table's edge and wrote 7KD with a blocky neatness that made her think of evidence lockers and stupid, awful rooms with fluorescent lights. "Direction?"

"Paused, then turned toward the main road heading out of town." She gestured vaguely toward the window.

"People telegraph more than they think." His pen tapped once. "There's more to that phrase and that case." He didn't look away from her.

Fallon didn't move. "We never talked much about the case when we texted and the deeper you got into it, the less we chatted."

"Things got dark, and before I made the arrests, I was on this twenty-four-seven," he said softly. "It was what they said to each other when a girl slipped their net or when one didn't matter—only a single word was different. It was, you can't *have* them all."

Her hand tightened around the cup. "Jesus, that's creepy."

"I don't like coincidence. But I like panic less. We'll treat it like a thing. We won't give it more than it earns."

"We," she said, before she could stop herself.

One side of his mouth kicked up. "Yeah. We."

They sat with that—staring at each other with an intensity that had nothing to do with unknown texts and muscle cars and everything to do with the heat and the fan and the quiet weight in the room.

"You saw the news about the Jane Doe rescue," she said, because easier topics were still topics and she didn't know where to file Buddy when he used the word we and stared at her like he might want something other than conversation.

"Stacey has a type," he said. "It's called 'Stacey.'"

"She asked Trent for an interview, but he said no on principle."

"Good for him. He'll give in tomorrow."

"Probably," she admitted. "He's allergic to being bored."

"And you're allergic to being handled," he said. "Which is what Stacey would've tried if she'd interviewed you."

"I'm not a performance. I'm a job." She groaned. "That didn't come out right."

"Perhaps not, but it landed."

The air shifted. Not because the fan changed speed. Because he didn't look away when he should've, and she didn't when she should've, and then he inched closer. His breath hot and his gaze hotter.

"This could be a bad idea," she said softly.

"Definitely."

He reached for her hand, knuckles grazing the inside of her wrist, right where her pulse fluttered. It wasn't dramatic. It wasn't even long. It still set something in her alight, hot and clean.

She leaned a fraction forward.

"Fallon," he whispered, like her name was the only argument he had left.

His lips brushed hers like a spark igniting a fire in her belly. It was the kind of kiss that felt less like risk and more like an agreement they'd both been making in their heads since he'd rolled into town. Maybe longer.

When it broke, the fan sounded louder than it had before.

"I'm not sure where that came from." He ran his thumb across her cheek.

She continued to stare into his dark, smoldering eyes. A million things raced through her brain, but only one stuck. "You haven't wanted to do that for a while?"

"I haven't seen you in two years."

"We've texted and..." God, her ego couldn't handle this.

"I know," he said. "I didn't mean it that way. It's just... Hell, I don't know."

"Your muffin is going to get cold."

"Tragedy."

She stood because if she didn't, she might say something she'd regret. "I've got a meeting with your office at eleven and then a ton of things to do for my fundraiser after that. Fletcher and Baily said I can store some things at the Crab Shack as well as the stuff I already have at the marina." She had no idea how either of them did it between owning the marina, being part owners in the Crab Shack and Everglades Overwatch, *and* being parents. She was exhausted just thinking about it.

""I can help. I can carry heavy things."

"You don't have to—"

"I know how to lift boxes and arrange storage stuff."

She glanced around at all his boxes. "I have my doubts."

His mouth tipped upward into a quick smile before fading just as fast. "Don't forget to send me a copy of that text." He took her hand and led her to the door. He released his grip and placed his hand on the frame, as if he didn't want to touch her multiple times in the same morning. "If you see that Charger again—"

"I'll call you," she said. "Before I pretend it's nothing."

"Good."

She reached for the door, but he stepped in front of her and gripped her hips.

"I've been attracted to you since we first met."

Her stomach dropped. Or lifted. She wasn't sure which, only that something in her chest went sideways and her breath caught somewhere between her lungs and her throat.

"I can list a dozen reasons why I've kept my distance—the Ring Finger case and all the other cases that brought me to town. I was here for a job, and it was temporary. I lived an hour away. I'm a little over ten years older than you. I've had one failed marriage and a couple of relationships that—"

"You don't have to explain. We're friends. I get it." Of course he had a list of all the reasons why he wouldn't act on whatever he was feeling. He was good at making lists.

"It's not an explanation. It's more like a... oh hell." He yanked her to his chest, wrapping his strong arms around her waist. His gaze was so intense, it burned through her like a pod re-entering the earth's atmosphere. His lips crash landed on hers in a wild kiss.

She gripped his shoulders, letting the rush of adrenaline flowing through her body take over.

His tongue twisted and twirled around hers. He tasted like coffee, oat milk, and sunshine.

When he pulled away, she wondered if he was going to regret that one, too. But instead, she was greeted with a smile and his fingers threading through her hair. "You'd better go. Otherwise, you're going to end up being late for your meeting with Sterling and Dove." He turned and opened the door.

She struggled to swallow. To breathe. To collect her thoughts, which pooled at her feet.

"I've got calls, so I won't be attending, but I should be done by the time your chat with my colleagues ends. I can follow you to the Crab Shack," he said.

"Okay."

She stepped into the bright Florida sun with her heart pulsating in her throat. The sign in front of Harvey's Cabins across the way blinked OPEN at no one in particular. A hose hissed. Somewhere, a kid squealed—the kind of sounds that made her wish summer was a thing she could bottle.

She touched her lips, wondering what the hell had just happened, and what it meant.

Scurrying between the yards like a teenager racing home after her first kiss under the bleachers, she headed for home. Once safely tucked inside her kitchen, she leaned against the sliding glass doors and let out a breath.

Of all the things she thought, or expected, could happen this morning. That kiss wasn't it.

Her phone vibrated in her back pocket.

Buddy: *Don't forget to send that text. Muffin was delicious. Company was better.*

She blinked. The room spun. Jesus. She was a

fucking grown-up. Thirty years old. Kissing a man wasn't a big deal. Hell, she'd lived with a guy for a few months. Didn't matter that she didn't love him in a romantic way. Trent had been there for her when she needed someone the most. That counted for something.

But this was Buddy Ballard. A man she'd been fantasizing about for years, and that turned her insides to mush.

She fumbled with her phone, found the text image, sent it to Keaton and Dawson with a quick note about what had happened, then attached it to a text to Buddy.

Fallon: *Sent to Keaton and Dawson. Here you go. See you soon.*

Buddy: *Looking forward to it. Text if anything odd happens—even if you think it's nothing.*

She typed: *Bossy.*

Deleted it. Typed: *Will do.*

Outside, the Everglades kept humming. The heat pressed down. The strange message sat in her photos like a bruise. The past crept up like it did every year, reminding her that she could've been the one to be a ghost.

Fallon told herself she was fine.

She didn't believe it. But she could carry it because she had to.

Chapter Five

The Crab Shack's back room trapped the kind of heat that stuck to a man. Fryer oil lived in the walls. Salt lived in the wood. The faint tinge of lemon mixed with a cleaning agent lingering in the air indicated someone had run a mop earlier, and it did nothing to mask the scent of last night's fresh catch.

Buddy braced a shoulder under a plastic bin marked TESSA PROJECT—CENTERPIECES and slid it onto the top shelf Fletcher had cleared. The shelf groaned. So did his back.

"Careful," Fallon said from the step stool, palm up to steady. "If one more starfish sheds, I'm going to cry in front of witnesses."

"You wouldn't dare. I know you're stressed, but everything's going to be fine. You've got this down to a science." He glanced at her, and a mix of emotions swelled in his gut like a storm brewing over the ocean. The bin settled, but his heart didn't. He'd sworn off the kinds of feelings that tangled him with women in a way that meant he cared—meant that he wouldn't have a wandering eye—meant that he'd actually be willing to give a real relationship a shot.

He'd known that Fallon was special the second he'd laid eyes on her, nearly four years ago, the first time he'd set foot in this town. Ever since then, she'd haunted his dreams. He hadn't been prepared for what moving here would do to him physically, mentally, but especially... emotionally. He stepped back, hands open. "What's in it?"

"Glass cylinders wrapped in a fishing net and my last nerve." She hopped down, caught the step with her hand, and straightened. Glitter dusted her hairline like she'd leaned into a constellation and brought some of it home.

Boxes were everywhere: BUNTING, LANTERNS, SIGNAGE, DONATION FORMS. The tub of zip-ties was already half-empty—Fallon organized an event like a crime scene. Everything was bagged, labeled, and placed where it wouldn't get stepped on.

"The marina took delivery on the stage," she said, pointing her chin toward the back door where light cut the room into stripes. "Fletcher texted me a picture, which is how I know he read his email for once."

"Must be love," Buddy said.

"More like fear. He knows I'll kick his ass." Fallon shoved a crate of teal ribbon toward him with the toe of her boot. "Second shelf. And don't crush the bows."

"I would never crush a bow. That would be criminal,"

He lifted the crate one-handed and slid it in beside a stack of lanterns. "Your theme is dangerously cheerful."

"That's the point." She wiped her brow... and then the side of her face. Only, he could tell the swipe of her forehead was a ruse to remove the tear that had escaped and dripped onto her cheek.

He decided to let that be the end of it—for now. He'd seen grief build shrines. He preferred the way Fallon did it—lamps, pie, a dunk tank to make a town laugh at something that shouldn't be funny and remember a girl who shouldn't have been lost. While Fallon tried to bury the idea that she should've been the girl to vanish into thin air, never to be seen again.

The kitchen line clattered on the other side of the swinging door. A radio turned low leaked a chorus everyone knew whether they wanted to or not. Someone chalked the daily board: FISH TACOS • CUBANS • KEY LIME PIE (YES, YOU WANT PIE).

"You two redecorating my storage room?" Fletcher leaned in the doorway in his Parks and Recreation uniform, holding a pair of tongs in his hand. The man had the face of someone who'd fought the world to a draw and decided to feed it anyway. He was the heart of the community—the hero who'd returned home with three other SEALs and quite literally saved the town from itself. He, Keaton, Hayes, and Dawson all held different service jobs. They owned Everglades Overwatch, an airboat tour company, and now they were the proud owners of the Crab Shack. They were the glue, the protectors, and trouble, wrapped in one tight-knit group that would do absolutely anything for their neighbors.

"We're curating." Fallon crossed the room and gave Fletcher a big bear hug. "It's different."

"Mm-hmm." Fletcher squeezed her shoulder as he stared at all the shelves filled with boxes. "Second shelf will hold if you don't stack the entire ocean on it. And I put paper down because glitter travels faster than the gossip in this town."

"Too late." Buddy swiped at his shirt, and the colorful stuff flew off like fairy dust. "Fallon's hair is turning pink, purple, and green."

She swiped her hairline and held up a palm that sparkled.

"Ah, that's evidence," Fletcher said.

"Of absolutely nothing." She laughed.

Baily, Fletcher's wife, slid in behind Fletcher with a tote tucked under her arm. She had that particular glow of a woman who was tired and fine with it—belly rounding under her soft Crab Shack tee, eyes bright, hair in a messy twist that shouldn't have looked as good as it did. On her hip—Kendra, two years old and all opinions, a wooden spoon clutched in one hand like a scepter.

"Volunteer hour check-in," Baily said, tilting the tote toward Fallon. "And if I find glitter in my hush puppies, I'm razing your booth fee to infinity."

"Send me the bill," Fallon said, taking the tote. "I'll pay by working a few swing shifts when you need help either here, at the marina, or at Everglades Overwatch."

"Acceptable currency." Baily kissed Kendra's cheek. "Say hi to Buddy and Fallon, sweetie."

Kendra considered Buddy with the solemn, negotiating stare toddlers saved for strangers who might be in charge of snacks. Then she lifted the spoon and declared, "Cookie. Want cookie."

"So do I," Buddy said. "We have a lot in common."

Fletcher reached out to tap the spoon. "In a little bit, pumpkin."

"Okay, DaDa." Kendra rested her head on her mother's shoulder.

Buddy sighed and grabbed another tub, and the room fell into a rhythm he liked—work that didn't require talking—to toddlers. Not that he didn't like kids, he did. But it brought up emotions he didn't want to deal with.

"Come on, sweetie. You can help Mommy with that box over there." Baily moved across the room.

Tape squeaked off a roll. A fan somewhere clicked every third rotation. Fallon crossed to the list she'd taped to the wall and drew a line through three items with the quick stroke of someone who understood momentum. Fletcher moved more boxes, and Buddy welcomed the silence.

The door swung again, and Keaton stepped in with his Fish and Wildlife hat in hand. He had the rested-unrested look of a man who got enough sleep to function and not a minute more.

"Looks like you all robbed a craft store," he said.

"We left them a note." Fletcher lifted another box and hauled it to one of the shelves.

"Hey, Keaton," Baily said. "You hungry? I have some pre-made salads for anyone who dared to help with the glitter mess."

"My wife would like me to say yes to that salad," Keaton said, mouth tipping. "But I'd rather have a hush puppy."

"Now you're speaking my language," Baily said, jumping to her feet, hiking Kendra to her hip.

Keaton stepped further inside and clocked the room the way a trained military man would.

Buddy went very still. He knew that stance. He practiced that stance a million times. Keaton had something serious to say.

"Dawson got a hit on that partial plate." Keaton turned to Fallon and then Buddy. "Came back to an LLC out of Fort Lauderdale—Blue Heron Boat Tours. Mean anything to you?"

Buddy's chest went tight around a breath. Blue again. He didn't move because he'd trained that response out of himself, but the word crawled up the back of his skull and sat there anyway.

"Never heard of them." Fallon shifted her gaze between Keaton and Buddy, as if she understood what the word Blue would do to him. "What kind of tours?"

"Waterway. Intercoastal. Looking at the big houses. A couple of Tiki party boats. Charter fishing boats. It's a decent-sized operation from what I can tell." Keaton pulled out a piece of paper and handed it to Buddy. "Nothing appears strange about the company. But a muscle car under an LLC? That's suspect."

"If it were a four-door sedan, or an SUV, it might not concern me, but between that text and the girl, it's got my hackles high," Buddy said. He kept his voice as even as he could. "I think we should run tech on Fallon's phone. I can get someone to do it."

Fallon inched close to him. Her arm pressed tight against his. It was subtle and maybe no one noticed.

"Aegis tech? Or old FBI friend tech?" Keaton asked.

"Mia Sarich," Buddy said. "Logan's wife from the Orlando Aegis Network office. She's good. I'll reach out later. I'm sure she can look at the phone remotely. If she can't, it's only a two-hour drive."

Fallon curled her fingers around his biceps and squeezed but said nothing.

"I think that's a good idea. Dawson's gonna want to see that report," Keaton said.

Baily reappeared with a plate that would offend a nutritionist and a personal trainer. Hush puppies and some strawberries to make it legal. She handed it to Keaton and set a sippy cup on the low shelf where Kendra could find it. "I meant to ask earlier, is Trinity over the morning sickness yet?" she asked. "She's been in the second trimester for a while, but I know that part lingers for her."

"Oh, she's past that and on to the stage of eating anything and everything at all hours of the night and complaining she's getting fat, only she's barely gained any weight. She never does." Keaton ran his fingers through his dark, curly hair. "She's also reminded me that this baby better come out as quick and painless as Petra."

Fletcher burst out laughing.

"It's not funny, man. That was thirty-three hours of pure hell. Trinity said things I haven't even heard a drunken sailor say. By the time she agreed to the drugs, it was too late. And then when Petra was finally here, Trinity looked at me and told me that we weren't having another one."

"And yet, here you are." Baily patted her belly. "She's really forgotten what labor was like?"

"I don't think it's that. She wants a princess—a sweet little girl who wants to wear dresses and play make-up. Not toss mud pies and play alligator wrangler with Victor and Max. I keep reminding her that we could also be having a boy and in true Trinity fashion, she looks at me like I stabbed her in the belly." Keaton sucked in a breath and sighed. "I love my wife. She's the sweetest, kindest, most generous woman in the world. Once this kid is here, she's not gonna care if it's a boy, a girl, or an alien. She certainly won't give a..." he glanced at Kendra, "... it won't matter what the kid is into as long as he or she is happy and healthy. This weird thing during pregnancy is Trini-ty's only flaw and it lasts nine freaking months."

Buddy leaned against the far wall and tried to push the conversation into white noise. These people were more than his friends. They'd become family when he had no blood left.

But they were pumping out kids faster than the no-see-ums attacked his ankles at dusk.

"That's true, and being a tomboy doesn't mean Petra won't be interested in girly things as she gets older," Baily said. "Look at Audra. When Dawson takes her out on a romantic date night, she cleans up nice."

"Petra is three and a half going on criminal—like her Aunt Audra," Keaton said, taking a hush puppy like a grown-up closing on a deal. "She started a new class and the first thing she did was smuggle in a baby snake."

"I might've done that once." Baily chuckled. "On a dare by Audra."

"Petra is a born leader and an independent thinker." Fletcher shifted another box.

"She's a born something," Keaton said, but his prideful tone told its own story. "She's certainly giving us a run for our money."

It was in these moments that Buddy remembered one of the biggest reasons he'd walked away from meaningful relationships. Being a family man wasn't anything that was going to happen to him. He'd given up that concept at... Jesus. Fallon's age. Damn, that hit a little too hard in the chest.

"Sorry to change the subject," Buddy said. "But any word on the girl?"

"Still sedated." Keaton shifted his stance, no longer relaxed. "Vitals are steady. Lab's backed up—but Dawson's asked for a rush. We'll see if he gets it. No ID. No one's called looking."

That was a sentence Buddy had heard too many times, in too many hallways that smelled like disinfectant and death. It didn't land softer here.

"Alright," Fletcher said after a beat, like he'd reached

the end of a list and hadn't found what he wanted on it. "We'll feed people and string lights in the meantime."

"Pie solves more fights than it starts," Baily said.

Keaton lifted his hat and adjusted it. "Text me when your tech is set. Fallon's my best officer. I need to know the vehicle has nothing to do with the text, and I have nothing to worry about."

"You got it," Buddy said.

Keaton left. The kitchen hummed louder, like the room had been holding its breath.

Fletcher clapped Buddy on the shoulder. "Dinner's on the house. I'll let the staff know." He looked at Fallon. "And you need to take more than a ten-minute break, for once in your life."

"You're so freaking bossy," Fallon said.

Kendra announced, "cookie," again for emphasis and tried to drink from Fletcher's tea when no one was looking. Baily caught her mid-slurp and redirected to the sippy cup with the ease of a woman who'd intercepted a thousand toddler crimes.

They finished three more boxes in the time it took the fan to click twenty times. Buddy liked the work—lift, stack, check the label, move to the next thing. The Tessa Project banners were folded in neat piles, white letters stenciled clean: HOPE STARTS HERE. Hope was an odd word for a man who'd spent a career measuring how much of it people had left. He didn't hate it today.

"I'm going to stretch my legs." Fallon pushed through the back door and the heat poured over him like a second shirt.

Buddy followed her out to the dock, knowing something triggered a response about Tessa. Boards gave slightly under his boots but held. The water beyond the pilings threw sunlight back in hard, white sheets. The channel markers were weathered from years of sun and rain, the numbers long faded. Ropes creaked. Someone out on the bay gunned a motor and then thought better of it—a pelican watched from a post like a man who'd seen every bad decision and expected another.

Fallon stopped halfway down the dock where the stretch between the Crab Shack and the marina opened up. From here, a person could see all the places a girl could walk off and disappear.

She stood and stared down the river. She didn't move. She didn't touch the rail. She just looked. "She took my shift. She covered for me so I could meet my boyfriend. My parents hated him, and for good reason. It was so stupid, because they were gonna find out anyway. Someone would've told them I wasn't working." Her voice didn't hitch. It narrowed. "I still come stand here anytime I'm at the Crab Shack during planning. Or at the marina. It feels wrong not to. Even when the Crab Shack was a run-down piece of crap or had closed down because of the fire and the murder and the fundraiser was at the community center, I still came."

Buddy set his hands on the railing because he needed to put them somewhere. "You built a thing that fills the space she left with people and noise and light. That isn't nothing."

She blew out a breath and stared out at the Glades as

if they had the answers she so desperately needed. "I saw the twitch of your eye and your shoulders shift when Keaton said Blue Heron. That's twice in two days."

"Three," Buddy said before he could stop himself. His voice stayed easy. He didn't let the word snag. "Text yesterday. Blue on her wrist at the hospital. Now this."

Fallon looked over, eyes green and steady. "You put those men away. It's a coincidence."

"I don't believe in them." The truth felt like the only valuable thing he had to offer right now. "Just because they're in prison doesn't mean they don't have power. They could still have people on the outside. What I don't understand is why a car would be looking at you."

"We don't know that."

"Come on. You're smart. Don't pretend a vehicle that slowed enough to get a good look at you, or make a statement that you're being watched, then take off, isn't something. It was enough that you tried to remember the plate number. And then there's that message that is too similar to what Simon, the asshole I put away, taunted me with. There's just too much."

She reached up and twisted her hair between her fingers. A tell that it worried her.

"I'll make sure Mia pulls the text clean. If there's anything tied to it, we'll see it."

She nodded like he'd given her a to-do list and not a promise. That was Fallon. Give her a thing to carry, and she'd carry it. Give her a town, and she'd carry that, too.

Down the dock, one of the Everglades Overwatch tour boats slid past the channel mouth, wake braiding behind it. Buddy watched the water settle and thought about names. Blue as an operation. Blue as a stamp. Blue as a company.

"You ever feel like the universe is unsubtle?" Fallon asked, mouth tipping without humor.

"Every day," he said. He kept his hands where they were, didn't reach for her because Keaton's printout was still hot in his pocket, the word blue wouldn't get out of his head, and the emotional rollercoaster of love, loss, and babies settled too deeply in his chest. "We're going to be careful."

"We?" she said softly.

"Yeah," he said. "We." For half a second, he tried to push her away. Tried to shove her out of his thoughts because of his past.

And he failed.

The we part just kept slipping out.

But maybe that was just his protective nature, not a man who wanted to start over or believed in second chances.

She bumped her shoulder lightly into his arm. Not much. Enough to say she'd heard him, and she'd hold him to it. Sunlight glinted off the water. The dock hummed underfoot. Inside, Fletcher shouted something about tea, and Baily laughed like the world wasn't tilting, which was its own kind of anchor.

Fallon straightened first. "I need to check on the stage and where Fletcher wants to put it."

"Alright."

"You coming?"

"I'll be up in a second," he said.

She started toward the door, then paused and looked back. Whatever guarded thing he'd seen in her the first night at Massey's wasn't there now. In its place was something steadier. "Let me know when you've set up your tech person because I really can't go without my phone right now," she said. "And if you think of or learn anything knew about the girl."

"I will."

She went inside. The door swung once and thumped shut, and the smell of frying fish slipped out and faded.

Buddy stayed on the dock, hands on the rail, watching light scatter across water that refused to hold still. His head felt the same—thoughts breaking apart before they could form anything whole. The name sat heavy against his ribs—Blue Heron—and every time he turned it over, it was still wrong.

Too many blues.

Too fast.

Not a coincidence.

He breathed once, slow, the way he'd learned to do when the floor moved, and he needed it to stop. Then he pushed off the rail, squared his shoulders, and went back inside to lift the next box because he'd promised Fallon he could be part of "we". He knew it wasn't what she really wanted, and he was going to have to find a way to either settle the rollercoaster or get off the ride.

Without hurting her.

Chapter Six

The Everglades shimmered like sweat on sick skin.

Even after years on patrol, Fallon still hadn't learned how to breathe properly in the dense heat only the Glades could provide. It bored down, thick and unrelenting, like the swamp had decided functioning lungs were optional. Cicadas droned in waves. A heron rose ahead of her skiff, beating silver off its wings before vanishing into the sawgrass.

It had been five days since they'd rescued the girl.

Five days of waiting for lab results that still hadn't come in.

And two days, since Buddy had kissed her like he meant it—and then gone quiet. So quiet, it was as if he'd ghosted her without completely ignoring her.

She told herself it hadn't been that long, and they were both busy with life and jobs. That she'd been the one who slipped out of the Crab Shack two days ago with barely a goodbye. But would it have killed him to reach out to see if she was okay?

He hadn't.

And out here, where the airboat's engine was the only sound and she didn't have to pretend to be fine, the silence between her and Buddy scraped harder than she wanted to admit.

She reached for her cell, which was in its holder mounted on the helm. She tapped the screen.

No text from Buddy. Not that she'd expected one. They were friends. Nothing more, and he didn't owe her anything.

She'd seen him twice yesterday and the first time had been when she'd brought her phone to his office for Mia Sarich to connect to it remotely. But he'd had to leave to meet a client, and Dove finished the job. The second time had been late that afternoon when he showed up at the marina to help with the stage. He'd committed, and if he was anything, he was a man of his word. But by the time he'd arrived, she was about to head out and they barely exchanged glances.

On the plus side, Mia had confirmed her phone was clean. No trace software, no virus, no ghost number embedded in the message. Which left her with one conclusion—someone had wanted her to see those words.

You can't save them all.

Fallon adjusted her sunglasses, cut the throttle, and let the airboat glide. The water here was glass. Still enough to see minnows flick like silver sparks beneath the surface.

She'd come farther than usual—Sector Six, where the channels grew narrow and the mangroves closed in like fingers. Officially, she was checking for illegal net traps after a tip came through on her cell from a local number. She didn't know who, but it was local, so worth checking out. Unofficially, she was chasing an itch that had been crawling under her skin since they'd found the girl.

She rubbed her nose. The Everglades had a rich scent, like a greenhouse full of moss and algae. But there was something in the air that didn't belong—and it wasn't just the fuel and bilge water wafting off her boat.

Pushing her glasses on top of her head, she narrowed her stare and scanned the area and that's when she saw it. A slick of oil floating between two roots. Her gut tightened.

The oil spread from behind a tangle of mangroves, where the cut line was wrong—like someone had forced their way through. She lifted the binoculars from the dash. The lens caught a hunk of metal—half-hidden, low in the water. Not a prop.

A barrel.

She reached for her radio. "FWC Four-One-Two, checking possible illegal discharge—Sector Six, south edge of the run—"

The rest of her call drowned under the roar of another engine.

Louder. Closer.

Fallon whipped her head around just in time to see a dark airboat blast from the cover of reeds, wake curling behind it like claws. Two men. No markings. Mounted rifle gleaming under the sun.

"Son of a—"

The first shot tore through open air. The second hit water a foot from her hull, spraying mud and algae. Fallon slammed the throttle. Her boat screamed forward, spray pelting her face. Bullets pinged off the stern rail.

"FWC Officer Reeves—under fire—Sector Six," she shouted into the mic, but static swallowed her voice. The other airboat's roar was too close.

She ducked as another round shredded the canopy above her head. Her fuel gauge blinked. The needle dropped fast—too fast.

"Damn it." She jerked the handle, skimming the edge of a narrow pass. Roots blurred past. The smell of gas cut through the rot and salt.

The channel opened, and she caught sight of movement to her right—another airboat, smaller, familiar. Trent.

He was with Harley Mavis, the new mangrove trimmer, the one who didn't know when to quit asking questions. They were maybe fifty yards away, parked along the edge of a flat where the sawgrass turned gold in the sun.

Trent stood when he saw her boat fishtailing. His arm shot up. The bastard had no fear.

"Get down," she shouted, though he couldn't hear her.

Her hull slammed a wake, ricocheted. The steering yoke jerked hard, nearly sending her into the mangroves.

Behind her, the man holding the mounted rifle fired again. The crack echoed across the marsh like thunder.

Fallon swerved into open water. Her boat coughed, then caught, then coughed again. The smell of gasoline thickened. She was running out of time.

Through the blur of adrenaline, she saw Trent climb back into his seat, spin his airboat, and gun the engine in the opposite direction.

What the fuck was he doing?

She glanced between the tiny island and the wider open waters. Neither option would provide safety.

An engine whine cutting from in front startled her. She turned just as Trent's boat flew into view, screaming past hers like a missile.

No one was at the helm.

"Trent," she yelled, but the word tore apart in the wake.

The seemingly empty airboat veered toward the gunmen. For a heartbeat, Fallon thought it was going to crash straight into them. Instead, a flash of motion on the deck—a shape—then something thick and alive launched through the air. Long, with a large, raging mouth wide open.

A python.

She blinked, disbelieving.

The snake hit the gunmen's deck in a writhing coil. One of them swore and fired reflexively, but he'd already lost control. The boat pitched sideways as the python twisted, angry and loud.

Fallon didn't waste the chance. She gunned her throttle, trying to outrun the chaos, but the cough of her engine came back worse. The gas smell bit at her eyes.

A new roar rose in front of her.

Keaton.

His airboat barreled through the reeds, lights and sirens blazing.

Fallon risked a glance back. The gunmen fired again —wildly this time. One shot caught Trent's hull. The other—

Her heart stopped. Trent staggered.

"Trent," she screamed.

The gunmen peeled off, their airboat limping but moving fast, disappearing down a side channel.

Keaton's boat closed in. Fallon cut her engine and coasted hard into Trent's line. Harley was already kneeling beside him, hands slick with blood, pressing down on his abdomen.

"I told him not to—he wouldn't listen—" Harley's voice cracked.

Fallon jumped across the boats, boots slipping. "Hold pressure. Do you know if the bullet exited?"

"It did," Harley said. "Clean pass, but it's bad."

Trent's face had gone gray, sweat shining across his forehead. His eyes fluttered open. "Did the snake hit its target?"

"Yeah," Fallon said. "Ten points for accuracy."

He tried to grin. Failed. "Told you I had good aim."

"Save your strength." Harley wiped her chin on her shoulder. "You're going to need it for that hot date of yours, tonight. Though, it's gonna happen in a hospital room."

"That can't be sexy." Trent coughed.

Fallon stared at Trent. "Please tell me you don't actually have a date with Dove?"

"Of course he does," Harley said. "He's gone through all the locals."

"You haven't dated me." His voice was barely above a whisper.

"That's because I'm smarter than everyone else in this town." Harley held one hand on his gut, the other on his back.

"Not true. You've just got the hots for Cullen Monroe," Fallon said.

Harley didn't confirm or deny, and that spoke volumes.

Keaton came in hot, bumping his hull alongside hers. "Chopper's inbound—fourteen minutes out and docks are twenty, so we hold here."

Fallon cut Trent's shirt, pressed gauze and wrapped. Harley kept pressure. Blood-soaked fast, dark and too much.

Trent wheezed. "Hey, Reeves..."

"Yeah?"

"Tell Buddy he owes me a beer."

"You'll tell him yourself."

The air throbbed with heat and the rot of churned water. The Everglades were too quiet. No birds, no gators close enough to break the surface. Just the low, distant hum of an approaching helicopter.

Fallon looked east, into the sun, until the glare turned white.

She wasn't religious, but she found herself praying anyway—half to the swamp, half to whatever gods watched over fools who threw snakes at gunmen.

The blades hit first, chopping through the air, the sound growing louder, closer. Fallon's hair whipped against her face.

"Hold on, Trent," she said, voice barely audible over the wind. "Hold on."

The medevac chopper crested the cypress line, sunlight flashing off its rotors. Keaton signaled with a flare. The wind beat down, scattering sawgrass and spray.

Fallon stayed low beside Trent, hand pressed to his shoulder, the swamp wind hammering every inch of her skin.

The world narrowed to noise, blood, and the smell of jet fuel.

The helicopter dipped low, wind beating the swamp into submission. Keaton braced against the gust, shouting over the roar as the medics lowered themselves onto the boat—two of them, lean and efficient, gear bags slung across their chests.

"Male, late thirties," Keaton said. "Gunshot wound—entry right lower abdomen, exit right flank. Conscious but fading."

One medic nodded and dropped beside Trent, assessing fast. The other passed Fallon a roll of gauze without looking, already unwrapping saline.

Fallon took it. Her fingers were slick with blood. It

felt tacky, too warm. She didn't realize she was shaking until she tried to press again and Keaton's hand steadied hers.

"Hey," he said, softer now, voice pitched for her alone. "You did good."

She swallowed hard. "I didn't do anything."

"Sure you did. You lived, and so will he."

Trent groaned as they lifted him onto the basket dangling from the chopper. His eyes cracked open. "That... snake's gonna need a raise."

Harley let out a strangled laugh that sounded more like relief. "You can argue with him about it when you're not bleeding on my boots."

Trent's mouth twitched. "Deal."

The medics secured Trent in the basket and signaled thumbs up. Seconds later, the basket was inside the helicopter, and a ladder dangled from the opening. One of the medics climbed up. Then the second. Wind howled across the flats as they lifted. The noise turned her chest hollow.

Fallon shielded her face from the spray, watching as the blades of the chopper beat the air until it felt like her heartbeat had synced with them.

Then it was gone—just the echo, and the smell of gas and salt and swamp.

Keaton shut off his radio and leaned against his console. "That didn't feel completely random. Not when we found a girl out here five days ago."

Fallon nodded. "I know."

He looked at her, jaw tight. "We'll run it down. State,

Feds, whoever. I've already sent a message to Dawson and Buddy—"

Her head snapped up. "Buddy knows?"

"He was with Dawson when the call came through. I gave them an update, and he's been blowing up my phone ever since." Keaton paused, side-eyeing her. "I bet yours is too, and if you don't respond soon, he'll just show up like a beast."

"I'm fine," she said, too fast.

"Didn't say you weren't."

Keaton checked the channel again, then climbed back into his airboat. "We'll need to tow you in since you've got no gas left. And we'll need to check the hull back at the docks."

"Copy that."

"Harley, Dawson will want a statement. You good to drive Trent's boat in?"

"Yeah." Harley nodded.

"Alright. Let's go before someone else shows up. Coast Guard is gonna send someone back here and will add in patrols now." He tossed Fallon a line, and she tied it to the bow cleat before easing back behind the helm. "Be careful what you touch, Dawson will need to check the boats over, see if we can find any wedged bullets anywhere."

"Copy that," Harley said.

Fallon stared at her cell, and a message from Buddy stared back.

Buddy: *Heard what happened—worried about you. Check in, okay?*

Nine words, and she felt them land low and steady, the way his voice had sounded when he'd whispered her name right before he'd kissed her that first time.

She could almost see him in her head—jaw tight, eyes dark, pacing in his kitchen because sitting still never was his thing.

Another text.

Buddy: *Don't make me drive out there. Because I will.*

Her throat caught. A laugh wanted to come up but died halfway. She typed, I'm fine, and stared at the words for a long second. Then deleted them.

Fallon: *I'm fine. Chopper just left with Trent.*

The three dots pulsed.

Buddy: *Good. But don't tell me fine if you're not.*

That one got her. Because he would know. He always did.

She wiped her palm on her pants and tucked the phone away, staring out across the water as Keaton slowly navigated back toward the FWC docks. Somewhere under the sound of cicadas and her own heartbeat, she thought she heard the echo of gunfire again—the mechanical stutter that didn't belong in her swamp. Only it wasn't real—not this time.

Fallon drew in a breath, held it until her ribs hurt, and slowly let it go.

She could almost hear Buddy's voice in her head. We'll be careful.

"Yeah," she murmured to the swamp. "We better be."

Chapter Seven

The lights at Harvey's Cabins glowed low, a handful of porch bulbs cutting through the night like memory—warm, tired, and just bright enough to remind him how late it was.

Buddy parked in front of Fallon's place, shut off the engine, and sat there long enough for the crickets to fill the silence. The air hung thick with salt and swamp—Florida's version of grief.

Trent was stable.

The doctor had said it three times, like Buddy wouldn't believe him.

He'd seen the man himself—gray, pale, still managing to charm two nurses and make Dove blush hard enough to color the entire room. That was damn near impossible to do. But if those two lasted more than a week, it would be a miracle.

Buddy half expected to find Fallon at the hospital. Of

course, he'd been late getting there, and she'd already left. So he came here—because he had to see her. Had to make sure she was actually fine.

Her house sat quiet except for the low hum of her AC unit kicking on and off. The porch light was still on, a habit she'd picked up after the night her friend disappeared. She'd told him that once, offhand, like it was nothing. But he knew better. People left lights on for ghosts.

He stepped onto the porch, boots whispering over the wood, and knocked.

A second later, the door opened. She stood in cutoff shorts and a thin tank, hair in a messy knot, eyes tired but alert. She looked like someone who'd spent the last few hours replaying every second of her near miss—and then kept going because that's what she did. She was strong that way. One of the strongest people he knew. He admired her. Adored her.

The last thing he wanted to do was hurt her. But he knew he'd already done that, and he couldn't do it again.

"Hey," she said quietly.

"Hey, back." He shoved his hands in his pockets. "I didn't mean to wake you."

"You didn't." She hesitated, fingers still on the door. "I was just watching some stupid reality show. Women screaming at each other. It's a lesson in mental health and my guilty pleasure."

He chuckled. "I can't picture you watching that crap."

Fallon's lips curved to a smile that didn't quite make it to her eyes. "Oh, it's freaking hilarious. It's better than watching Silas and old man Peters play chess while waving guns at each other."

"That is something," he said, holding her gaze. "I wanted to see you."

She blinked, that slow kind of blink that tried to hide too many thoughts. "You could've texted."

"That would be communicating through words. I wanted to see you with my eyes while I had a conversation with you. Not the same thing."

"Semantics." She opened the door wider. "Come in."

The house smelled faintly of cider and cinnamon. Her boots sat by the door, next to a half-unpacked crate marked TESSA PROJECT—SUPPLIES. He followed her into the kitchen, where she reached for two glasses and a dusty whiskey bottle with a peeling label.

"You look like you need this more than I do," she said, pouring generously.

"Probably true." He took the glass when she handed it over. Their fingers brushed. Warm. Comfortable. Familiar. And yet, utterly frightening.

They drank in silence for a while, the kind of silence that had shape—thick with things neither wanted to say first.

She set down her glass with a soft clink. "Trent could've died today—for me."

"But he didn't."

"He didn't have to do anything but call it in," she

said. "What he did was just plain crazy and his mother was in tears when they brought him in. I was waiting for her famous lecture about being reckless, but then she turned to me and told me how grateful she'd been that he'd been there. That he'd done the right thing, just like his father would've done if he'd still been alive. What a mind fuck."

"Fallon—"

She held up her hand. "I keep thinking what if he hadn't been there. What if Harley hadn't been there? What if I hadn't seen that oil slick? It's just luck. Dumb, stupid luck that any of us made it out. Change one thing and we're having a completely different conversation ."

"You can what-if yourself until the cows come home, but one thing will still stay the same. You could've died out there today."

Her mouth curved into a humorless smile. "You ever try telling your brain that when you've been shot at, and someone you care about takes the bullet for you?"

"More than once," he said. "It doesn't listen, but eventually, it settles. It has to."

Her gaze flicked up, sharp and searching. "You've been avoiding me."

He couldn't deny it. He wouldn't. That would make him a bigger dick than he already was. "I have."

"Why?"

He rubbed a hand across his jaw, the rasp of his stubble grounding him. "Because you scare the hell out of me."

"I don't know how to take that."

Buddy poured another two fingers and sipped, letting it burn. "You're thirty. You've got this whole life stretched out ahead of you. I've already lived mine. Or at least the part that mattered."

"That's crap," she said with the kind of sharpness that cut a little too deep.

"It's truth." He leaned back against the counter, glass hanging from his fingers. "You ever tell someone you'd give them everything, and then realize you already gave it all away to a job that didn't give a damn if you lived or died?"

She frowned. "Careers aren't people. They don't have feelings. They're what you do, not who you are." She lifted her tumbler to her lips

She had him there. He stared at the whiskey. "I'm talking about my marriage."

Fallon coughed on her drink. "You mentioned that once in passing, but you've never talked about it."

"Not many people know I was ever married, especially in this town. Hell, I never told Chloe, though she probably knows since she and I met shortly after Callie and I divorced."

"That's a shocker. She's a close friend. I'm surprised it was never discussed."

He shrugged.

"You brought it up, so I take it you want to tell me about it."

That was insightful. And true. "We met right out of

Quantico. She wanted kids. I wanted to save the world." He chuckled. "She got tired of sleeping alone, tired of me chasing monsters while I became one. One morning, she told me she was leaving. Said she didn't love me anymore. Said she was pregnant with another man's child."

Fallon's expression didn't change. Her eyes did. Softer. Sad. But there wasn't an ounce of pity. Nor was there resentment or anger. Emotions he'd gotten used to the few times he'd told the story.

"I didn't even fight her," he continued. "Because she was right. I'd already left. I just hadn't had the decency to pack a bag."

He polished off his drink and set it aside. "I fell apart. Got sloppy. Almost got fired. Almost got killed—more than once. It took over a year to crawl out of it, and I swore I'd never do that again."

"You mean fall apart," Fallon stated rather than questioned.

"No. I mean the whole love, commitment, marriage thing. It gutted me and not in the way you think. It's not that I didn't know what I had until I walked out the door, because I did. Callie was—is—an amazing woman. But I was the job. Needed the job more than I needed her, and that's why I fell apart."

"I don't believe that," Fallon said. "A man doesn't dive into a stupor for that long for nothing. You were mourning."

"Maybe, but I was also accepting something about myself. That I wasn't cut out to be a family man. I never had it in me, and I nearly stole that from her." He'd told himself that for so many years that he believed it, besides parts of it were true. He could've given up his job if he tried. But he never really tried to be a good husband. That was the part he could never say out loud. "You want to know the messed-up part?" he asked. "You're the same age Callie was when she walked out. Same damn age. And I'm standing here wanting something I shouldn't. I don't have anything to give you that isn't temporary. You deserve more than that."

Fallon's hand tightened around her glass. Her eyes didn't leave his. "That's not your decision to make."

He opened his mouth, but she cut him off—quiet, steady.

"You tell yourself it's noble. That you're protecting me or saving me from heartbreak, but it's fear. You're scared of losing again, so you left before I could even decide if I wanted to stay. Before we knew if one kiss meant anything at all."

That hit him harder than he would have expected.

She took a slow step closer. "You don't get to make that choice for me. That's not noble. That's unfucking fair. Not to mention selfish."

He stared at her—words locked somewhere behind the ache in his chest.

For a second, he thought about saying it—about admitting that she wasn't just someone who'd gotten under his skin, that he'd started to believe maybe he could have something again. That she'd been part of the reason he pushed so fucking hard to open the south office in Calusa Cove. Not the entire reason, but his attraction—

feelings—had factored into that want—that need. But the truth sat like gravel in his throat.

He couldn't promise her anything. So he didn't. "I'm sorry."

Fallon's jaw clenched. "Then you should go."

That landed like a gut punch.

He nodded once, slow, and stepped toward the door. He opened it and paused on the threshold, half expecting her to say something—to stop him. She didn't.

The screen door clicked shut behind him, soft as breath.

The night hit like a fist of humidity and regret. Crickets sang, frogs croaked, and his heart felt too loud in the stillness.

For a long moment, Buddy just stood there on the porch, staring out across the cabins toward the shimmer of the Glades. He could almost hear his ex-wife's voice, all those years ago. You're going to end up utterly alone and broken.

Maybe she'd been right.

He made it to the steps before something inside him cracked. He turned. Went back.

He hit the door with his fist once. Twice. Hard enough for the wood to rattle. "Fallon," he called.

Nothing.

He slammed again. "I've got something to say and I'm not leaving until you open the door."

Another second. Then the handle turned. She stood there, hair loose now, eyes bright and furious. "What the hell do you want?"

He exhaled like he'd been holding his breath for years. "I can't make promises," he said, voice low, rough-edged. "I've been broken for a long time. I can't promise I won't hurt you."

Her chin lifted, steady, defiant. "That's fine. I'm not built for picket fences and decisions past today. Besides, I can't promise I won't crush you."

The air between them snapped—charged and alive.

He moved first. Closed the space between them in two steps. His hands came up, cupping her face, and then he kissed her—hard, hungry, desperate in a way that felt like both surrender and survival.

Fallon didn't hesitate. She met him halfway, fingers gripping his shirt, pulling him closer. The kiss was heat and apology, whiskey and want, a collision neither of them tried to avoid.

When they broke apart, they were both breathing hard, foreheads pressed together.

"This is a bad idea," he whispered.

"Definitely," she said. "But I've had worse." Her lips curved, soft and dangerous. "So much worse." She tugged him inside, slamming the door shut.

The cool kiss of the air conditioning was a jarring contrast to the heat simmering off them, breathing heavy, their bodies pressed closer than they had ever been. He let out a slight, broken sound at the feel of her softness against him, the brush of fabric against fabric before their bodies inevitably drew together.

In his mind, this was all kinds of wrong. He wasn't good for her. He wasn't suitable for anyone. Yet, he was selfish enough to want her, to take what she was willing to give.

"Bedroom's this way," Fallon whispered, a thread of laughter coloring her voice. She slipped from his grasp, and Buddy trailed after her like a man who'd follow her anywhere.

His gaze flitted across her back, the way her hair brushed against her back, the expanse of taut shoulders, and then the sway of those shorts as the space between them grew. She moved like a woman who knew her power, who understood the impact she had.

Her bedroom was filled with the glow of the moon through the partially opened blinds. Her eyes flickered to him, uncertain for a moment before she turned towards the bed, pulling off her tank top without hesitation.

His breath hitched, caught between surprise and desire, as the smooth plane of her bare back met his skin, casting shadows that danced over and highlighted each dip and curve of her frame. This was Fallon—raw, vulnerable, but undeniably fearless.

She tossed her top aside, her bare skin glowing in the soft light diffusing through the window. His heart pounded an unsteady rhythm, echoing the throbbing pulse that had taken up residence in his veins. The air seemed to tighten around him, the scent of her—vanilla and coconut—sweet and maddening, wrapping itself around every atom in the room, setting his senses ablaze.

The moment hung suspended, stretched between heartbeats as he stood there, frozen, caught between the urge to retreat and the visceral pull towards her.

"Are you just going to stand there?" Her voice, sultry and amused, cut through his hazy thoughts, prodding him back into fevered reality.

In response, he reached for her, his hands finding her hips. His fingers dug into the soft fabric of her shorts, grounding him in the present— this was Fallon, alive and warm, beneath his touch. "I'm here," he murmured, his voice barely rising above the deafening beat of his own pulse.

She chuckled softly, a sound that did unthinkable things to his insides, before her fingers were on his shirt, her touch searing through the cotton, plucking at the buttons. Her lips found his in the darkness, their bodies aligning in an intoxicating dance that was now becoming familiar yet remained utterly terrifying.

Her lips were molten silk against his, a fervent promise that sent a shockwave coursing through his veins. Wordlessly, Fallon guided his hands to the waistband of her shorts.

He moved slowly, nerves wreaking havoc on his usually steady fingers. The button popped open, and he tugged the zipper down gently. The shorts slipped down, pooling at her feet, revealing her in her intimate glory.

There was no further hesitation as he urged her back onto the bed, her body sinking into the mattress. His hands traced the curve of her hip, the dip of her waist in a journey of revelation, each touch filled with his raw worship and desire. His lips left a trail from her collarbone down to her naval, each kiss punctuated with a gasp or writhe of pleasure from her.

He pinched and plucked at her tight nipples with one hand, while the other toyed gently with her clit, circling before slipping inside and repeating, all while he watched her in suspended awe.

Fallon arched into him as his mouth found her clit, a moan tearing from her throat that shot straight to his groin. The wet heat of her was overwhelming and drove him into a frenzy that matched the heady pulse of her body beneath his.

His hands skimmed under her, fitting snugly around her ass to pull her closer, granting him further access into the bittersweet paradise that was her scent and taste. Her fingers tangled in his hair, tightening sporadically in time with the flicks of his tongue. The tiny gasps and gentle bucking of her body were pure music to his senses, stirring a profound longing within him that he'd been denying for far too long.

"Buddy," she breathed, her voice shaky and gasping.

He flattened his hand over her taut belly as she quivered under his touch, on the verge of exploding. She tasted like honey, and he couldn't get enough. He lifted his head for a second, catching her gaze.

"Yes," he encouraged. His fingers worked faster and his thumb strummed her clit.

She bucked against his hand, squeezing her eyes shut as she rode out the wave. Her breath hitched for a second before her body trembled, every string pulled taut before snapping.

As the shudders began to subside, he slid back up her

body. "I should've asked this sooner," he whispered. "Birth control?"

"On the pill," she managed. "But there are condoms in the drawer if we need..." she blinked a few times, catching her breath. "... do we need them?"

"I don't. Clean."

"Me too." She wiggled underneath, and he nearly came undone.

He pushed himself into her, and everything tilted. Steadying himself for a moment, he stared into her eyes.

She clenched around him, her walls contracting again. He groaned, his own release dangerously close.

The world narrowed to just them, their heavy breaths, the slick sound of skin on skin, the soft squelch every time he thrust into her, the delicious friction driving them both to the edge.

"I'm close," he warned her, his voice a choked whisper as he struggled to hold onto his control. He wanted to feel her come apart beneath him one more time before he allowed himself the same pleasure.

"D-don't stop," she said, her legs wrapping around his waist and pulling him deeper.

He adjusted his angle, his thrusts changing into a deep grind that made him see stars. She clenched around him as her second orgasm ripped through her, her cries muffled in the crook of his neck where she'd buried her face.

The feel of her squeezing him, the sweet friction of her body milking him, was too much. He let out a low groan as he followed her into oblivion.

Exhausted and sated, but not wanting to crush her with his weight, he slid to the side, pulling her into his embrace. He traced lazy circles on her bare skin and stared at the ceiling fan as it rotated above.

She draped an arm and a leg over his body as she tugged a sheet over them. "You're not going to sneak out in the middle of the night, are you?"

He pressed his lips against her temple. "Not my style. When I leave, you'll be kissing me goodbye at the door, or kicking me out because I snore."

"And what if I snore?" She glanced up and smiled. "Because it's been known to happen."

"I guess I'll have to wake you up and find a way to quiet you."

"That's a promise I can get on board with."

"I'm an old man. Twice in the same night is not happening."

"Maybe not for you, but no reason you can't do things—"

He covered her mouth. "Don't tempt me. Now, close your eyes and get some sleep."

"On one condition."

"I'm not sure I want to hear this."

"More like a question." She rested her chin on his chest. "When was the last time you tested the theory on whether or not—"

"Years," he admitted. "But I know morning will work, and I like shower sex, so let's not ruin that for me, okay?"

"Jeez, you're demanding."

"You have no idea." He kissed her sweet lips and then closed his eyes.

His last coherent thought before he drifted off was that he'd deal with the consequences of this night sometime—probably in the near future. For now, he'd just relish having her in his arms.

Even if it was only temporary.

Even if he didn't deserve her.

Chapter Eight

Fallon gasped, jerking awake, her heart pounding hard enough for it to hurt.

She blinked, unable to focus on anything but darkness. It was thick, quiet, and wrong. She slowed her breathing, hoping it would steady her racing pulse. Buddy's warmth registered as her eyes adjusted to the thin light of the moon carving through the window. The sound of something dragging against wood tickled her ears and every muscle stiffened. Then came a shatter, muffled, but no mistaking the source. Glass.

She flung aside the sheet and was halfway upright when Buddy's hand closed around her wrist, steady, quiet. She gasped.

"What?" he whispered.

"I heard something—like glass breaking."

He was out of bed in a blink, the mattress lifting with his weight. He reached for the nightstand. "Shit. Gun is in the truck."

She slid open the dresser drawer, fingers shaking only a little, and pulled out her Glock. "There's another weapon in the closet."

Buddy raced toward the side of the room. The low light cut over the muscle in his shoulders as he moved. He yanked open the door. "Where?"

"Shelf. Pink shoebox."

He reached up, snagged the box, pulled out the weapon, then spun and snagged his cell. His face lit up under the dimmed screen as he thumbed at it one-handed.

"What are you doing?" she asked, hiking up her shorts and pulling her shirt over her head.

"Sterling. Dove. Dawson," he said. "Better safe than sorry." He found his pants and managed to stumble into them as if this were his normal routine.

Fallon's heart drummed in her ears—the kind of pulse that made sound feel thick and close.

They moved fast—barefoot, practiced, silent. The floorboards were cool underfoot. The faint scent of pear from her candles filled the air. The AC kicked on, and she nearly jumped out of her skin.

Buddy gave her a hand signal, pointing toward the left. Then he moved right.

They swept through the hall. Bedroom—clear. Bathroom—clear. The silence thickened with every step.

In the kitchen, the clock over the fridge ticked far too loud. The blower for the AC had kicked off five minutes ago. The air had already turned damp with the kind of humidity that made her skin feel slick even without sweat.

Buddy's flashlight from his cell cut across the counters, caught a glint in the window. He paused, listening.

Outside, something shifted—quick, sharp, then gone.

Fallon's throat went dry. "Front door," she whispered.

Buddy nodded once. They moved as one like they'd done this a dozen times together.

He eased the lock open, slow and quiet, gun raised. The door swung with a soft creak.

The night spilled in—wet, warm, and wrong. The air carried swamp and mud and the faint tang of leftover fried catch of the day from the pub down the street.

Buddy stepped out first, scanning the shadows beyond the porch. The cicadas hadn't come back. Even the frogs had gone still. The only sound was the slight rustle of the palm leaves dangling in the breeze.

Fallon followed, her weapon steady.

That's when she saw it—white, too bright under the light of the moon.

An envelope. Centered perfectly on the table next to her rocking chair, her name was written clean across the front. FALLON REEVES.

Her stomach flipped. "Buddy."

He followed her gaze, then froze.

"Don't touch it," he said. His voice was the kind of low she'd learned to listen to—the one that meant danger had a face, even if they couldn't see it yet. "And don't move. Not until I've had a chance to look around." He crouched, examining the wood floor of the porch, his gaze scanning every inch.

Her eyes slid past the porch to his truck parked in the drive. The sight knocked the air out of her lungs.

The windshield was spiderwebbed, the side windows punched clean through. Glass glinted across the gravel like ice under the streetlamp.

"Jesus," she whispered.

"What?" Buddy stood and glanced over his shoulder. "Shit." He was down the steps in a flash. "Stay there."

"Like hell—"

He turned and glared. "Please."

That one word stopped her cold.

He moved with the controlled precision of someone who'd cleared too many dark scenes. He bent to one knee, phone to his ear. He rattled off her address first, then said, "Vandalized truck, personalized note left on the porch. No signs of entrance to the house. All doors locked and secure. No other evidence. Send a unit."

He tucked his cell in his pocket and glanced toward the road, every line of him wound tight. "They're gone. But not long gone."

"How do you know?" she asked.

He pointed to the truck. "If they were still here, and this was more than a message, we wouldn't be vertical anymore." He tiptoed back to the porch, dodging broken glass. "Do you have gloves and a letter opener?"

"Gloves and a pocket knife."

"Get them," he commanded.

"Shouldn't we wait for—"

"Just do it." He held her gaze, and not just any gaze. It was a stare she'd seen before—four years ago—during the Ring Finger case. The look was focused. Determined. And it demanded people listen.

She turned on her heels and raced inside. Her breath uneven. Her pulse wild. She'd been in dangerous situations before. Not often. It wasn't a regular thing in her job. She dealt more with citations when people fished or hunted in the wrong places—or tried to skirt the laws. The most hazardous parts of her job came from dealing with reptiles in need of rescuing.

But she had never had anyone vandalize anything on her property and leave her a mysterious note. Or been under fire.

All those things happened in the same day.

She found the knife and the gloves and headed back outside. "Here." She handed them to Buddy.

He snapped the gloves in place and reached for the envelope, careful, using two fingers, even though his prints wouldn't be left behind. However, she knew enough about evidence that this was about not disturbing anything the perpetrator left behind.

Fallon stood next to him, leaning over his shoulder as he slowly pulled out a single piece of paper. She stared at the words on the page.

He couldn't save them all.

He won't be able to save them all.

Blue 42.

A gasp caught in her throat. Tears burned her eyes. "Does *he* mean you?"

"I'm pretty sure it does," he said quietly. "But whoever left it obviously wanted you to see it." He set both the envelope and the note on the table. Easing off the gloves, he stuffed them in his back pocket.

The events of the last few days rolled through her mind like a movie on fast-forward. She couldn't slow it down. She couldn't stop it. And she sure as hell couldn't make sense of it.

Abruptly, Buddy stood and marched across the porch. He gripped the railing and stared across the street. "Someone's been watching me. They're fucking with me, and now they're fucking with you." He turned. His eyes were dark and full of rage. He pointed to his truck. "They knew I was here."

"Okay." She swallowed her pulse. She wanted to take a step back. This was not the man she'd been with just a few short hours ago. This was a man who held pain and anger too close to his heart. She knew how that felt. Knew that if he didn't find a way to let it go, it would not only continue to rule him, but it would destroy who he was at his core.

She wasn't going to let that happen. Not on her watch. Not while whatever this was between them still existed. She inched closer. "But I got that first text before any of this happened. Before, we spent any real time together."

"You're forgetting we've known each other for four years. Whenever I could get back to town, we managed to see each other."

"Nothing ever happened."

"No. But we did have some interesting text conversations that indicated we were interested."

"Mia said my phone was clean."

"It is, but you said it's a new phone. That you got it six months ago. We don't know what's on the old one."

Her stomach churned. "And I traded it in."

He ran his fingers through his hair. "Not to mention, I had a job to do in the location you found that girl. A job that was a bit of a waste as the client won't be coming through the Glades after all." He crossed his arms. "Whoever did this wanted me to find her. You just got there first."

"Are you saying this has to do with that case?"

"It's all language from it, except Blue 42. I don't know what 42 means. But Simon Court, one of the men I put behind bars, was—is—a ruthless man with no soul. Two victims died the day I slapped cuffs on him. He smiled at me, knowing they were dead, and told me that I couldn't save them all. That I'd never be able to save them. That's when it hit me, I stopped one massive pipeline, but trafficking is endless. He's not the only monster out there."

"So, you think this is someone else, and whoever it is, is targeting you the same way Simon did?" It made sense. Sort of. "Doesn't the FBI and other law enforcement agencies keep things from the public for that reason and others?" It wasn't really a question, because she knew the answer.

"Simon's a powerful man. We arrested seventeen people, but that doesn't mean there aren't others loyal to him out there. Or he could've found a way to pay some-one. Pulling strings from prison isn't impossible."

The air shifted. A car engine filled the silence. She shivered, but she wasn't cold.

Images of Tessa, wearing Fallon's jacket, walking out of the Crab Shack, waving goodbye to old man Tomey and Silas, never to be seen again.

A Calusa Cove patrol cruiser rolled up, headlights throwing a harsh light across the drive.

Jasper Newton stepped out, flashlight in hand. "I got a report of vandalism and a possible break-in. Everyone alright?"

"Not exactly," Fallon said.

Jasper's beam caught the truck and to his credit, he didn't even flinch. Not bad for a young rookie. "I'll need to call the crime scene unit from State, and I'll also need to wake up the Chief."

"I don't think that's necessary." Buddy pointed toward Harvey's Cabins. "I texted him, and there's his SUV."

Sure enough, Dawson's vehicle was coming down the access road from the bed and breakfast and turning onto the main road. He pulled up in front of the house and was out of his SUV in seconds. He jogged over barefoot, T-shirt and jeans, pistol holstered at his hip. "That's an interesting place to park your truck. Kind of makes a statement."

Fallon's cheeks heated from a combination of pure embarrassment and unchecked frustration.

"I didn't get you out of bed at three in the morning for

wisecracks." Buddy ran his hand through his hair—again. "You need to see this."

Dawson made his way up the porch and stared at the piece of paper without touching it. His brow furrowed as his lips drew together in a tight line. "Jasper, call Detective Lester from State. Don't go through the office, contact him directly."

"On it, Chief," Jasper said.

"Lester's not gonna like the Aegis Network working on this, and I won't tell my team to stand down. This is personal. Not to mention they brought Fallon into it... because of me. All because of that fucking case."

"You don't know that." Dawson planted his hands on his hips.

"I've been incredibly vocal when it comes to human trafficking," Fallon said. "I speak at schools. I do volunteer work. I have my fundraiser. I could've pissed someone off. Stepped on someone's toes."

"What you do is incredible and most definitely needed." Buddy's hardness had softened slightly, but that darkness was right under the surface. She could feel it radiate off his skin. "But has anyone ever targeted you? Or sent you a message warning you to stop?"

"Well, no."

"This isn't about you," Buddy said.

She glared. "It is when someone tries to kill me."

"Someone has a target on both your backs, and it's my job to protect you." Dawson shifted his gaze toward Jasper, who was doing a perimeter check of the truck, light sweeping the gravel. "The Jane Doe case has been handed off completely to the FBI."

"I'm not surprised. Who's lead?" Buddy asked.

"Special Agent Liam Flagler," Dawson said. "Chloe gave him high praises."

"He's a good man. Great agent. I've worked with him before." Buddy leaned against the railing. "What changed that the FBI now has jurisdiction?"

"Her prints don't come up anywhere. We did facial recognition. No hits. But her labs came back and there were benzos in her system. We also found out what that substance was under her nails." Dawson rubbed his temple. "It's a mixture of marine epoxy resin and fine blue-gray silica dust. It's the compound used to seal false bulkhead panels on boats and shipping containers."

Buddy turned and kicked the railing. "You've got to be fucking kidding me."

"What is it?" Fallon raced to his side and rested her hand on his bare shoulder.

He shrugged it off as if she'd burned him. "It's a rare compound that Simon used to create walls inside the vessels he used to transport his victims across oceans. There are only a couple of companies that make it, but we never could connect one of them to Simon." He squeezed the railing so tight his hands turned white. He dropped his head and let out a snarl. "We got court orders to search records—every detail. We had forensic accountants in there. The best of the best. And we couldn't find a single one that sold to Simon."

"Could he have made it himself?" Fallon asked, her

mind rapid-firing on the information, but unable to file it in a way that made sense. She understood everything. Knew what it meant. But somehow it didn't track.

"Anything's possible, I suppose." Buddy pushed from the railing, turned and started pacing. "Anything else I should know?"

"That's all I got."

"Hey, Chief," Jasper called. "Lester said he'll be here in twenty. Crime scene unit will be here as soon as they can. I can tape it off and wait for them, if someone can come in early and cover the rest of my shift."

"I'll cover it. It's only a few more hours. I just need to put on some shoes and proper clothes," Dawson said. "But I want to take a look around first."

"Be my guest." Fallon wrapped her arms around her middle. Tears burned the corner of her eyes. It wasn't just the events of the last few days. She didn't know how to help Buddy. How to ease his tension. His suffering. His self-torture.

She'd spent the first year after Tessa disappeared trying to get abducted. Wanting to know what it was like. Needing to feel and experience whatever her best friend had. Then came the depression. The overwhelming sadness that consumed her, followed by anger and self-hatred. She lashed out, self-harmed, and self-medicated.

And then her parents died, and her world flipped again.

That changed everything. She saw how much she'd been missing. How much she needed to live.

Buddy wasn't living. Probably hadn't been since his

wife left him. But this case had come close to destroying his humanity.

She stood on the porch, next to Buddy, while Dawson and Jasper circled the truck.

"No footprints. Too much loose stone," Jasper said.

Dawson crouched beside the front tire. "They hit it with a bat or pipe. All inward strikes."

Fallon rubbed her arms against the damp chill. "Do you think whoever did this could still be watching from a distance?"

Buddy's gaze stayed on the dark tree line. "I'd bet my life they have eyes somewhere."

The Everglades was a sheet of black water under the moon, silent and infinite. The swamp swallowed people. The swamp kept what it wanted. And what it didn't want eventually surfaced—bloated and unrecognizable.

The porch light flickered, then died, plunging them into half-dark.

"Perfect," Fallon muttered. "An omen."

Buddy shouldered closer. "We're not going to be able to stay here tonight, and I don't think you should be alone until this is figured out." He grabbed her waist and turned her. "Whoever's doing this, whether it be Simon from prison, or someone I've pissed off and who knows this case, has connected you to me. If I thought it was safer to send you somewhere else, I would. But unfortunately, I think we're better off together."

"That sounds like you don't want to be anywhere near me." She curled her fingers around his wrists, easing his grip, and pushed his hands away. Meeting his gaze, she took a step back.

"Not true." He rubbed the back of his neck. "Things about that case affect me in the worst way. I'm sorry I was such an asshole."

"Oh, I understand how those words on that page tore through your heart. Or what seeing that girl did to you." She placed her hand on the center of his chest. "You hold that case right here. Every piece of it. I get that. I still carry Tessa with me. And every year, I still think it should've been me, not her." Tears rolled down her cheek. She dropped her hand to her side and let the tears wet her face. "I let myself purge those emotions. I have to. Or I become a hard person who no one wants to be around."

"Are you saying that's who I am?"

"No. Not yet," she said softly. "I'm not upset with you because of how you responded to what feels like, and probably is, a personal attack. It scared me. I didn't know how to help you. But what hurts are your words. 'Send me somewhere', and 'unfortunately'." She palmed his cheek. "I get this is temporary. I haven't had a relationship that wasn't. I also haven't gone into one thinking this is it. This is going to be my man." She shrugged. "I don't live my life looking for permanence. Nothing lasts forever, and none of us is getting out of here alive. I live to honor those I've lost and to be the kind of person they'd be proud of. The rest is icing." She turned and strolled toward the front door on shaky legs.

She'd always fallen hard for men. Caring about

someone was the easy part. And she welcomed it. She'd been in love a couple of times. Or, at least, she thought she had. The breakups were never easy. Never fun. But she'd learned that life wasn't always fair. It was often painful. And if you tried to avoid the things that hurt, you missed the truly good parts.

Like last night. She wouldn't trade that for anything.

She glanced over her shoulder. "I'll pack a bag because I know being alone would be dumb as fuck. I'm a lot of things, but stupid isn't one of them."

Chapter Nine

The office building, owned by a local land and real-estate developer, had a smell all its own—old plaster and humidity, faint mildew baked into the paint, and the faint trace of furniture polish someone had used a decade ago. It was the scent of things that had survived the Florida coast a little too long.

Buddy shifted the box under his arm, felt sweat start at the back of his neck even though it wasn't nine a.m. yet. The air inside carried the hum of window units that never quite kept up. He passed a flickering fluorescent light and caught the sound of a voice up ahead—low, familiar, full of good humor.

"Hey, Decker," Buddy called, stepping into the light. "Heard you're finally getting married. Congratulations."

Decker Brown, the owner of the building, turned from his office door with a grin so bright it made his face look ten years younger. He wore a crisp shirt, sleeves rolled to his forearms, tie loose like he'd already survived one meeting. Truth be told, he'd survived a lot more than that, and this town, especially Fletcher and Baily, owed him a bit of gratitude for his role in taking down a crime family and securing the future of their marina and the Crab Shack.

However, Decker didn't see it that way. No, he believed this town saved him.

"Thanks. Be on the lookout for an invite. It's not gonna be a big wedding. Or all that formal. Just the good people of Calusa Cove at the community center."

"Silas will love that. He says that place doesn't get used near enough."

"He's been doing a potluck dinner there every other month for the last six months. Seems to be working out. We've gone almost every time. It's fun. I think this next one he's trying to get a band, but knowing him, it will be swing music."

Buddy smiled. "Nothing wrong with that."

"I suppose, but I can barely move across the dance floor without tripping over my own feet." Decker pocketed his keys. "Got a meeting—redevelopment project for the old theater on Main. Whole place smells like mold and nostalgia, but we'll make something out of it. Calusa Cove needs a little more hope."

Buddy nodded once. "We all do."

Decker pointed at the box in Buddy's arms. "Looks heavy. You building your own theater?"

"Just rattling some old skeletons," Buddy said.

Decker laughed like he hadn't heard the truth in it.

"Well, if you ever decide to trade security work for construction, I'll put you on payroll."

"Not my skill set." Buddy shifted the box. "I break things. I don't build them."

Decker clapped him on the shoulder and headed out into the sunlight. "I see the beauty in broken things. And then I like to take the cracks and fill them with sunshine."

Buddy tossed his head back and laughed. Hard.

"Yeah, I heard how corny that was."

Buddy turned down the hallway, past an insurance agency that smelled like cheap aftershave and printer toner, until he reached his office. The frosted glass bore no name—kind of the point.

He pushed through the door.

Inside, the air was marginally cooler. The old ceiling fan wobbled as it rotated. The walls were lined with corkboards and whiteboards—ghosts of old cases still faintly visible where the marker hadn't fully erased.

Sterling sat on the edge of the desk with a cup of coffee that smelled faintly of burned chicory. Dove perched on the windowsill, sunlight through the blinds cutting stripes across her arms. She was barefoot, hair tied in a knot that said she hadn't slept, tablet balanced on her knee.

"Morning," Buddy said, setting the box down on the table.

"Right back at you." Sterling stared at the box. "Is that what I think it is?"

"Yeah." Buddy pried the lid open. "Simon Court. My own notes. The stuff I kept when I shouldn't have."

Dove raised an eyebrow. "Define shouldn't have."

Buddy gave her a look. "Let's call it professional insurance."

Sterling leaned forward. "You're sure you want to dredge that back up? You didn't exactly come out of that case whole."

"I resent that statement." Buddy stared at the papers, the curling corners, the black ink of names that still knotted his chest. "Besides, either this bastard is back, or someone wants me to think he is," he said quietly. "Might as well face him on my terms."

He started pulling out folders—his handwriting on half the labels, tight and precise, because somewhere down the pike, he'd learned the art of being a perfection-ist. Drove Chloe crazy. Drove everyone he worked with half nuts. "These are my field notes. Cross-checks. Map overlays. Unofficial witness statements. Copies of images I really shouldn't have snapped from FBI files."

Dove stood at the edge of the desk and stared. "I thought you were a rules man."

"I am, until someone pushes me too far. Simon kicked my ass off the fucking cliff." He spread the files across the desk like cards in a hand he hated holding.

Dove bent over, hands behind her back, and closed one eye like she was looking through the scope of a rifle. "You've got a hell of a system for a guy who hates paperwork."

"I used to love it," he admitted. "It helped me make sense of things. Only, how can you make sense of girls who vanish without a trace?"

They worked quietly for a while, tacking photos and notes onto the corkboard. The hum of the fan filled the silence, along with the faint sound of gulls over the water. Outside, Calusa Cove went about its routine — engines, distant laughter, the low moan of a boat horn cutting through humidity.

Sterling broke the quiet first. "Who's watching Fallon?"

"Cullen," Buddy said, not looking up, because he couldn't. He needed to focus and thinking about Fallon would break that. Only, it had been broken the second she was out of his arms and out of sight. He'd wanted to tell her to call in sick. To come to work with him.

But that would make him look like a total prick, and he was on thin ice as it was.

Consequences were already playing out, except they weren't the ones he'd expected. He thought he'd get squirrely. That he'd need more space. More room to breathe. That he'd want to sleep alone. Be alone.

But all he wanted was her, and that realization was more than he could handle.

Dove snorted. "Cullen Monroe? The guy with the twitch and the thousand-yard stare?"

"Yeah, that one." Buddy's gaze went from the files to the corkboard and back.

"I'm not sure he's completely there," Dove said.

Buddy turned, one corner of his mouth ticking. "He's earned the right to twitch. You'd have one too if you'd lived through what he did. But he's a good man. His dad is a native of Calusa Cove. Cullen's working on himself.

And more importantly, he'll protect Fallon. He's a Marine. And I've seen him in action. He'd take you down."

"Still," Dove said. "He stares like he's trying to remember if I'm real."

"He's solid," Buddy said, pinning up another photo. "Where it matters."

Dove smirked. "So, you're not worried he'll try anything?"

Buddy stopped mid-motion. "What?"

"Come on. You spent the night at her place. Don't play dumb."

Buddy grabbed a tack and pressed it into the cork with more force than necessary. "That's none of your business."

Sterling let out a heavy sigh. "I'm apparently the only one not getting any in this entire town."

Buddy shot him a dry look. "Heard you tried with the new owner of Massey's Pub, Juniper. How'd that go again?"

Sterling groaned. "Not a total crash. She just said she was 'rebuilding' and not ready for distractions."

"She meant you were the distraction," Dove said.

"Funny." Sterling pointed at her. "Says the woman who stayed at the hospital with Trent. Whole damn town's gossiping about that one."

"Let them gossip," she said. "I like attention, but that's over, although it never really got off the ground."

"Not even a week, and yet, I'm not surprised." Buddy took a step back and stared at the board. "You're all exhausting." And they were. But Timothy White, the head of the Jacksonville Division of the Aegis Network, had let Buddy pick his team to open this office. It was his choice and as nutty and opposite as these two were, they were exactly who he wanted to have his back.

"And you're deflecting," Dove said. "Classic Buddy move."

He ignored her and nodded toward the whiteboard. "Write this down. The words on the notes, and anything we know so far."

Dove pulled the cap off the marker, her handwriting looping fast across the board:

MESSAGE:

—He couldn't save them all.

—He won't be able to save them all.

—Blue 42.

DETAILS:

—Marine epoxy resin + blue-gray silica dust

—Blue Heron Boat Tours, LLC—Possible Simon Court connection

Buddy leaned against the desk, crossing his arms. "Sterling, start calling manufacturers who use that compound. There might be new ones since this case ended—distributors, boat builders, sealant suppliers— anyone in Florida who moves either compound, or both. Find me someone off-book. Do whatever it takes. They're not getting this stuff legally, and when I was with the FBI, my hands were tied way too tight. I had to go in with court orders and all that shit."

"I know that feeling all too well." Sterling nodded. "Got it."

"Dove, find out what Blue 42 could be—call sign, boat name, coordinates, anything. Also, comb through the files and see if Blue and 42 come up in a combination that I might have missed."

"On it," she said.

Buddy rubbed a hand over his jaw, the scrape of stubble grounding him. He hadn't slept more than a few hours, and he could feel the edges of exhaustion in his bones. But he couldn't stop. The need to fix what was coming—it was the same impulse that had ruined his marriage and nearly killed him after.

He'd told Fallon the truth, mostly. But he hadn't told her how the shattered glass around his truck had felt too familiar. How it had taken him right back to the night his wife left—door slamming, his reflection in the mirror, battered and broken, as he tried to understand why he hadn't fought harder.

But he knew why.

He'd loved Callie, with everything he was, and he'd wanted to protect her. But he couldn't do his job, the thing he was born to do, and love her at the same time.

One had to go.

And he'd forced her to make that choice.

He'd been a coward.

Now, the ghosts were back, and it was Fallon in the crosshairs.

The door opened. Keaton and Dawson stepped in.

Both looked like they'd been running on caffeine and fumes.

"Morning," Dawson said. "You all look like a crime scene waiting to happen."

Buddy straightened. "We're halfway there. Tell me you've got something."

Keaton rubbed a hand through his hair. "Depends on what you call something. I went out to the mangroves where Fallon spotted that oil slick. No barrel. No trash. No sign of discharge. But there's a break in the mangrove roots—clean. Like a cut, not natural. Something was there."

Sterling leaned forward. "Boat?"

"Could be," Keaton said. "Or something dragged through. We also found blue paint on the roots. Sample's at the lab."

Buddy felt his pulse hitch. "Blue again."

Dove went to the board, without Buddy asking her to, which is why he'd brought her with him, and added the details.

"I also traced the phone that texted Fallon. Burner. Deactivated," Dawson said.

"That means someone lured Fallon out there on purpose," Buddy swore under his breath, running a hand through his hair. "Alright. I'll talk to Flagler. He owes me a favor."

Dove arched an eyebrow. "You sure that's such a good idea. I get Dawson and maybe even Chloe. But an active Fed? Don't care if you know him or not. We've got sensitive—"

"Part of why our company works is because of our contacts." Buddy pointed at Sterling. "CIA, and someday, we'll need some inside that alphabet agency. Besides, I know Flagler. He's a bend the rules if you can kind of guy."

He pulled out his phone, thumbed Fallon's contact. She picked up quickly, engine hum in the background.

"Buddy? Is everything okay?"

"Yup. How about you?" he asked.

"Fine. Cullen's riding my bumper. Sometimes that man sure knows how to talk. He's like his uncle that way."

He could picture her — sunglasses, ponytail whipping in the wind. "Be careful," he said.

"I always am."

"Docks at four?"

"Promise?"

"Yeah," he said quietly. "Promise."

He hung up and pocketed the phone.

Dawson inched closer to the board. "We've still got nothing on the girl in the hospital. You think she's connected to all this?"

Buddy looked at the board, at the two faces he hadn't saved, at the words that wouldn't leave him alone. "She has to be," he said. "We just haven't seen the pattern yet and whether it leads to Simon or some other asshole that I crushed during my career."

"Blue 42," Keaton said softly. "That's a quarterback call at the line of scrimmage."

"I know what it means. I played football in high

school. But this isn't a football game. And Blue means something else in this situation." Buddy ran a hand over the top of his head and stared at the board.

"I don't know." Keaton moved closer. "When the quarterback uses Blue, it could be simply to change the play, and then the number corresponds to the play, whether it be a run or a pass. But Blue 42 could also be a dummy play, depending on the team." Keaton waved a finger at the words on the board and glanced over his shoulder. "Whoever is doing this is signaling to you that he's changed the game, or he's changed the something specific in the game, or this is just to get you to focus on something that doesn't matter. It's a distraction so they can do whatever's next without you seeing it coming."

Sterling took a step back and folded his arms. "I hate to admit it, but that makes sense."

Buddy leaned back on his desk and continued to muddle through it all. He couldn't argue that it didn't fit. But he couldn't argue that they should toss it out, either. "Even if it references football, it's got a deeper meaning."

"If you figure that out, let us know," Dawson said. "We have to get going. Call if you need anything."

Buddy waved his hand aimlessly. He glanced from the whiteboard to the corkboard, and back again.

The fan ticked overhead. A fly circled near the window. Outside, the light shifted—Florida morning bled into noon, the world carrying on like it didn't care who'd been left behind.

Buddy stared at the photos until his eyes blurred. He could feel the humidity sinking into his skin, the ache behind his ribs that started when he thought too long about what might come next.

He stepped up to the board and uncapped the marker Dove had used. Beneath all the notes, he wrote in block letters:

THE PAST DOESN'T DIE. IT WAITS.

The marker squeaked against the surface, the smell of ink filling the air.

He stood there a long moment, staring at the words until they looked like they might burn through the whiteboard.

Then he whispered, almost to himself, "Not this time."

Chapter Ten

Fallon hated hospitals. Not only did they remind her of death. They smelled like dirty feet and rotten eggs. Not even the Florida humidity mixed with antiseptic could mask that stench.

It also reminded her of the day her parents died.

Buddy's hand was warm against hers as they walked the long corridor, past muted voices and the soft ping of heart monitors echoing behind closed doors.

She didn't pull away.

Maybe she should've, but the truth was, she didn't want to. She needed his strength.

He stopped just outside Trent's room. "You've been quiet since I picked you up."

"We didn't get much sleep, and it's been a long day."

"That's not what I mean."

She glanced at him, and he caught her with that look —the one that saw through every layer she tried to hide behind. His eyes were softer than usual, less shadowed, and maybe more caring.

"You've been distant since last night," he added.

"I'm processing."

"Or avoiding." His thumb brushed the back of her hand. "I want you to know that I heard you. What you said about me sending you away—about being in the same house was unfortunate. I understand it wasn't just the words—it was what they felt like, especially because of what's happening."

The lump in her throat tightened as a nurse passed them in a hurry. "Not the right place," she whispered.

"I've never had good timing. But I needed to tell you, and I want to discuss it."

"After I've seen my friend."

"I'm not going anywhere." He leaned down to kiss her—just enough pressure to make her heart skip, not enough to make her forget the words he'd used yesterday that cut deeper than she wanted to admit. "I'm going to walk around a little, but I won't be far."

She stood there a beat longer after he let go, trying to remember how to breathe. She watched him stroll down the hallway with that sexy swagger he had. Every bone in her body knew he wasn't going to abandon her when she needed him most. He was that kind of person. But he was also running from ghosts and hiding from the past.

Something she knew a little bit about.

She pushed all that out of her mind, turned, and pulled the door open.

Trent looked like hell—but a defiant kind of hell. His

color was better, the bandages on his side were fresh, and the nurses had probably already surrendered to his charm. A vase of flowers sat on the tray table, and a half-eaten pudding cup balanced precariously on his chest.

"Well, look who it is," he said, voice rough but cocky. "I thought you'd be out saving the world—or at least trying to figure out who took a pot shot at you."

"Taking a coffee break from heroism," she said, easing closer. "You look good for a guy who took a bullet for me."

"Just another day in the swamp. Heard you had a little more excitement last night."

She winced. "Word travels fast."

"Small town. And a few of the nurses were talking about your little sleepover. They might have been disappointed that Buddy's now off the market and commenting on your choice of bed partners."

Her cheeks went hot. "Jesus, Trent."

He smirked. "I'm just saying, you do have interesting taste in men and sometimes that puts you in precarious situations."

She sank into the chair beside him, elbows on her knees. "It's not funny. Somebody's toying with him—with us. And I don't know what comes next."

His teasing expression softened. "I'm sorry. I shouldn't've poked fun—before I asked if you were okay. Are you?"

"Not really." She rubbed her palms together, staring at the scuffs on her boots. "I think I'm falling for him, and I don't know what to do with that."

He chuckled. "You mean like you fall for all the guys, or like you fell for me?"

That pulled a laugh out of her. However, there was a distinction between the men that made her rethink her life for five minutes, and the only man who'd made her consider a different path, except Trent hadn't been prepared for that storm. "You loved me a little."

"Only because you could wrestle a gator. and my mom still asks about you." He smiled, a tired, real smile. "We were good, you and me—while we lasted. But we were meant to be friends."

"I figured that out—eventually." She leaned back, arms crossed loosely. Trent had been the only man to put a real ache in her chest. He hadn't broken her heart because he was right, they weren't supposed to be a couple. Given enough time, they would've killed each other. But he'd been the first man she'd truly fallen in love with.

He lifted a brow. "What is it with you and older men?"

"Daddy issues?"

"Another thing we've got in common," he said. "Only my shrink says mine are more authority issues because I'm pissed off at the government and how I perceive what they did to my dad."

She and Trent had bonded over loss more than once. He'd been a kind older friend when Tessa had vanished. That's probably where the crush had started. And he'd been a shoulder to cry on when her parents had died. It was rare that Trent opened up, but when he did, he cracked wide. "Since when do you see a therapist?"

"Since my mom was diagnosed with cancer, and the doctors say it's terminal, and the thought of losing another parent is messing with my desire to be a good person."

That was a lot to unpack. It was also honest, raw, and pure Trent. He'd been doing a balancing act between being misunderstood and crossing the line since puberty. But being looked at as a person of interest in a serial killer case? That had changed him. "I'm so sorry. I had no idea. What can I do?" She leaned forward and took his hand.

He squeezed. "You're here. That's enough. Cullen and Harley are helping out with Mallor's Landing while I'm stuck in here and during my recovery. Silas and his wife are helping with my mom." He swiped a hand across his mouth and down his jaw. "My mom won't do chemo. Or radiation. Doctors say it will only prolong her life by a few months anyway and she doesn't want to be sicker. She wants to enjoy what little time she has left, which they tell me isn't long. Three months tops, if we're lucky."

Fallon didn't know what was worse. Knowing your parent was going to die or having them ripped from you in the middle of the night in a freak accident. "If you need anything, I'm always here. And if you don't ask, I'm showing up when you least expect it, and I don't care if I interrupt you and Dove."

He chuckled. "That ended before I could make her a decent breakfast."

"Seriously?" She lowered her chin. "Why? She seems like your kind of girl."

"My mom needs me right now, and while Dove is fun, she doesn't understand shit about the Glades, and she freaked out when I brought her to Mallor's Landing."

"Yeah, well, most women would. You've got a pond full of gators in the back yard."

He shrugged. "I do have a favor to ask of you."

"Name it."

"Try not to treat my mom differently. Let her keep doing what she's always done with Tessa's Project."

"I know what it's like to have this town smile and wave as you walk by, but their eyes are full of something else. Then, the second your back is to them, they whisper. They all did it when they found out I was the one who was supposed to be working at the Crab Shack the night Tessa went missing."

"No one ever blamed you for that."

"Her parents did," Fallon said. "They still do. While they permitted me to use Tessa's name and donate every year because it's a good cause, they won't come and don't speak to me. Honestly, I don't blame them."

"Because you still blame yourself." He tapped his index finger on the back of her hand. "Just like I hold the government responsible for my father's death."

"We're quite the pair, aren't we?"

"I know you don't want to hear this."

"Then don't say it." She folded her arms, knowing exactly where this conversation was circling back to. She'd opened herself up the second she'd called them a "pair".

"You fall in and out of love like some women change

their hair color. But I can see in your eyes, he's different, and don't try to tell me otherwise, because I know you better than anyone. I just want you to be careful with your heart. This one has the potential of breaking it."

"Why do you say he's different?"

"Because of the way you look at him. The way you've always looked at him. And he's looking back, but I see some of myself in Buddy. It's what I see in Cullen. Those deep wounds that are so hard to come back from. I'm working on it. So is Cullen. What is Buddy doing?"

"We all have demons. We all have something we have to carry. But we're barely a thing. It's way too early to even have this conversation."

"My parents met and were married three weeks later. They were madly in love and had a great relationship. I know I was young when all the crazy shit went down and he died, but I still have memories." Trent lifted her hand and kissed the back of it. "People with bruised souls like you, me, Cullen, even Buddy, we find each other. I don't want to see you hurt, or I'll have to kick his ass."

"He's weirded out that we dated."

"I would be if I were in his shoes." He dropped her hand, shifted and grimaced.

"Yeah, well, he's a better kisser," she said, trying to lighten the mood and change the subject.

"My lips are offended." He reached for the tray, snagged his water, and sipped. "So, any clues about what happened last night? Any leads?"

"Only that Buddy believes it's tied to his last big FBI

case. He's so worried about it that he's got Cullen playing babysitter when he can't be with me."

"That's a good idea. But what about Cullen? How's he holding up with that protection detail? That could be triggering for him, and I know Silas. He'll be on all our asses if we do anything to upset that balance. He's incredibly protective of his nephew."

"I think Cullen's fine, and I'm happy to tell Silas that," she said. "Cullen was excited about the opportunity."

"I'm sure it makes him feel useful."

"That, and he likes being around Harley, who we see out there often."

"Oh, he likes her a lot," Trent said. "It's good to see him have interests other than making things out of wood." He shifted again, groaned, and grabbed his side. "Promise me you'll be careful."

She reached out, squeezing his arm. "I promise."

He smiled. "Good. Now, go, before the nurses catch me flirting with you and revoke my pudding privileges."

She laughed, wiped under her eyes, and stood. "Try not to charm your way into another bullet."

"I never want to see the inside of a hospital again."

She left the room with her chest tight and her heart heavier than before.

Buddy waited in the hallway, leaning against the wall, arms crossed. The man looked like he'd been constructed from worry and coffee.

"Any change since I saw him this morning?"

"Still cocky," she said. "Still himself."

"That's something."

"I could use some coffee, and I don't care if it's crap."

"We can get some here."

They walked toward the cafeteria, the sound of squeaking soles and rolling carts filling the hall. The hospital had that clean-but-tired look—fluorescent lights too bright over hallways too worn. When they reached the cafeteria, they grabbed coffee—and Buddy even managed to find almond milk, which was good enough— and locate a table in the corner.

Not exactly candlelight and wine, but it was private enough.

Buddy stirred his cup, eyes fixed on the swirl. "I'm scared," he said finally. "Not easy for me to admit, but it's the truth and you should know that."

That caught her off guard. "Of what? The case?"

"That does concern me, but I've been dealing with danger my entire adult life." He lifted his gaze. "For the first time since my marriage ended, I feel something real. And I can't help the timing. The chaos. You, me—this. It was below the surface when I was working the Ring Finger case. I thought about you every time I came to town. Always thought about asking you to dinner or out for a drink. I just didn't because I don't know how to separate what's happening in my head from what's happening in my heart."

She leaned forward. "I don't understand." For her, relationships weren't complicated. Not even with Trent, especially not with Trent, and he was a man with a ton of baggage. Most people thought Trent was just someone with a chip on his shoulder. But he had deep emotions that stemmed from personal pain.

"There was a guy I worked with—Gino. Good agent. Smart. Funny. Married to a woman who lit up any room she walked into. Two kids who were as adorable as could be. He was investigating a cartel, one of those mid-tier traffickers with too much money and not enough conscience. Gino thought he was careful. But they found him. Broke into his house while he was out getting gas. His wife and kids never made it to morning."

Fallon's throat tightened. "Oh, God."

"He never came back from that. Not really. And I watched it ruin him. That's why I pushed Callie away. I thought I was doing her a favor." He gave a small, hollow laugh. "Turns out, she didn't need saving. She just needed someone who wasn't already halfway gone."

Fallon stared at the black liquid. "You ever stop feeling responsible? For everything and everyone?"

He met her gaze. "That's an interesting question, and I could ask the same of you, especially about Tessa."

Her chest ached. "Not sure I'll ever be able to let go of all the self-blame."

They sat there a moment, surrounded by the hum of vending machines and the clatter of trays. It reminded her of high school. Not the good parts, but the parts that haunted her dreams. It brought her back to the lonely days of sitting by herself. To all the kids whispering about what had happened. About her jacket being found by the marina. About how it could've—should've—been her.

"When Tessa disappeared," Fallon said, "I thought if

I could just understand what she went through, I could bring her back somehow. So, I started putting myself in bad situations. Hitchhiked once with a guy who could've been on every wanted poster in the state. Spent nights going to biker bars, known criminal hangouts in cities where I didn't know the terrain, places chicks shouldn't go alone, hoping something—someone—would happen. When it didn't, I hated myself for wishing it would."

Buddy's jaw worked, but he didn't interrupt. He was often good at listening.

"It took losing my parents to pull me out of that spiral. Grief on top of grief. You either drown, or you eventually learn to float." She let out a breath. "Sometimes, I feel hardened by all of it. Like I'm too used to loss. Like I expect it. Or anticipate it."

"You're not hard," he said. "You just know how deep the water can get."

She smiled faintly. "That's poetic."

"Don't tell Sterling. He'll never let me live it down."

She reached across the table, brushing her fingers against his hand. "I've always chosen men who aren't going to be around forever. Trent—"

"I can't believe you dated him."

"Correction," she said with a half-smile. "I lived with him for a few months. It was right after my parents died. He was there when I needed him. It was more convenience than anything, but we did have a connection. A bond. And we both cared—still do—for each other. He saved me from myself."

"You should know that I have jealous tendencies."

She laughed, the sound shaky but genuine.

He squeezed her fingers gently. "Whatever this is— whatever we are—it's good. It's real enough for now."

"There's a part of me that wonders if this is more about you needing to protect me, because you feel more responsible than anything else." She considered herself a good reader of people. And she'd figured out some of Buddy's tells. But his expression gave away nothing.

"I won't pretend that I don't want to take care of you. Make sure nothing bad happens. I'm sorry if I've made that feel like the only reason, because it's not. I do care for you. But my career has always been about protecting people. I can't change that part of me."

"That's fair, and for now, that's enough."

"And until whoever's behind this mess is caught, that's all we can ask for."

Fallon looked at him, really looked at him—the gray at his temples, the tired eyes, the man who carried too much. "You sure you can handle me? I'm told I'm extra."

"Not a chance." There was warmth in his words. "But I'm dumb enough to try."

They sat there in the cafeteria with their bad coffee and worse timing, holding hands across the table like the world wasn't still coming for them.

And for that one fragile, ordinary moment—it almost felt like peace.

Chapter Eleven

Massey's was thinning to a hush when Buddy slid into one of the back booths—lunch rush fading, TV on mute over the bar, forks clinking in twos and threes. Sterling sat across from him, scanning the room with the kind of focus that only a trained operative used until his gaze landed on Juniper.

She was an attractive woman in her early to mid-thirties. Buddy was told she'd come to town a month ago and offered Holly Massey a deal she couldn't refuse. This was long after Holly had given up selling and taken it off the market. Part of Buddy found that odd. Too good to be true.

But Juniper seemed to fit into the town like chocolate chips fit into ice cream.

Juniper wiped down the far end of the bar with the brisk, no-nonsense rhythm of someone who'd already broken up one argument today and wouldn't tolerate another. On some levels, it contradicted her bubbly, always-happy personality. This place could use someone like Juniper. Someone who could handle a rowdy, drunk fisherman while wearing a smile and carrying a rainbow. The only thing that really made the situation odd was that Sterling had become interested.

Not that the women he dated weren't inherently easy-going or happy. They just weren't over-the-top about it, and Sterling had a type. Sophisticated, high-heels, designer everything—the kind of woman who demanded things be perfect and pitched a fit when they weren't. They drank dirty martinis, ate caviar, and went to the country club for weekly gossip.

Juniper wasn't that.

"He's late." Sterling shifted his gaze to the front door and stared at it as if a magical puff of smoke might appear and seconds later, Flagler would walk through it.

"He's FBI," Buddy said. "Late's a performance choice."

Flagler came in a second later, as if on cue—tall, tailored, the same unflinching eyes Buddy remembered from when he'd been a special agent, and they'd worked together on a few cases. Flagler clocked exits first, then them, and crossed with the easy stride of a man who'd been told a bar was a perfectly acceptable interview room.

"Buddy Ballard." He shook once, firm. "And you must be Sterling."

Juniper showed up out of nowhere and dropped off water without being asked. "You need menus?" She smiled sweetly—at Sterling.

Maybe he hadn't crashed and burned as hard as the man had thought.

"We're good, thanks," Buddy said.

"So, how's the private sector treating you?" Flagler leaned back, loosened his tie, as if he needed to breathe a little.

"I like it," Buddy admitted. "Especially the part where I don't have to file paperwork to save lives."

Flagler cocked his head. "We get the job done."

"Some days. But I didn't ask you here to discuss my exit from the FBI or to try to recruit you to the Aegis Network—though, you'd be welcome."

"Alright. Why am I here?"

"I want to know about Jane Doe. About the case. And I want to know if you're looking into connections to Simon."

"Well now, that's a mouthful." Sterling reached for his water and took a few gulps.

Juniper appeared again. Buddy always found it fascinating how she picked specific tables to wait on. She was the owner. She didn't have to, but she always seemed to wait on the perceived important people of Calusa Cove.

"Can I get you boys, a drink? Something to eat?"

"Just coffee for me," Buddy said. "Oat milk, please."

"Coffee for me as well, black." Sterling flashed his million-dollar grin.

"I'll have the same." Flagler leaned forward, resting his hands on the table. He waited a few seconds after Juniper left and then said, "I shouldn't tell you anything. But I will—on one condition."

"What's that?" Sterling asked.

"I need you to keep me in the loop on anything you find, because I know you're not gonna let this rest. And I'll do the same. We work together, or I work alone. Deal?"

Buddy nodded. "We can live with that."

"First, I'll agree there are too many similarities to Operation Blue Eden to ignore. But you know how the Bureau works. Fucking slow. Not to mention, you made so many damn arrests and shut down one of the biggest pipelines of human trafficking they'd ever seen."

"Are you saying they won't even consider Simon's setting something up from prison. That he's still got people on the outside?" Buddy asked.

"Not yet. But I've filed the paperwork to talk to him."

Buddy swore under his breath. He hated all the red tape.

"You should know, the girl's finally awake. Came too early this morning. Seven days of being either unconscious or sedated. She woke up screaming. Tried to yank out her IVs. Kicked and thrashed at the nurses. But they were able to calm her down." Flagler stared at his water with a distance in his eyes that Buddy recognized. It was that emotional detachment that was required to do the job. The one that Buddy never wanted to have again. She gave us a name when she finally calmed down. Tannette Runon."

"I'm glad she's awake." Buddy leaned back. "What did you find out about her when you ran her name through the database?" Buddy asked.

"Absolutely nothing," Flagler said. "No state record. No federal. Nothing with HHS or DHS. She has a bit of an accent, but it's not thick. I'm leaning Vietnamese—maybe Khmer. Could be Thai. She's terrified. Won't look men in the eye. Anyone in a uniform, or with a badge and gun, makes her shake like a building's about to collapse on her."

"What about bringing Chloe in?" Buddy said. "No badge. No gun. No uniform. Just a nice woman with a friendly face."

"Did that two hours ago. She's the one who got her name." Flagler finally lifted his gaze. "Chloe thought she could be undocumented."

Sterling tapped his fingers on the table, something he did when he was thinking, and it drove Buddy up the wall. "Do you believe she was trafficked into this country? Because the pipeline Buddy shut down was internally run, or girls were shipped overseas. While Simon did have a flow coming in, it wasn't his main business."

"But it happened. And while Simon did work mostly inside the US, I've worked a case where hundreds of kids were brought in to work our version of sweatshops—rich white dudes who want a young foreign girl. Nothing shocks me anymore," Flagler said. "We're running foreign queries. It'll take time."

Juniper stepped to the edge of the table with a tray. She placed their coffees in front of them and slid a basket of fries onto the table like a peace offering. "You boys look like you could use some think tank food."

"Thanks," Buddy said. His phone vibrated against his pocket. He pulled it out and stared at the screen.

Unknown number. No preview.

He opened it.

If you want to save Fallon, you'd better hurry. He's out there again, and he wants her.

The blood ran cold as the words sliced clean through him.

"What's going on?" Sterling asked.

He raised his cell so Sterling and Flagler could see the text.

"Fuck," Sterling mumbled.

"Buddy typed a message to the unknown number.

Who is this? Where?

It went underlived.

He hit call. Disconnected.

"God damn it."

"It's a trap," Sterling said.

"I know." Buddy stood, tucking more than cash under the basket of fires to cover at least a couple of meals they hadn't ordered. "Doesn't matter. We can't just leave her and Cullen out there, even if we do warn them."

Flagler was already up. "I'm coming."

"Follow me to the marina," Buddy said. "And call Dawson on your way. Tell him I need to borrow a boat and that he should meet us there. Tell him what's going on."

They were out the door in a line—Buddy first, Flagler two steps behind, Sterling the anchor. The afternoon heat radiated off the sidewalk. Buddy climbed into his borrowed truck—courtesy of the Aegis Network. Flagler followed in his four-door sedan that screamed federal agent.

He set his cell in the carrier and tapped Fallon's contact information.

"Hey, what's up?" she said, picking up on the first ring.

"Listen, I need you and Cullen—"

"Sorry, call coming over the radio. I gotta go. I'll call you back as soon as I can." The line went dead.

"Fuck." He smashed his hand against the steering wheel and pressed the gas pedal, just a tad. Lots of people out walking. "Take my cell and text her."

"And say what? Run? Hide? She's answering a work call."

"I get it. But ask her to text me back her location."

"Okay, but let's face it. This isn't about her, and we both know if they wanted her dead, they could've killed her. Harley told us she thought they missed Fallon on purpose. That they were aiming for the boat. The water. Not Fallon, and the only reason Trent got shot was because he tossed a motherfucking big ass snake at them. They wanted to scare Fallon and send you a message, and that's what this is, too. Or maybe they just want to kill you." Sterling spoke faster than Buddy had ever heard before. And when he spoke quickly, it meant he wasn't thinking about the words. He wasn't choosing carefully. His instincts were kicking in.

And maybe—just maybe—he was right.

"Besides, Keaton will know where she went if it's a work call."

That was true, but it didn't make Buddy feel any better. Whoever was targeting Fallon—targeting him—was going to pay.

He was going to make damn sure of it.

The stillness of the Everglades usually brought a sense of serenity to Fallon's aching heart—especially this time of year, when the air turned heavy with memory. Out here, surrounded by cypress and sawgrass, something in her settled.

The water sat dark and slick, reflecting light off its surface like polished stone, despite looking like liquid mud. Gators floated in the distance, half-submerged kings of a realm that didn't care about human grief or its anniversaries. Her father used to say the swamp had a soul—that if you were quiet long enough, you could hear it speak.

He'd been right.

This was her sanctuary. Her church. Her reminder that life went on, even after loss.

But today, the stillness weighed too heavy. The air felt thick. The water looked darker, denser, like oil pooled beneath the surface. And no matter how hard she tried, she couldn't shake the feeling that someone was watching.

"Here." Cullen handed her a cold bottle of water

before dropping the cooler behind her seat as he stretched out on her bow. His skiff bobbed beside her FWC boat, the line between them taut and neat. "You look deep in thought."

"And you got a haircut." She twisted the cap open and forced a smile. Her mother used to say she had a bad habit of redirecting conversations when they got too close to her heart.

Cullen wiped his mouth with the back of his hand. "You noticed." He ran a palm over his shorter hair, the gesture easy, unbothered. It barely brushed the back of his neck now.

"Been slowly cutting it shorter and shorter," he said. "Needed to stop scaring the tourists. My uncle has been giving me a hard time about it. So has my aunt. But the real reason is I want to see my son, and my ex-wife won't let me unless I show real effort in change, and looking like a human is part of that agenda."

"How old is your son?"

Cullen smiled—prideful. "He's six. Looks like me, but smart and kind like his mother. They moved to Jupiter with her family when I was medically discharged from the Marines. Tamara told me that as long as I'm working on myself, I can have supervised visits, so I go there twice a month. I'm hoping that soon, Tyler can come here and stay with me. But I need to deal with the nightmares."

"Baily told me Fletcher had them. That all the guys had them after being tortured and Ken being murdered."

"Dawson's had more than one conversation with me

about it. So have Hayes, Keaton, and Fletcher." Cullen shook his head. "My uncle's been putting me in their path ever since I came to town. All I want is to be a good father."

"I'm sure you are."

"I don't know. I got so messed up in the head that I didn't know reality from fiction." He tapped his temple. "But I'm getting the help I need. My Uncle Silas and Aunt Opal are amazing people. I'm so lucky to have family like that."

She took a swig of her water. "Well, I like this hairstyle on you. Fits your face. Did you get it done in town?"

"Harley's been doing it. We swap services. I'm making her a couple of pieces of furniture, and she's been giving me free haircuts for a while."

"That's nice." Fallon lifted her feet and stretched out her legs across the bench. "You two have been spending a lot of time together."

"I've been out on the water a lot lately." Cullen leaned back on the bow of the boat. "The addition to the bed and breakfast is done. Decker doesn't have any local work for me right now and I don't want to relocate to Fort Myers for his next job. That's too far from my son. Fletcher and Baily have me building some furniture, and Buddy, well, he hired me for this. But outside of that, Harley lets me hang out with her and help. She can't pay me, but that's okay. She bakes me cookies."

Fallon chuckled. "You could get work at the pub. There's a help-wanted sign hanging in the window. It's washing dishes, but it's something."

"I don't mind hard work." Cullen stared out into the water. "But I still jump at certain sounds. Don't like enclosed spaces, except my trailer, and even then, sometimes I still end up sleeping outside. Drives Silas and Opal crazy. They wish I felt comfortable inside their home. I keep telling them it's not about their hospitality or anything about how I feel about my relationship with them, because they've always been awesome. It's just being in enclosed spaces and wondering when something's gonna explode."

"I can relate."

"While I know you're an outdoorsy type, I don't see you wanting to sleep under the stars every night."

"I'm just saying I can understand what it's like to feel closed in by walls and convention." Her cell buzzed from its perch on the console. "It's Buddy. I'd better take it." She dropped her feet to the bottom of the airboat and leaned forward. "Hey, what's up?"

"Listen, I need you and Cullen—"

Her radio crackled to life and Keaton's voice boomed over the airwaves.

"Sorry, call coming over the radio. I gotta go. I'll call you back as soon as I can." She snagged the mic. "This is Officer Reeves."

"Reeves, I've got a report of a distress call from a kayaker," Keaton said. "I need you to go check it out. Sending coordinates."

"Got it. I'll check in when I get there."

Cullen was already in his boat, untying and firing up his engine.

Fallon eased the throttle forward, following the GPS marker Keaton had sent. The sun sat low enough to make the water glare white-hot, and the air settled thick against her neck. They cut through a narrow channel where the mangroves bent low, their roots curling into the shallows like black claws. This part of the narrow strait always reminded her of Sleepy Hollow.

"This isn't a popular spot for kayaking," Cullen called over the engines.

"Which means either they got lost, or they're in trouble." She squinted ahead. "Either way, we find them."

The coordinates dropped them into a wide bowl of still water framed by cypress. Spanish moss hung low, stirring just enough to look alive. She slowed the airboat and pointed. "There. In the reeds."

A lime-green kayak half-hidden by tall sawgrass rocked lazily with the current. No person. No paddle. No life vest.

"Great," Cullen muttered. "That's not ominous."

Fallon shut off the engine, letting the boat drift the last few yards. "Hello?" she yelled, cupping her hands. "FWC officer. If you can hear me, call out."

Nothing—just the buzz of insects and the creak of branches shifting overhead.

Cullen coasted up alongside her. "Kayak's wedged in there pretty good. Doesn't look overturned."

She scanned the shoreline. A gator eased across the water. Another set of reptilian eyes settled on hers from the port side, not far from the kayak. Frogs sang that deep throaty twang that reminded her this was their world, not hers.

Then it came—a voice, faint and frayed, threading through the air like a whisper.

"Help... please..."

Fallon froze. "You hear that?"

Cullen nodded once, his eyes narrowing. "Direction?"

She turned her head, trying to track it. "Could be anywhere. Sound bounces off the water."

"There's a hut on the point," he said, nodding toward the bend in the river. "If anyone dragged themselves ashore, that's the only shelter. And it's not safe to go wading in these waters. I'm not even sure Trent would dare. I've counted six gators so far, and they ain't small ones."

They grounded the boats and climbed out. The mud sucked at their boots as they moved up the bank. The hut looked abandoned—a wood and grass structure. "My dad took me back here when I was a kid. We'd sit with the Seminoles, and they'd tell us stories. They consider these huts sacred because their ancestors built them."

"When I first came back from the Marines, I came out here. I heard about another Marine who lived out here for a while. That the Seminoles let him. Someone—broken—like me," Cullen said.

"That would've been Cole Delany. He left town before you returned," she said softly.

"I wasn't too good at listening back then and I didn't

people too well. I heard this Cole guy was slowly easing back into society."

"He kind of jumped right back in one day when his daughter showed up with a couple of grandkids. He hadn't seen her in like seventeen years. It was a beautiful thing. Four months later, he left to go live near her. Dawson, Hayes, Keaton, and Fletcher all hear from Cole every once in a while. They get Christmas cards. Cole still has some issues, but he's doing well."

"That gives me hope." Cullen stopped, raising his hand.

"FWC!" Fallon called again. "Help us find you?"

Another whisper. Closer this time. Faint but definite. "Help... me..."

"That's not wind," Cullen said.

She felt the hairs rise on her arms. "Maybe it's coming from inside and muffled by grass." She rested her hand on her sidearm. She pushed it open slowly. The hinges screamed.

Empty. Dust, a few scattered tools, a half-broken chair. No sign of anyone.

Cullen went still beside her. His entire body changed—the subtle coiling of instinct. Eyes wide. Jaw clenched.

"Fallon," he said quietly. "You hear that?"

Before she could even breathe, the heat hit, sharp and consuming and the air turned to fire. A sheet of flame raced up the wall and leapt to the ceiling.

"We've got to get out of here." Cullen did a one-eighty. "Now."

Fallon threw an arm up over her face.

"Go," Cullen yelled, already shoving her toward the door.

She stumbled as the heat clawed at her back, the roar of flame deafening. They didn't run—they dove, straight through the mouth of the blaze, out onto the scorched grass beyond.

The ground hit hard. Fallon rolled, instinct taking over, smothering sparks that clung to her clothes. Beside her, Cullen was beating at his pant leg where it smoked.

"You good?" he shouted over the sound of the fire chewing through the hut.

"I'm not dead." She stared at Cullen. His eyes had darkened, and underneath were the same shadows that had been present when he'd first come home. Not as clear, but they were there. Haunting him. Driving him.

She turned her attention to the hut—it was already engulfed by the flames—roof collapsing, sparks leaping into the sky. The fire spread into the dry sawgrass, crackling outward in rings of orange.

"Damn it." She scrambled to her feet. "We've got to stop it before it jumps the waterway."

Cullen had already grabbed the cooler off her boat and dumped the contents, racing to refill it from the canal. Fallon hit her radio, voice hoarse. "FWC Four-One-Two. We've got a structure fire off Sector Five, near the tribal boundary. Possible accelerant—repeat, possible accelerant. Request immediate response."

Static answered, then Keaton's clipped reply: "Copy that. Fire unit and rescue en route."

She tossed the mic aside and grabbed a bucket.

They worked in tandem, throwing water, sloshing mud, anything to slow the spread. The flames hissed but refused to die. Heat pulsed in waves, making her vision ripple. Cullen's arm was red and blistering, but he didn't stop.

"Get back," he shouted as a plank from the roof fell and shattered.

Fallon stumbled to a halt, chest heaving. The entire clearing was orange now—glow on water, fire on dried grass.

Cullen jumped to his feet, grabbed the cooler, and raced back to the waterline. He was a man on a mission, only she wasn't sure if it was this one or shadows of the past.

The wind shifted, blowing smoke into her face. She coughed, eyes streaming, and in that split second, she thought she heard it again—faint, high, and wrong—a woman's voice, echoing across the water.

Help me.

She turned toward the sound, heart hammering, but there was nothing—only fire and the endless, watching swamp.

Chapter Twelve

Buddy pulled into the parking lot of the marina and skidded to a stop in the first available parking spot.

Mitchell's Marina was busier than usual for a weekday—guides swapping gas cans, deckhands coiling lines, gulls calculating theft. Dawson was waiting at the far slip in a Calusa Cove police boat, sunglasses on, posture loose enough to fool anyone who hadn't worked with him.

"Thanks for coming," Buddy said.

"You couldn't've kept me away." Dawson shoved his glasses on top of his head.

Sterling peeled off for the Everglades Overwatch shed. "Keys?"

Baily met him outside and tossed a ring the size of a fist. "You break it, you bought it."

Dawson stepped in close. "All our airboats have trackers. If this is bait—and it is—I can ride quiet on your signal. No lights. No markings. We'll shadow you in a plain hull, and since I'm the chief, I can pretty much write my own rule book."

Buddy's phone buzzed again.

Unknown Caller: *Come alone, or all three die.*

He swallowed hard. "Text says three will die if I don't come alone?"

Sterling met his eyes. "Fallon, Cullen, and...?"

"Harley? She's out there trimming mangrove." Buddy's stomach knotted. "Where the hell are they?"

"Keaton said there was a distress call from a kayaker, and Fallon hasn't reported back yet. That area isn't scheduled for mangrove maintenance. I think Harley's doing private contracts today," Dawson said.

Another ping.

Unknown Caller: *I am trying to help. If I'm caught, I die too.*

Buddy scanned the rooflines, the pilings, the stacked crab traps. He felt watched because he was watched. "Cameras?" he asked over his shoulder.

"Fletcher did a sweep an hour ago," Dawson said. "Nothing funny, and we regularly check the software in all our systems because of the trouble a couple of years ago. It hasn't been hacked. No one's watching from here."

Buddy looked from the text to Dawson. His mouth was already making the call his brain hated. "Give me ten. Then you come the long way around Hoag Island, no decals. If you're inside five minutes of my wake, they'll smell you."

"Copy," Dawson said. "Martyrs make paperwork." He held Buddy's gaze. "Don't be a martyr."

Buddy tapped the screen on his phone—Fallon, then Cullen. Both went to voicemail. He didn't leave one. Words were a weight, and he wouldn't drop any that might be found by someone else.

Sterling had two airboats ready—tanks topped off, hulls clean, radios checked. "Yours is number four," he said. "Tracker pinged. Dawson's got you."

Flagler stepped into the second without ceremony. "The Bureau appreciates the loan," he said dryly to no one. "I'd better not see an alligator out there. I hate those creatures, and I've seen enough of them already."

Buddy swung onto the deck, fired the ignition, and the fan screamed to life. He didn't look back. He pulled out, nose down, and let the river take him, white wake unrolling like a dare.

The Glades grabbed heat and flung it back. Sawgrass hissed against the hull; dragonflies stitched green lines in the air. Sector markers flew by in quick slashes—painted poles, numbers Buddy had memorized long before he'd admit this place felt like home. Sector Five meant narrower cuts, mangroves with knuckles for roots, the kind of water that ate mistakes and called it a light snack.

He watched everything at once. The glare, the dark seams that meant deeper channels, the margins where a boat might sit with its prop out and a man with a long gun could think about range and wind. The text rode shotgun, words repeating in a rhythm he couldn't escape.

If you want to save her.

He had failed to save two. Their faces lived in a box

in his closet, and on the bad nights, behind his eyelids. He said their names out loud every day.

Maya. Sophie.

He'd never forget.

And he'd never be able to forgive himself.

Wind shifted left. Smoke threaded the air, thin at first, then thicker, dragging its own shadow. Buddy opened the throttle, and the boat leapt, as if grateful to be told what to do.

Buddy banked hard around a curve, and the world opened to brightness and wrong—an old Seminole shack at the waterline, dry boards stacked under a grass roof, the whole thing licked orange and then swallowed by flames.

Two boats rode at the edge of the reeds—Fallon's FWC airboat and Cullen's patched skiff, both nosed in ugly like they'd been shoved into the reeds. Fallon and Cullen were a blur—bucket, throw, bucket, throw—steam rising where muddy water hit heat.

Buddy cut power before the last turn and let momentum carry him in with a quietness that felt like respect. He put a hand to his radio, making sure he was on the proper channel. It crackled to life before he could press the mic.

"Buddy, this is Keaton. There's a fire in Sector Five. Same coordinates I sent Fallon."

"I know. I'm staring at it."

"Fire rescue on the way," Keaton said. "Sending everyone in. This takes precedence. For now."

Buddy cradled the mic and dropped anchor against

the mangroves, hopped down, and his boots hit muck with purpose.

"Fallon!" His voice was bigger than the space could hold. She turned—face streaked with smoke, hair caught under a cap, eyes steady—the right arm of her uniform charred.

"There's another bucket over there," she shouted over the roar, pointing. "We've got to get this under control. Fire department at least ten minutes out."

Sterling brought his boat in tight, Flagler's hull just behind.

The shack's beams groaned. A corner fell, and the roof punched smoke into a low ceiling over the water. Heat bent the air. Buddy moved Fallon back two steps with a hand on her shoulder—gentle, no argument in it. She resisted, then gave him those two steps because she'd seen the roof list, too.

"Anyone else here?" he asked her.

She shook her head once. "I don't know." She raced to the waterline, dipped her bucket in and ran back to the flames, tossing what looked like a droplet onto a raging inferno.

As Cullen marched toward him, Buddy stood in his path. "That's not going to do anything." He looked Cullen up and down. Shirt torn up. Parts of his pants were burned away, but the exposed skin looked unharmed. Silas was first going to be grateful that both Cullen and Fallon were okay.

Then he was going to kick Buddy right to the moon.

Cullen blinked. His eyes locked in on something that

wasn't in the Glades. Something far away. Ghosts from his past that haunted his present. His nostrils flared with each breath. His lips drew into a tight line.

For a brief moment, Buddy thought Cullen might either shove him out of the way or clock him.

But he did neither. His features softened. He dropped his bucket, and his shoulders slumped. Yet, he said nothing, and that was okay.

Buddy squeezed his shoulder. "You tried. That's what matters."

Fallon came rushing back. "Don't just stand—"

"Dumping buckets isn't going to stop that." Carefully, he placed his hands on her shoulders, making sure he didn't touch any of the burns. "Listen." He raised his hand. "Sirens. Water Fire Rescue is minutes away. Let them handle this."

Tears poured out of her eyes like rain.

"It's okay. I've got you." He wiped them away, leaned in, and kissed her forehead.

"We got a call—someone in trouble..." she managed through a sob. "We went in, and it flashed. But no one was there. Just... nothing."

Cullen inched closer. "Do you smell that?" he asked, voice hoarse. "I should've noticed it when we got here, but we heard someone calling for help. I swear, it wasn't just me who heard it."

"He's right. I heard a faint whisper. A girl. It was a girl calling for help. There's a kayak in the reeds around the bend."

Buddy's muscles went cold and rigid.

You can't save them all.

He made himself catalog what he had. Of what Dove had put on the whiteboard. He visualized it and added this scene.

"There's a girl out here somewhere. Somewhere close." He placed his hands on his hips as the water fire boats approached. Hoses pointing toward the flames. Men shouting. Dawson and Sterling pulled up and jumped off their boats, racing toward him. "This was a test," he said to no one in particular.

"What?" Fallon asked.

"I was focused on you. On Cullen." He ran his hand across his mouth and down his chin. "When I couldn't save Maya and Sophie, Simon taunted me after I arrested him. He told me that if I thought more about the victims and less about him—that if I'd done that, they might have lived."

"Only, he'd still be out there."

"Which is always the catch-22," Cullen said as he eased in next to them. "My old staff sergeant used to tell me collateral damage is unavoidable. I've always hated that term."

"So have I. But whoever this is, he wants to see how I react—to choices." Buddy squinted, scanning the waterway. A gator floated in the center, as if it were the one watching. Studying him. "He told me there were three people out here who could die. He wanted me to choose who could live. Friend and lover? Or victim?"

"You don't think this is about your old case anymore?" Fallon asked.

"Oh, it is. I'm sure this prick is trafficking girls. And he has something to do with Simon's pipeline. They all know each other. Honor among thieves and shit." Buddy rubbed the back of his neck. "That was the ruse to get me to come out and play this fucked up game."

"Buddy." Cullen stepped closer to the waterline. His boot sank in the muck. "What the hell is that over there?"

The channel across from them sat like a black eye. The mangrove on that side had a split—wide enough to take a man sideways—total disrespect to the beauty of the Everglades.

Buddy squinted into the tangle, and the shape that didn't belong resolved: fabric where there shouldn't be any, a body handing at an odd angle, a hand turned palm-out, as if asking and not receiving. He let his eyes adjust to the green and the black, then saw it whole.

A body, strung up in the roots, five feet in. Clothing painted with block letters, slashed across the chest.

BLUE 42.

The world went distant—and then knife-sharp.

"Sterling. Flagler. Dawson. Get over here."

They were at his side in seconds. He didn't say a word. He just pointed.

"Jesus," Flagler said. "No one contaminates that bank. We do this by the book. The FBI book. I need to go in and see if she's alive."

Buddy nodded, even though he wanted to argue. The FBI rules often sucked. But this time, he had no choice. He'd brought Flagler out here, and this was his case. His jurisdiction. And Buddy wasn't a fool. "I'll mark the channel and rope off the reeds in front of the scene," Buddy said, because doing something was how he remembered how to breathe.

Flagler hopped on Dawson's boat, and they moved just past idle. But no matter how careful they were, the swamp would destroy evidence faster than gravitational waves.

"Fallon and Cullen, I want both of you to get checked out by the paramedics." He waved a hand toward the water. "EMT boat just pulled up." Fallon opened her mouth. "Don't argue with me. I know you want to help, but let's make sure that the only thing that got burned is the hair on your arms or legs."

"What about Harley?" Cullen asked, wide eyed. "Anyone see her? She's in this area."

"I'll ask Keaton to make sure someone has eyes on her," Buddy said. "I'll let you know as soon as we find her."

"Thanks." Cullen stepped away, Fallon following.

Buddy signaled to Sterling. They climbed aboard his boat and went to work. Systematically and quietly, they stuck poles in the water. He took a coil of line and two bright bumpers from Sterling's hull, waded to his knees where the muck gave reluctant permission, and set the floats wide so the water units wouldn't chew up the evidence with their prop wash.

Sterling handed him a roll of yellow tape. Crime scene tape.

His pulse had long since returned to normal. Adrenaline no longer controlled his movements. Now, it was a simple action based on years of experience. Years of too many dead bodies.

He shifted his gaze toward Dawson. He shook his head.

Shit.

Flagler held his cell phone, taking pictures and mapping the scene. The body hung in a way that didn't make sense if the person who'd put her there had a soul. The letters on the shirt were almost neat. That pissed him off more than the fire.

Dawson waded toward him, shoulders square, head held high. It was the sign of a man who knew how to keep the demons at bay, but behind that heavy armor—if someone cared enough to look deep into his eyes—they'd find a man who carried the burden of his town. Not because it was the honorable thing to do. Or even the right thing to do. But because he didn't know how to do anything else.

Buddy understood that better than most.

"She was still warm," Dawson said his voice tight. "Don't need to be a medical examiner to know she died on those roots, and it wasn't that long ago."

"Somehow, I was supposed to see her, and that fire at the same time." Buddy couldn't take his eyes off the young girl. She couldn't have been more than eighteen. Had her entire life ahead of her. "But she's hidden pretty well. I can only assume that whoever did this was hoping she'd last a little longer and scream her lungs out, so I'd hear her. Fallon and Cullen heard something."

"That's fucked up," Dawson said.

Buddy's phone vibrated against his hip. He pulled it out and stared at the screen.

Unknown Caller: *You can't save them all.*

His teeth met hard. He held up his cell phone, showing it to Dawson, then tried to send a message back.

Who are you and what do you want?

"It fucking went undelivered again."

He put a hand on the side of the boat and breathed once, twice, three times—slow in, slower out. He made a list in his head because lists were the only prayer he knew how to say.

—Track origin of the text to Fallon.

—Track this burner.

—Blue Heron Boat Tours—touch every shell company, every captain, every fuel slip.

—Marine epoxy supplier list from Sterling by nightfall. Cross-ref with purchases in Broward, Monroe, Miami-Dade.

—Every shack marked on old charts—find the ones not on maps.

He glanced at Fallon. She was watching him that steady way of hers that didn't ask for promises he couldn't make. He wanted to go to her, to put a hand on the back of her neck and tell her something that would make sense of this. He stayed where he was because there was a dead girl five feet into the trees and he knew better than to touch the living when the dead needed naming.

On the far side of the channel, a blue heron stepped once, slow, and then lifted into the air with a crank of its wings like an old hinge. It cut across the glare and was gone.

Buddy stared at the place it had been and thought about coincidence.

He didn't believe in it.

"Whoever he is," Flagler said, low, "he thinks he's winning."

Buddy kept his eyes on the water until it stilled around the bumpers he'd set. "Until we catch him, he is."

Chapter Thirteen

The next day, Fallon stood just outside the back door of the Crab Shack. It carried a strange kind of gravity—half comfort, half ghosts. Slowly, she walked toward the water. The planks of the dock were worn under her boots, and the sunlight was sharp enough to make her squint. The channel stretched vast and endless, a mirror of brackish water broken only by the dark slashes of mangrove roots. No clouds on the horizon. No storms creeping in off the Gulf. Just the still, breathless heat that made the air heavy as syrup.

A gull cried overhead, circling lazy arcs, waiting for scraps. The smell of butter and frying crab drifted from the kitchen window, tangled with hickory smoke from the pit out back. The same scent had clung to this place since she was a kid—back when she and Tessa used to sneak fries during their shift and swear they'd never leave Calusa Cove.

That memory used to make her smile. Now, it pressed against her chest like a bruise.

She rubbed the back of her neck and forced herself to breathe.

Tessa's Project. Every year it brought people together—families, fishermen, retirees, kids running barefoot down the boardwalk—but it also pulled at something deep inside Fallon. A crack that refused to seal.

"Don't tell me you're hidin' out again." Leroy's voice rolled out from behind her, warm and teasing. The Shack's head cook wore his usual grease-splattered apron and had the kind of charm that could calm a hurricane.

"Not hiding," she said, forcing a smile over her shoulder. "Just thinking."

"Ah. Dangerous habit." He leaned on the railing beside her. "You got all your ducks in a row for Saturday?"

"Pretty much. Food's sorted, band's confirmed, volunteers lined up."

"Good," he said with a satisfied nod. "'Cause I've got my kitchen crew fightin' for braggin' rights. Mrs. Culver's coleslaw might actually kill a man this year."

Fallon laughed softly. "She swears the secret is in the vinegar."

"Yeah, and the pound of sugar she 'accidentally' dumps in." He handed her a small plate with a pair of golden crab cakes. "Try these. New batch."

The scent hit first—buttery, spicy, alive. She took a bite and closed her eyes, the taste bright and familiar. "Leroy, these are ridiculous."

"Secret spice," he said.

"Old Bay, lemon zest, Worcestershire sauce, and extra butter?"

He snapped his fingers. "Damn. Ruined my mystery again."

For a moment, the world stilled. The laughter, the heat, the ghosts—all of it faded under the comfort of something simple.

"You doin' okay?" he asked softly.

She looked out over the water again. "I'm fine."

"You sure? You got that faraway look. The one you get when you're talkin' to the shadows that live in the swamp."

Fallon exhaled, steady but quiet. "Some shadows don't listen when you tell them to leave."

"Yeah, well," Leroy said, resting his elbows on the railing. "Some people don't know how to stop fightin' for the ones they lost. Ain't the worst problem to have."

Her throat tightened. Showing up—again and again—wasn't courage. It was survival.

The sharp buzz of her phone cut through the still air, dragging her back to the moment.

Baily: *Got a delivery for you at the marina.*

Fallon frowned. The tension that had started to ease, coiled tight again.

"You look like the world just cracked open. What's wrong?"

"A package came for me at the marina, only I wasn't expecting anything."

Leroy arched an eyebrow. "You always order so many

164

different things, maybe you lost track. Maybe this will be a good surprise."

"With my luck lately?" She pocketed her phone. "That's doubtful." She handed him back the plate.

"We make our own luck," Leroy said. "I'm sorry, strange things have been happening to you. Buddy will figure it out. He's smart that way. He helped Hayes and Chloe bring in a serial killer. One that was hiding in plain sight. He'll catch whoever shot at you." Leroy smiled. "And he'll probably run away with your heart, too."

"Please. No one can do that."

"Your red cheeks say otherwise."

"It's hot out here."

"It's barely eighty, but you can tell yourself that." Leroy looped an arm over her shoulder. "I'm happy to see you with someone who not only challenges that personality of yours, but who can handle your grit."

"Oh, trust me, he can't handle anything about me." She chuckled. "But I'll give him credit—he's trying." She strolled up the dock toward the walkway that led down to the marina. "I'll see you later."

"I'll be here every day." Leroy waved. "Anything for you." He pushed open the door to the Crab Shack and disappeared.

She sighed. Time to go find out what extra goodies she ordered. It was like finding a twenty in the washing machine.

The boardwalk along the canal hummed with cicadas. The water stretched dark and glassy, stirred only by the lazy churn of an airboat somewhere downriver.

She passed the old crab pots stacked by the shed, the faint clang of tools carrying from Fletcher's workshop next door that he'd built for Cullen.

Calusa Cove was alive in its usual way—murmuring engines, distant laughter, the sound of her hometown breathing. It should've been comforting. Instead, it all felt too bright, too fragile, like one wrong step might shatter the illusion of safety she'd been pretending existed.

She waved at Silas as he unloaded tackle from his skiff. "Afternoon, Fallon," he called. "How goes things with the final prep this weekend? Anything I can do last-minute?"

"You've done so much already. I appreciate your generosity each and every year."

"If there's anything else you need help with, don't hesitate to call me. Day or night. I want to help." Silas stepped onto the dock. "Tessa was such a bright soul. I know it's hard for you, but you do so much to keep her memory alive.

He didn't know the half of it.

A memory twisted in her mind—Tessa laughing as they'd raced along this same stretch of dock, barefoot, wild, invincible.

"It's necessary." She smiled. "I'll see you Saturday." She continued walking toward the main building of the marina—the memory of Tessa rusting in her chest like an old, beat-up truck left in a vehicle graveyard.

She pulled open the door and found Baily behind the counter, paperwork spread across the desk. The smell of oil and burnt rope hit first—real, grounding.

"Hey," Baily said. "Package is on the table." She pointed. "Showed up about a half hour ago."

Fallon eyed the plain box on the counter. "I'm pretty sure I've already received everything I ordered."

"It came by special courier. I had to sign for it, so I figured it might be important."

"That's just weird." Fallon lifted the box from the table by the coffee machine and stared at it. Her name was written in bold block letters.

They stared at it together for a moment. The silence thickened, heavy with what neither of them wanted to say.

"Maybe it's a donation?" Baily suggested.

"Maybe." But Fallon's stomach had already gone tight, a deep pull low in her gut that said, *no, this isn't right.*

She pulled out her phone. "I'm calling Buddy."

He answered on the first ring. "You okay?"

"No one's shot at me, so that's a good thing," she said, hoping the sarcasm landed well. "But a package came to the marina today by special courier with my name on it, no return address."

"Don't open it." His voice was sharp, clipped, and low. That tone—controlled but edged—always set something in her chest off balance. "I'm with Dove. We'll be there in ten."

"Buddy—"

"Ten." He hung up.

Baily leaned over the box. "That man doesn't waste words now, does he?"

"Not often," Fallon said. "He hordes them like Halloween candy, but when he gets going, he can't stop."

Baily leaned her hip against the desk. "You really like him, don't you?"

Fallon hesitated for a moment. She was used to people knowing about her relationships. That didn't mean she didn't do her best to keep them private. But this was Baily. She'd been Fallon's babysitter and then her friend. "He's... mostly steady. I trust him. Which is probably why it scares the hell out of me."

"He's what—ten years older?"

"Give or take."

"Older doesn't mean broken."

Fallon gave a humorless laugh. "No, but it means he's lived through more wreckage. And I have a bad habit of running when things start to feel real."

"Maybe this time you stay," Baily said simply. "See what happens if you don't bolt."

The words hit harder than they should've. Fallon wanted to tell her she wasn't running, but the truth was, she'd always run. From loss. From guilt. From anything that might make her remember how much it hurt to lose the people she loved.

Before Fallon could answer, the door opened.

Buddy stepped inside, all focused movement and quiet tension. Dove followed, gloved and already scanning.

"Show me," Buddy said.

Fallon pointed to the counter. The box hummed with wrongness.

Dove leaned in, turning her head. "No ticking noise."

"Still, take it slow." Buddy inched closer.

Fallon wrapped her arms around her middle.

Dove slit the tape with a pocketknife. The blade made a sound that raised the hair on Fallon's arms. She held her breath, pulse thrumming in her throat.

Inside—fabric. Blue, soft, folded with care.

Fallon's knees weakened.

Dove reached in and gently pulled out a jacket. The lightweight navy material caught the light. The gold piping was new and across the back—her name stitched in bold white thread. REEVES.

It wasn't the same jacket Tessa had borrowed the night she vanished—but it was identical.

Her voice came out in a whisper. "That's a spirit school jacket. Just like the one Tessa borrowed the night she vanished." Fallon couldn't breathe. Her throat closed, her lungs refusing to expand. "My jacket was found on the side of the road by the marina parking lot," she said. "How... why... I don't understand."

"Is your jacket still with the police?" Buddy asked with a soft but steady voice.

"Tripp said it had to remain with what little evidence they had, so I believe so." Fallon pressed her hand against the center of her chest, as if to calm her heart rate.

"Who's Tripp?" Dove reached into the box again, tweezers pinching a folded note.

"He was the police chief here a few years before Dawson took over." Buddy took out a pair of gloves and snapped them in place before taking the note that Dove handed him.

His jaw tightened.

"What does it say?" she asked.

"It should've been you. Blue 42." Buddy placed the note back in the box, along with the jacket. He ripped off his gloves and swore under his breath. "Dove, call Dawson and Chloe. We need to get them down here. Then call Flagler. We've got to loop him in on this, even if I'd rather work this angle without the FBI breathing down my neck."

"On it." Dove stepped aside.

Fallon rubbed her shaky hands up and down her thighs. "Why is this happening?"

Buddy palmed her cheek. "Whoever is doing this is trying to get to me through you. It doesn't take but an internet search to figure out your connection to Tessa's Project and what happened. This asshole has been watching since you found that body in the Glades. I was there, and then we made it even easier by being together. He's trying to break me by hurting you where it will hit the hardest."

"Then he's getting what he wants." A tear rolled down her cheek. "Because I'm crumbling," she whispered.

"I'm not going to let this prick destroy you, me, or anyone else. My team is the best, and I don't have the constraints I used to with the FBI. I've got you." His voice was a low, steady anchor, but she could hear the strain underneath. He was trying to hold it together for her. She hated that part of her almost wanted him to fall apart too —just so she wouldn't feel so alone in it.

"You believe this is only about you?"

"I think everything about this screams 'personal'— unfortunately, anyone in my life is going to be collateral damage in this jerk's game. And I don't mean just you. They could've targeted anyone on my team. Or Chloe. Or anyone they thought I was close to." He pointed toward the box. "They're using what they can to send me a message. I just don't know exactly what it all means, yet."

"So, me, my fundraiser for Tessa, that's just the bait?"

"I'm sorry." He thumbed away the wetness on her cheeks and stared deeply into her eyes. The gesture was kind, caring... but she could feel the guilt and torment in his touch.

"Don't apologize for something neither of us did."

Wind pushed through the open door, carrying swamp heat and the smell of sunbaked wood. The flags along the dock snapped once, like punctuation.

"Everyone in this town remembers when Tessa went missing. But what I don't remember is if it was reported that the police found Fallon's jacket," Baily said.

"It wasn't." Fallon wrapped her arms around her middle. "But I don't know anyone who doesn't know she was wearing it. Silas was the one who found it. And this town can't keep a secret."

"What kind of person sends something like that?" Baily asked.

"The kind that wants to remind you they still own

the story." Buddy pulled Fallon close to his chest, holding her tight in his strong arms, as if no one else was in the room.

But she couldn't breathe and she needed air. Needed space. She stepped back and looked inside the box again. The note open. The words echoed—*It should've been you.*

She felt the air shift, the world narrow until all she could see was that single cruel line. She'd been telling herself the same damn thing since Tessa vanished. And someone had gone to a lot of trouble to let her know they agreed.

Buddy's hand brushed hers, lacing his fingers through hers, squeezing tight, as if to anchor her to him. "You're safe."

She wanted to believe that. She really did. But safety had betrayed her before, and trust didn't come easy anymore. When she glanced out the window toward the water, the reflection in the dark current rippled—and for half a second, she thought she saw movement in the mangroves.

Her pulse jumped.

And for the first time, the Everglades didn't feel like home.

It felt like a warning.

Chapter Fourteen

The conference room in the Calusa Cove Police Department wasn't big enough for this many shadows—not when half of them belonged to Buddy. They circled the chairs, clung to the walls, breathed in the quiet between words.

He leaned against the edge of the table, arms folded, watching Dawson spread out the old file like it was a fragile relic. He pushed a piece of paper across the table with a gentle finger. Placed an image of Tessa in the corner. He barely touched the sides of the photograph. With gentle hands, he laid a crime scene report in the center of the table—just a single page with only a few words about where the jacket had been found, which Dawson had sent to the lab to recheck DNA. It was a long shot, but worth a try.

Buddy scanned the information a second time. Not much of a crime scene.

The overhead lights hummed—too bright, too clinical

—bleaching the room and making everything feel sharper than it needed to be.

Chloe stood beside Dawson—her dark hair scraped into a no-nonsense knot with a few stray strands escaping the elastic band. It was a far cry from the perfect ponytail or bun she wore back when she'd been an FBI agent. Motherhood, marriage, and a badge had brought forth a more relaxed, a more alive version of Chloe. And she wore her new life with pride and a happiness that Buddy, oddly, envied.

She smiled faintly—one of those "we're in the shit again" smiles they'd shared when they'd worked the same halls but different units with the FBI. They often passed files that in the beginning seemed unrelated but somehow always managed to be tangled in their respective cases. She was one of the best, and from the moment he'd met her, he knew the second she'd found her sister's killer, she'd be turning in her badge and walking out the door and moving on to something more peaceful.

He just never expected she would've traded it in to be a cop in a small town. Then again, he never thought he'd be working for a security firm that took on a wide variety of missions. It wasn't the job that was a shocker. It was the fact that Buddy, the rules guy, was willing to skirt a few as well as bend some laws to get the job done.

Flagler stood near the whiteboard, sleeves rolled to his elbows, and tie gone—which almost never happened. When it did, shit was about to get real. He looked like he'd walked straight out of Quantico and into a sauna. Florida humidity was not his friend, and neither was this case. Flagler was the kind of man who was not only married to the job, but the job was also his mistress. However, this was the kind of case that changed a man.

Buddy knew that firsthand.

Silas sat stiff in one of the metal chairs, hat in his hands, knuckles white against the brim. He was the heart of Calusa Cove—the man who knew every crack in every street and every secret worth keeping.

Flagler eyed him with suspicion. He hadn't wanted him in this meeting for one simple fact—he didn't carry a badge, nor had he previously worked for the FBI. However, in this town, sometimes that didn't matter, and Silas knew more about this case than anyone... except maybe Fallon.

But she needed a break and was currently basking in some good old-fashioned girl time with Audra, Dawson's wife, Trinity, Keaton's wife, and Baily, Fletcher's wife. Fallon had balked at the idea at first but gave in quickly. She might be a bit younger than that group, but they were her friends and among the best women in this town.

Buddy pushed all that out of his mind. No distractions. He needed to focus.

He stared at the papers on the table—the Tessa Blake file.

Old. Thin. Too thin.

Dawson set the folder aside. Its edges were soft to the touch, worn by years of being opened and closed without ever finding an answer.

"Alright. Let's walk through it." Dawson glanced at

Silas. "I know you've told this story a few times, but I've never heard it in an official capacity."

"It's strange. This town talks about Tessa all the time. About what happened, but after a few years, the authorities just stopped asking." Silas ran a hand over his scruffy white face. "I'm not casting judgment, I'm just saying there's never been a lead. Never a single clue. Not one piece of evidence. The cops never had a direction, and no one ever believed that the child ran away. She wouldn't have done that."

"We're listening." Dawson pulled a chair out, sat down, folded his hands, resting them on the table and leaned forward. "And I promise you, I will do what I can to find a lead. To find answers."

"We appreciate you coming in and doing this," Chloe said gently. She spoke in that calm voice—the one she used with victims and shaken witnesses. "Take your time."

Silas nodded, eyes dropping to the papers on the table as if they might bite. "Tessa was at the Crab Shack the night she vanished. This was before the place started to fall apart completely. Before the fire. Before Dawson here and the rest of his team rebuilt it and made it a booming business it again. Back then, the Crab Shack had character. The tables had gum stuck under them. The vinyl on the booths was cracked. But our town has always loved that little spot, and old man Tomey tried real hard to keep it going. And he loved hiring local kids. Those girls were willing to do anything. Wait tables and bus them. Do dishes. Cook. Clean the fryers. Heck, one year they even helped wash out the dumpsters. What a nasty job."

"I know this isn't easy," Dawson said. "But can we keep the focus on Tessa?"

"Sorry. It's hard for me not to go down memory lane when I think about all this." Silas sighed. "Anyway, Tessa wasn't supposed to be working that night, but none of us knew that Fallon was scheduled for the shift. Tessa picked it up so Fallon could go see her boyfriend."

Buddy felt something hitch in his chest—not surprise, not shock. Just the reminder that Fallon had spent every year since that night drowning in guilt for making that choice.

"They were always together. Those girls... they were wild in the way good kids can be. Loud. Full of life. Loyal. Always giggling. I pretended to give them a hard time. Like I did with Fletcher and Ken. Or Trent and Cullen. It's supposed to be my thing, but those two always had a special place in my heart. Kind of like Baily and Audra." Silas swiped at his eyes.

Chloe flipped a page in her notebook and scribbled something down. "You were there that night. Did you notice anything strange about Tessa's behavior? Was she unusually nervous? Talkative? Did she seem preoccupied? Or did she leave early?"

"She was bright and bubbly as always. Snuck us an extra basket of onion rings. She and Fallon were always doing that, and not for a bigger tip. They just did stuff like that. I once saw them pool their tips to help a family who couldn't buy ice cream sundaes for their kids." Silas shifted his gaze toward the small transom window. "She left right at closing. Walked out with me, Hondo's dad, may he rest in peace, and Monty, Trinity's dad. We all split off at the lot." Silas lowered his chin and shook his head. "I should've waited for her parents to come get her. I should've insisted when she told me that she'd be fine and to go home."

"Hey." Chloe reached out and touched Silas' hand. "We live in one of the safest small towns in South Florida. You couldn't have predicted what happened any more than I can predict the next time Max is going to try to shove something up his little sister's nose."

Silas snorted. "You've got your hands full with that one."

"I know." She smiled.

Buddy had always admired the way she handled herself during interviews with witnesses. And she was damn scary when interrogating suspects.

"Please, continue," Dawson said.

"The next morning, before sunrise, but after we all knew Tessa hadn't gotten home, I found Fallon's jacket. Tessa had borrowed it—it was right by the marina parking lot. Hidden in the brush near the fence by the walkway. It was folded, nice and neat, which seemed weird."

"That *is* odd," Flagler said quietly, like the words tasted wrong.

Dawson leaned back. "Tripp noted that in the original report. He thought it meant staging, and they searched for days for a body, but one was never found."

Buddy had never known Tripp, but he'd heard

stories. A small-town police chief who didn't always do things by the book but never bent the law to the point of breaking it. "According to his report, he never believed she ran away, like some other experts did."

"A couple of the FBI agents who'd rolled into town to help believed she ran off. The state investigator did as well. But anyone who'd spent any time with Tessa knew she wasn't the kind of kid who took off," Silas said. "Tripp hated having nothing to hand Tessa's family. Hated even more when he knew there were a few other girls not far from here who went missing during that two-year period. But he couldn't connect the dots on his own, and no one would listen."

Flagler straightened. "I checked those cases. Two still missing. One body was recovered a month later near Coral Bay. Never solved."

"Same age range?" Buddy asked.

"Seventeen to nineteen."

Silas scratched at his scruffy face. "This town's been on edge ever since. Parents started checking windows twice before bed. Curfews. Kids didn't walk home alone after dark. Then Dewey, a man who'd basically lived here his entire life, ended up being the Ring Finger killer, and that didn't help."

Chloe snorted, then covered her mouth. "Understatement of the decade."

Buddy understood why Chloe might find the statement teetering on dark humor. Dewey had murdered her sister, among over thirty other victims. Not to mention, as it turned out, Dewey was her biological father. When everything was said and done, she found out she had a half-sister.

Talk about strange times.

Silas glanced between them all. "Look—Tessa's case—it's the one that this town never let go. I'm sure Tripp wrote about it in his private journal. He kept those pages separate from his reports. Like he was trying to solve it in his sleep. He did that with a lot of things."

"I'm well aware." Dawson lifted the leatherbound book, flipping through Tripp's sparse notes. "Not much here about the investigation. Just mentions of the families, Fallon's grief, and the fact that he hated dead ends. The rest is just his frustration over having no leads and nothing to give the family."

Silas's hands trembled on the brim of his cap. "Fallon did everything she could to help back then. She was just a kid herself. But she never stopped—fundraisers, prevention work, speaking at schools. All of South Florida knows who she is and who she lost."

Buddy's throat tightened because he knew exactly how many ways loss could twist a person.

And Fallon... hers was woven into everything she did.

"Thank you, Silas. That's all we need right now," Flagler said.

Silas stood. Paused. Looked at Buddy with something like an apology. "I hope you catch whoever's doing this. Fallon deserves peace. Been a long time coming."

"We will," Buddy vowed.

Silas tipped his head and headed toward the door. As he reached for the handle, he paused again. "Oh—

Dawson? I thought you should know that I told public works the channel markers from forty-one to forty-six need repainting. Faded to hell. Nearly put some idiot tourist in the mangroves last week."

Buddy's pulse raced, but he didn't move. Instead, he processed the information.

Red and green channel markers. Not blue.

But still.

"I know, but thanks. I'm pretty sure both Fletcher and Keaton have spoken to them as well. Keaton said he'd paint them personally."

"Just out of curiosity," Buddy said. "Where are those channel markers?"

"Forty-one's at the mouth of the channel into the bay. Forty-two is between the marina and Crab Shack. The rest move into the Glades toward Snake River." Silas glanced between Buddy and Dawson. "Anything else?"

Buddy shook his head.

"We're good for now," Dawson said.

Silas left, the door clicking shut behind him.

Buddy's pulse clicked higher.

Blue 42.

A call at the line. A shift. A signal before the play changes.

And now—a channel marker.

Right between the marina and the Crab Shack.

Part of Fallon's work patrol. Part of where she'd spent her entire life. Her sanctuary.

Tessa's last shift.

Could it be the place where everything began?

A cold, clean line sliced through his mind—clarity he didn't want but couldn't ignore.

He didn't speak. He couldn't. Not yet. He let Dawson and Chloe shuffle papers. Let Flagler rub his temples. Let his brain put the pieces in a line he wished didn't make sense.

"Buddy?" Chloe placed a warm hand on his forearm. "When you go quiet and still like this, your brain is turning something over. What is it?"

Buddy scrubbed a hand across his jaw. "I think I know what Blue 42 means."

"We're listening," Dawson said.

"Keaton was right. It's an audible change. I know Simon's behind bars and—"

"He's refusing to speak to me, but word has it, he's not running anything. That no one will talk to him from the outside," Flagler said. "That he's been blackballed from what was left of his own network."

"That may be true. But someone who either worked with him or knows him is making a play change to get me to come out and run defense." Buddy generally didn't like to speak in analogies, but this prick didn't give him a choice. "Blue could mean a lot of things, and whoever this is, knows it. That means they know Simon. They also know things about me. About the trafficking pipeline I shut down. But more than letting me know the game's changed, they were indicating a location in that statement."

Flagler straightened. "The channel markers that Silas just referenced?"

"Marker 42 is between the Crab Shack and the marina," Buddy said. "I bet if you stand where the jacket was found the day after Tessa went missing and looked out at the channel, you'd be staring dead center at channel marker 42. They've known all along about Tessa and Fallon, and that makes me wonder about a few things."

"Jesus." Chloe exhaled. "I've struggled with whoever this guy is using Fallon to get your attention. Tessa isn't related to your case. But it's all blending together, and that doesn't feel right."

"Agreed." Dawson frowned. "Not to put your personal life under fire, but you and Fallon, from all the chatter that's landed on my ears, didn't start seeing each other until after Fallon found the first victim."

"That's true. But we've been friends for a long time, and we've been in contact with each other for years. However, that's not the point. If the case I closed is somehow connected to Tessa, then whoever this is would've fucked with Fallon regardless of whether or not I spent the night at her house just because she's here and so am I."

Buddy shook his head, slow and grim. "This asshole is letting me know that I was only quarterbacking for part of the game, and that game isn't over—because I can't possibly save them all." The back of his neck prickled. His chest tightened. "And he's reminding Fallon it could've been her. And no matter how much awareness and money she raises, she can't bring Tessa back, and she can't stop this from happening to others."

He heard his old instructor's voice from Quantico in

the back of his skull. *When a predator knows your history, he weaponizes it.*

Dawson leaned forward. "Are you saying that Tessa Blake was trafficked through the same or similar pipeline as the one you shut down? That maybe this would've always found its way to my town?"

"I don't believe this guy would be here without me," Buddy said. "I'm the catalyst. Me moving here gave him more to work with regarding what happened with Tessa. He can weaponize both, putting me not only on the defensive but also in the role of protector. Blue 42 is also him saying, 'I know where your blind spot lives'." Abruptly, he began to pace. He needed to move. To think. He'd brought this right to everyone's doorstep. To Fallon. Now, he had to find a way to stop it before anyone else went missing.

Or died.

"I don't like it when you scuff floors," Chloe said. "It means you're not only pissed off, but you're on edge, and not in a good way."

He paused and shifted his gaze. "Before I left Jacksonville to open this office, I begged my boss to relocate. I worked him hard for this location. Everyone busted my ass because they figured it had to be because of a woman. They couldn't believe I willingly wanted to move to a small town like Calusa Cove. Not when I could live in Miami. Fort Lauderdale. Or even Tampa. Hell, I could've gone northwest to Destin or Pensacola. But if I was gonna do it, it had to be this town, or nowhere at all."

"And why was that?" Dawson asked. "Were you and Fallon—"

"No," Buddy said swiftly. "But we've kept in touch. Spoken to each other on the phone. Texted, and some of the messages might be considered explicit." He rubbed the back of his neck. "Before I moved, we hadn't seen each other since the grand reopening of the Crab Shack. But I was there. I flirted with Fallon, and she flirted back. I thought about her. About something happening, but it didn't. However, I want you to think about that timeline for a second." Buddy cocked his head, glancing around the room.

Dawson's body went rigid.

Chloe's jaw slacked open.

Flagler exhaled, loudly, as he fell back in the chair. "Jesus. You were still with the FBI—working that case."

"I was knee deep in it, and there was a very real part of me that didn't think I should come—considering the operation and where it was heading," Buddy said. "But I did, and it's very possible someone was watching, keeping track of the people I got close to here. I've also made donations to Tessa's Project since I learned about it. If someone's been tracking me and my ties to Calusa Cove, it's possible they've also been tracking Fallon."

"How often did you and she communicate?" Chloe asked.

"After the grand opening, it was probably four or five times a week for close to a year. But I felt like I was leading her on, and the case was getting difficult, so things slowed down. It became more of us checking in with each other. More of a proof of life kind of thing." Buddy leaned against the desk. "Fallon's gonna kill me, but I started only texting at work, to keep myself from making inappropriate remarks."

"Audra would hog tie me and feed me to the gators if I said anything." Dawson stuffed his hands in his pockets.

"Any chance someone at the Aegis Network could be dirty?" Flagler asked.

"Doubtful, but I suppose anything's possible." Buddy rubbed the back of his neck. "I'll have Logan Sarich and his wife, Mia, out of the Orlando office, check into it. They worked with Fletcher—"

"I know them well." Dawson nodded. "I'd trust the Sarich brothers with the lives of my kids. They're about as solid as they come."

Flagler stood, glancing at his watch. "I best get going. Check in with me regularly. I'll do the same."

"Thanks for coming." Dawson opened the door, stepping aside, then tugged it closed. He leaned against the wall and folded his arms. "Do you remember Bingo?"

"The dock hand that worked for Baily?" Buddy asked. "Didn't he join the Navy?"

"He did." Dawson nodded. "He's in SEAL training. He turned out to be quite the young man. We're very proud."

"I bet," Buddy said. "I remember he was pretty protective of Baily."

"He views her like a big sister." Dawson dropped his arms to his side and stuffed his hands in his pockets.

"Anyway, he's coming back to town for the fundraiser. Fallon doesn't know. He wants to surprise her."

"That's nice. I'm sure she'll love it." It always amazed Buddy how close this community was—even after residents left—they were still part of the town.

"How's Fallon holding up with all that's been happening?" Chloe gathered all the papers and the file and neatly stacked them in the corner of the table.

Buddy swallowed, a knot forming hard and unmovable in his chest. "She's tough. One of the toughest women I've ever known. But she's... she's showing cracks."

"Understandable," Dawson said.

Buddy stared at the wall as if he could see right through it and into the water beyond. "She and Cullen could've died in that fire in the Glades. She almost got shot, but instead, Trent took that bullet for her. Someone left that note at her house. Sent that jacket to the marina. Every hit keeps landing on her—but something tells me the messaging is meant for me." He exhaled. Slow. Controlled. Not enough. "I'm worried and not in the conventional way. Not in the way that gets my hair standing on end during a case. It's more than whatever our unsub is doing now... but what he's planning next because this is no longer just a case. It's personal."

Dawson drummed his fingers once on the table. "I keep circling back to you and Fallon and what would've happened if you hadn't come to Calusa Cove."

"Fallon's life would've gone on as usual. Her fundraiser would've continued. And there'd be no clues as to what might've happened to Tessa. And I'd still be dealing with this, but the audible call would be different. The game slightly different."

"So, Blue 42 is still a taunt, regardless of what it means."

"No." Buddy shook his head. "It's worse."

They all looked at him.

Buddy lifted the old folder with Fallon's name scrawled in the corner.

"It's the starting point. Whoever's doing this knew Simon. Probably did business with him, and I screwed that up. But I'm thinking this whole thing is bigger. Broader. That the second I came to Calusa Cove, I triggered something. That maybe I just reminded them of a girl they stole in the night and a woman who's trying to keep her memory alive."

And for the first time since he'd stepped into the room, Buddy felt the familiar weight settle in—determination sharpened by dread.

He wasn't just hunting a trafficker now.

He was hunting a man using the past as a blueprint.

His past.

Fallon's.

Tessa's.

And the girls he couldn't save.

He reached for the folder, opened it, sighed, then closed it, reverently, like closing a wound. "We need to move fast," he said, voice steady but dark. "Because what-ever this jerk is trying to say, he's not done talking."

Chapter Fifteen

The fire pit crackled like it had something to add to the conversation. Fallon pushed her bare feet closer to the warmth and let her head tip back against the Adirondack chair, the sky black and velvet, overhead. Nights like these were a contradiction. They pretended to be peaceful. They lulled a soul into a sense of serenity. They cut through armor meant to protect, while the beauty of the evening hid the shadows that stole the precious and innocent.

When she'd lived with Trent, she'd sit out under the tiki hut at Mallor's Landing, stare at the lily pads, and try to forget about grief, ghosts, and loneliness. And for a brief moment, it worked. Until the darkness crept into her mind like fog rolling across the Glades, reaching into the roots of the mangrove, reminding her that life had hardened her in ways she couldn't ignore.

Soft laughter filled the air and dragged her back to

the moment. She'd learned to live for the times when the world seemed to stand still, and she could allow herself the joys of what life could be. Of what she believed it should be.

The bed and breakfast Audra and Dawson owned sat tucked behind her and her friends. The old, rundown shell had been turned into a cozy rental with string lights, mismatched furniture, and a fire pit that smelled faintly of orange wood. Around the pit were some of the best women Calusa Cove had to offer. Audra was a native to the town, and she had a rich history that people still enjoyed whispering about under a bright moon around a fire much like this one. Then there was Baily. She'd suffered profound loss but managed to keep it all together while fighting for her family legacy.

Fallon shifted her gaze to Trinity and smiled, thinking about how odd it was, yet utterly perfect, that she'd formed such a tight bond with the other two women. Trinity had been born into money. She'd been raised by a mom who'd told her she was better than everyone in this town When Trinity had been younger, she'd tended to treat everyone as though she believed it—including Audra and Baily. But now, they were like sisters.

That thought brought Fallon right back to ghosts—to Tessa. Fallon lifted her tequila and gulped, doing her best to push the past into the flames and refocused on the conversation, which she'd missed the last few minutes of.

"... And then my lovely little Petra looked me square

in the eye, with her hands on her hips and asked me if this baby was going to come out of my vagina." She patted her belly.

"Now I know where Victor learned that word." Audra smiled. "Of course, he also knows the word penis, and he uses it at the strangest times."

"What I want to know is how she figured out how babies are born," Baily said. "Fletcher and I have had to explain all sorts of things to Todd and Chad, including how to make a baby." Baily smacked her palm to her forehead. "Hardest conversation... ever. Sadly, they already knew most of it. But Petra is only three."

"She found my baby birthing book." Trinity shrugged. "Keaton and I—well, mostly me—are looking into alternative options. Like water birth at home."

Everyone around the fire pit burst out laughing—including Fallon. Anyone who knew Trinity, knew that she hated being in pain, even though she didn't want drugs for fear of what it would do to her baby. She also didn't want stretch marks or scars.

Trinity was an awesome person. Kind. Considerate. Generous. But calling her vain would be the understatement of the year.

"It's not *that* funny." Trinity leaned over and snagged a cracker from the tray. "Even Keaton didn't laugh at me." She smiled. "But I did tell him about it while he was stuffing his face full of his favorite home-cooked meal."

Fallon's chest tightened, and a vision of Buddy from last night flashed across her mind. They were in his kitchen, making dinner together. It was light, fun, and simple. She hadn't put any context on it because she'd cooked with other men she'd dated before. She loved to cook. She loved food. It had always been her way of decompressing—of washing away a bad day—or just enjoying a quiet moment with someone she liked being around.

But all of a sudden, something clicked, snapped into place—and she realized this was different. This simple domestic task shared with Buddy filled spaces inside her that she hadn't known existed. This hadn't just been about fulfilling her body's demand for food while scratching an itch with someone convenient. They hadn't simply been going through the motions. Her connection with Buddy was honest and real—no pretense, no games, just something solid she could actually trust.

The image of her and Buddy flashing through her brain sent longing twisting trough her veins, and she wanted more—craved it with a hunger that terrified her. But in the strangest way, it anchored a truth she'd been running from for years—the idea that she could want someone and keep them. That wanting didn't have to mean losing.

Baily leaned over and placed her hand on Fallon's leg and squeezed. "I'm sorry. It's hard for us to sit around and not talk about families."

Audra lifted her glass. "Okay, new rule. No discussing husbands or kids unless it's absolutely hilarious or involves bodily fluids."

Trinity snorted. "In this group, that's the same thing."

Fallon laughed, the buzz of the tequila warming her edges. She'd needed this. Women. Laughter. Connection.

The word stuck.

Her chest tightened. When was the last time she'd let herself have this? Real friends. Real conversation. Not just surface-level politeness or professional courtesy.

Not since Tessa.

Buddy had cracked something open. These women—Baily, Trinity, Audra—were slipping through that crack, filling spaces she'd kept empty for years.

She'd had Trent once. But back then, she'd been too raw. Too aware that connection meant attachment and attachment meant loss. She'd pushed him away before he could leave first.

Buddy was different. Bigger. Brighter. Something solid she could actually hold onto.

Which made him just as terrifying as a gator waiting submerged in dark water—patient, invisible, ready to strike.

Trinity nudged her foot. "You've been quiet, and you're usually one to take a shot at Fletcher. And if Chloe were here, I know you'd have a good story about Hayes falling off his little fishing boat the other day."

"Yeah, that was a good one. But, right now, I'm enjoying the show," Fallon said, swirling the last bit of her beverage. "It's like National Geographic: Domestic Edition."

"Domestic?" Audra cackled. "Honey, have you met our husbands? Keaton once tried to convince me that using duct tape to secure Christmas lights was 'structurally sound.' And Fletcher wears Crocs in public."

"Those were a gift," Baily protested. "From someone he helped after falling on a trail. He was being polite."

"He kept wearing them," Trinity said. "That man does not need encouragement."

Fallon smiled, but something inside tugged—soft, uncertain. The warmth of the fire blurred into a sweetness she hadn't expected. Watching these women tease their husbands, talk about their kids, build this little community of chaos and comfort... it hit somewhere she rarely let herself look.

The future.

A real one.

A house. A yard. A dog. Maybe a kid—a little girl—with a stubborn streak and her father's eyes.

It wasn't a dream she chased. Never had been. Fallon had always lived moment to moment because she knew better than anyone how fast life could tilt. One second, she's making spring break plans with her best friend—the next, she's searching the Everglades for a body.

But lately...

Buddy had become a complication she hadn't seen coming. Older, sure. A little damaged, absolutely. But steady, and warm in ways that terrified her. And when she let herself look even half an inch too far into the future, she saw a white picket fence—something she didn't think she wanted until she could imagine wanting it with him.

Not that she was in love with him.

That would be ridiculous.

Dangerous.

They'd been dating for a week. It was intense. Wild. And the love making—well, just wow.

But if she wasn't careful, he was the kind of man she could fall in love with.

And maybe she wasn't being as careful as she thought.

"You're doing it again," Audra said gently, pulling Fallon back. "The thinking face. The one where you stare past the horizon into space like you're already on a rocket ship heading for the moon."

Fallon rubbed her forehead. "I don't have a thinking face."

Baily raised a brow. "Sweetie, your thinking face has a thinking face."

"We started these nights so none of us had to be lost in our own thoughts. So that we always had a safe place to land and say anything, no matter how outrageous we think it might be. So, whatever it is that's got you looking more constipated than Fletcher when he can't figure something out," Trinity said, eyes twinkling. "Just let it out. It's not going anywhere but up to the sky with smoke from the fire."

"Is it about Buddy?" Baily asked.

Heat crept up Fallon's neck. "I don't know what you're talking about."

"Oh, she's absolutely talking about Buddy," Audra said. "Because I've seen that look before. Trinity had it for a year before she and Keaton finally got together. It's the 'I actually like this man, but not sure how to deal with it' look."

Fallon lifted her tumbler, tossed her head back, and polished off her drink. "It's... complicated."

"Good complicated?" Baily asked. "Or run-in-the-opposite-direction complicated? Because this group knows all about relationships that don't have a clear path. We've all had to jump over things, crawl under them, and dodge a few bullets to get to where we are."

Fallon hesitated, collecting her thoughts. The alcohol loosened her tongue, but not enough to drown her senses. "It's... both. He kind of scares me, and that's pretty hard to do considering I lived with Trent for a few months."

"That one still blows my mind." Audra leaned closer. "I can't imagine it's his job that frightens you because you carry a weapon. And you've never shied away from things like that. So, I'm guessing it's the 'if I let myself feel this, I'm gonna fall hard' kind of fear."

"And maybe because Buddy's a bit broken?" Trinity asked. "Because we all know about broken men."

Fallon stared into the fire, letting the flames blur, while she tried to unjumble her thoughts and untangle the feelings she didn't quite know what to do with or where to file them. "I've never thought about marriage or kids or any of that because it's never been a priority for me."

"And Buddy's making you rethink your life structure?" Audra asked.

"I don't know. Maybe some of it's him, and maybe some of it is sitting here with all of you. Listening to you poke fun at your lives, that you obviously wouldn't change a single thing, and I realize how thick and strong my walls are." She swallowed the bitter taste of truth.

"We all do things to protect ourselves," Audra said. "We've all had to break out of metaphorical chains. You've had a lot of loss in your life and at a young age. I know what that's like. It hardens the heart and bleeds the soul. However, we've all learned that ghosts of our past don't have to command where we go in the future."

"Damn, that's poetic, and you're not even drinking." Trinity shifted, rubbing a hand over her expanding stomach. "Fallon, let me ask you this. Can you visualize the kind of life you want in five years? Does it differ from what you wanted before you and Buddy became a thing?"

Oh boy, that was a big question. Fallon wasn't sure she was prepared to be completely honest with these women, much less herself, with her answer. "Before, I couldn't see it. A life with a partner. With kids. I've always dated guys with the emotional maturity of a teenager. Or they're more damaged than I am and I can't do that anymore." She shifted, crossing her legs at her ankles. Her pulse kicked up a notch, and a bolt of adrenaline coursed through her like she'd downed a shot of fireball. "I look at Buddy, and everything inside me settles. When I'm with him, especially when chaos hits, I don't feel alone. While I know this town has wrapped me in a warm blanket ever since my parents died, I feel like an outsider."

"I'm sorry if I've ever made you feel like you don't belong," Baily said.

"You've never done that. No one has. It's me. It's like the day Tessa disappeared, I decided to torture myself for the rest of my life." She swiped at her eyes, hoping to keep the tears at bay. "If Tessa can no longer have it, then neither should I. And for years, I've told myself I didn't want it, anyway. That I could live out my days on 'good enough'. But now, it's like my brain finally stopped pretending I don't want someone to share my life with. I now want to be completely happy with all the messy parts that come with a family. I don't know what to do with that."

"That's not a bad thing," Baily said softly.

Logically, Fallon knew that. But knowing and believing were two different things. She'd spent so long convinced she didn't deserve happiness that wanting it felt like betrayal.

"Do you feel guilty for wanting all the things someone took from Tessa?" Audra asked.

"Yeah. Sometimes." The guilt had been easier to carry than the risk of actually living. Safer. Like if she stayed small enough, grief couldn't find her again. "But being around this. Being with Buddy. If it had been me who'd vanished, I'd haunt Tessa to the ends of the Everglades for not living her life. She'd tell me to stop being stupid and take it."

"So, what's the problem?" Trinity asked.

"The problem is, the guy I'm seeing doesn't want any of that. And he's made it clear he's temporary. And I agreed." Fallon shrugged. "At the time, I couldn't see past the bed sheets." Fallon tugged at a loose thread on her shorts. "Now, I'm not sure I want to let him go."

"You two are magnets," Trinity said. "And magnets don't do temporary."

Fallon opened her mouth to argue, but headlights swung across the yard.

Buddy.

Her pulse tripped.

He stepped out of his SUV, moving with the low, quiet confidence that always made something in her chest go warm and unsteady. He spotted her instantly, and despite the chaos of the world outside this backyard, he smiled.

A genuine one that made her stomach twist in circles like the beginning of a tornado.

"Hey," he said, his voice a low rumble that did terrible things to her insides. "You ready?"

Fallon blinked. "You're early."

"You texted me that you were tipsy," he said with a smile that was so kind and sweet. How could she see beyond the moment? "I thought maybe since this bunch is all pregnant, you were drinking for four."

Audra turned and glared. "It's just mean to remind a red-headed pregnant woman she can't have a drink."

Buddy laughed, and Fallon hated—hated—that the sound made her breath catch.

When she stood, he reached for her hand, warm and steady. She swayed the tiniest bit, and he tightened his grip. Protective. Careful. Too damn good.

And too damn fleeting.

He leaned in and kissed her cheek, letting his lips linger a little longer than necessary. Sweet. Simple. The kind of gesture you gave someone when you were keeping things casual, keeping things light.

Except her pulse kicked up, her chest tightened, and every nerve ending where his mouth touched her skin lit up as if he'd branded her. For something that was supposed to be short-lived that kiss sure as hell whispered forever.

"It's always good to see you ladies." He waved and they waved back, saying their good-byes, promising they'd do it all again.

The walk to his vehicle was strangely intimate—his hand around hers, her mind spinning with tequila and longing and danger. He opened the door for her, like he always did, and she climbed in, heart tapping too fast.

The drive was only five minutes, but she studied him the entire time—the strong line of his jaw, the way his hands wrapped around the steering wheel, the faint tension in his shoulders like he was constantly holding something in.

Even when he was soft with her, he held something back.

She didn't ask. Had never asked. She wasn't sure she wanted the answer. Or maybe she already knew it.

Temporary.

No promises.

This was just fun while it lasted.

Trouble was, she wanted it to last. For the first time in

her life, she wanted to find out what the possibility of a future was like, and she wanted it to be with Buddy. Granted, she couldn't force him to want that too. Besides, maybe she wouldn't fall...who was she kidding? She was halfway there.

They pulled into the rental and strolled up the path to the door. A million things raced through her mind, but she couldn't focus on anything but him. On being with him.

He barely had the door closed before she grabbed his shirt, fisting the fabric, yanking him down into a kiss that was hungry, hot, and desperate.

He responded instantly—hands on her waist, mouth claiming hers in a way that made her knees go weak. Their tongues twisting and rolling over each other, hungry and relentless.

She shoved him into the wall, needing him, needing this, needing the noise in her head to quiet.

He kissed her like he'd needed her, too—like the last twenty-four hours had exposed something raw in him. He lifted her off the ground and turned, slamming her back against the wall, his knee shoved between her legs. His fingers dug into her hips like he was staking a claim.

She glided her hand across his neck, down his back, over his hip, doing her best to wedge it between their bodies, and find... him.

Abruptly, he curled his fingers around her wrist, placed her hand on his shoulder, and cupped her face, his breath harsh against her lips. He held her still, staring down at her with eyes that saw far too much.

Her chest heaved.

His did too.

She brushed her mouth against his, voice a whisper frayed at the edges. "I need you." She swallowed hard, fingers curling into his shirt. "Just you. I need to forget everything else—everything happening out there. I need to lose myself in you."

Buddy's breath hitched at her plea, his gaze searing into hers, the intensity of it more intoxicating than any tequila. A flicker of something undefinable, more potent than lust, shimmered in the depths of his eyes. Or maybe that's what she wanted to see—hoped to see.

He leaned in, his lips brushing over hers, slow and deliberate. Each touch, each moment, was a question, an invitation, and an affirmation. All she wanted to do was strip them of their clothes and feel every inch of him inside her, stroking her, making her withe in his passion.

With a growl, he shifted his grip to her thighs, lifting her higher against the wall. The sudden movement forced a shocked gasp from her, but it morphed into a moan as his mouth traced a path from her lips down to the pulse beating wildly at her throat. Every nerve was electric, her body humming in anticipation.

He stepped from the wall and his hand slipped under the hem of her shirt, tracing the sensitive skin of her lower back. Her muscles jumped in response, her breath hitching as his fingers found the clasp of her bra.

This wasn't new territory. They'd had sex at least five times in this house. His bed. The shower. Even the kitchen. She'd always enjoyed the physical act. She'd never been shy when it came to her body. Or men.

But now that she'd opened up a little to the girls—and to herself—this felt so very different. It wasn't just physical anymore. It was intimate in a way that terrified and thrilled her. Like he wasn't just touching her body—he was touching something deeper.

He unhooked her undergarment and carried her, his arms securely wrapped around her waist, as he walked from the hallway and into the bedroom.

He paused, almost imperceptibly, at the threshold of the room. It was as if the air itself held its breath, their bodies silhouetted by the soft spill of moonlight through the window. The space was familiar, but the feeling was intoxicatingly foreign. With every step he took, her heart pounded louder, echoing in her ears. She clung to him, her fingers digging into the fabric of his shirt, craving the sensation of skin against skin.

Buddy set her down on the edge of the bed, his hands solid and warm on either side of her waist. Never breaking eye contact, he gently tugged her shirt over her head, letting it drop to the floor. He slid her unclasped bra off her shoulders, tossing it across the room. A sudden coolness licked at her skin, raising goosebumps in its wake. His gaze seared her with a tenderness, that fluttered her stomach.

He stood at the edge of the bed, staring down at her, and traced a finger across her jawline, down her neck, over the top swell of her breast, and circled her taut nipple.

She reached for him, unbuckling his belt, fingers fumbling in anticipation as she unzipped his jeans and pushed them over his hips and down his thighs. Swiftly, he ripped off his shirt and kicked off his pants. He stood, –a statue in the imperfect light. She drank in the sight of his form. Even in silence, every contour of his body whispered to her, each muscle a testament to a life lived in service and sacrifice that she was just beginning to understand.

The look in his eyes held a mix of lust and tenderness that made her heart pound. The way his brows furrowed when he looked at her, as if he were studying a work of art, made her feel cherished, valued. An unexpectedly powerful emotion that she didn't want to acknowledge welled within her chest. She'd loved before, or so she thought, but never like this.

She curled her fingers over the length of him, squeezing gently, stroking firmly.

As he fisted his hand in her hair, he continued to stare at her intently. A combination of lust and... something else. Something deeper. But that couldn't be real. She wanted it to be. Wanted him to feel that deeper connection the way she did.

Temporary. Can't promise you anything.

Leaning forward, she brushed the tip of him with her tongue, and he hissed. His muscles tensed, but his gaze never wavered. It never changed. She could handle passion, desire, all of that. But the other things frightened her—the things that she couldn't quite name lurking in the depths of his dark eyes.

Before she could take him into her mouth, he pushed her to the bed.

"These need to go."

She glanced down and he'd already undone the button on her shorts, lowered the zipper, and was currently yanking them and her panties toward her ankles.

He flung them over his shoulders and winked. "Much better." He knelt at the edge of the bed, lifted her legs over his shoulders, and licked his lips.

"Oh, God," was about all she could manage.

His tongue darted out and flicked across her clit with the perfect amount of pressure.

Her breath caught in her chest. Everything narrowed to the heat of his mouth, the pressure building low in her belly. She grabbed for something—anything—sheets, his hair, it didn't matter. Her hips moved on instinct, chasing sensation she couldn't control.

When he added his fingers, curling inside her while his other hand found her breast, the world went white at the edges. She was coming apart. Actually coming apart. And the terrifying part was how much she wanted to let him break her wide open.

"Buddy," her voice emerged huskier than she'd intended. She stared at him, watching him please her, and her climax hit her like an ambush—violent and consuming. She couldn't think, couldn't breathe, could only ride the wave as it tore through her in pulse after devastating pulse. A sound ripped from her throat—raw, desperate, nothing she could control. Her body arched, trembled, shattered. And still, he didn't stop, wringing every last tremor from her until she thought she might black out from the intensity. She worried it might never stop. The nerve endings on her clit were on fire.

Who needed multiple orgasms when that happened?

He curled his hands around her legs, prying them open with the gentle force only a loving partner could provide. He kissed his way up her torso, stopping at her breasts, giving each nipple attention, before landing on her mouth. He kissed her like a man desperate and starved.

His body pressed against hers—solid muscle, weight, heat. She couldn't get close enough. Couldn't think past the need coiling tight in her belly, sharper and more desperate than anything she'd felt before.

"Fallon," he whispered, his breath hot against her lips, his voice filled with an edge she hadn't heard before, something raw and unguarded. The sound made her shudder with a conflicting mix of euphoria and apprehension—should she pull away or let herself drown in it?

She opted for the latter.

It should have terrified her—this free fall, this complete surrender. Maybe it did. But she didn't pull back.

They shifted on the bed until he was pressed against her in exactly the right spot, but he didn't move. He didn't take her. Instead, he braced himself above her on his elbows, framing her cheeks with his thumbs, searching her face... for something. But she had no idea what.

And then, before she could say anything, he slid inside her, slowly, gently. Her breath released in a shudder. This. This was what she'd been fighting. Not the sex, not the physical—this sense of rightness, like something clicking into place she hadn't known was misaligned. She was open, vulnerable, completely his. Each stroke was unhurried, every thrust bringing them closer to the precipice. There was a connection between them—an undeniable pull—that went beyond the physical. It was there. No denying it.

She closed her eyes, surrendering to the pleasure building low in her belly. His weight pressed into her, the rhythm mesmerizing, relentless. The orgasm hit hard—her body clenching, shuddering around him. Above her, Buddy's breath went ragged. His fingers dug into her hips, his whole body going taut. He pulsed inside her, and she heard the broken sound he made against her neck.

Afterward, they lay tangled together, skin slick with sweat. Her chest heaved. Her mind spun between satisfaction and that thing she didn't want to name. She traced idle patterns on his arm, hyper-aware of how exposed she felt. How much she'd just given him.

It was as if they'd crossed an invisible line—the one he made abundantly clear could never happen.

Buddy gently rolled off her, but not without pulling her along, tucking her against his side. He stared at the ceiling, his chest lifting and falling in rhythm with his calm breaths. She tilted her head to look at him, his throat moving like he was swallowing words he couldn't say.

This—lying together, breathing the same air—this was what scared her. They'd just stripped each other down to nothing. No pretense. No walls. And now she was supposed to just... what? Pretend it didn't change everything?

His hand found hers, fingers interlocking, the gesture so tender a lump formed in her throat.

"Fallon," he began, his voice tight, and she could hear his struggle. Could see the conflict in his eyes.

"Yes?" she answered, her voice barely above a whisper, her heart pounding fiercely.

His expression was serious, searching, filled with an odd reluctance. "I don't... I don't know what this is," he admitted, his grip on her hand tightening. The intensity of his statement hung in the air, an unspoken possibility, a whisper of what could be.

His words echoed in her ears, a silent confession that mirrored her thoughts. He was confused. Lost. Much like her.

She squeezed his hand, a silent comfort, and swallowed the knot in her throat. "I don't either," she confessed, "But, whatever it is, or isn't. I... I don't... It's not..." her words trailed off, not finishing her statement. How did she tell him she didn't want a temporary relationship? That she wanted to take a risk? Put herself on the line? Her mouth went dry. She'd never told a man how she'd felt about him. It had always been about sex. That was it. That was all her relationships had been based on, except for maybe Trent.

"Yeah. I know," he whispered. For a moment, he

looked like he might say something else, his grip tightening on her hand. But instead, he pulled her into an embrace. An understanding comfort. Wordless reassurance. She wrapped her arms around him, closed her eyes, and waited for sleep. Whatever they were to each other would unfold at its own pace—or it wouldn't. And she had to accept that.

Chapter Sixteen

The Aegis Network field office in Calusa Cove felt too small for the size of the storm he'd dragged into it.

Buddy stood over the conference table—an ugly, government-issued slab of laminate that had seen too many late nights—hands braced on either side as he stared down at the mess he'd made. Not three neat folders. Multiple stacks. A full eighteen months of his life represented in paper. The Simon Court case files he'd printed when no one was looking, the photocopied reports he'd had no business keeping, his own cramped handwriting crammed into margins and across legal pads. Screenshots from databases he wasn't supposed to access anymore, emails from old contacts who'd told him not to use their numbers again, favors called in from people you didn't want to owe twice.

It looked less like an investigation and more like an autopsy.

Simon's operation. Tannette Runon. The nameless deceased victim. Tessa Blake. Fallon. Three timelines, a dozen cross-references, and one ugly pattern he hadn't been fast enough to recognize. Every page on the table was another reminder that someone out there was playing him like he was still green—making moves he should've seen coming, twisting his failures into weapons, and picking at the people he'd allowed himself to care about like they were loose threads he couldn't afford to have.

Dove perched on the edge of the table, boot tapping the leg like she was doing the two-step while simultaneously crushing peanut shells.

Sterling strolled into the office carrying a tray full of coffee mugs and a bag of something that smelled like apples and cinnamon.

"You're late," Buddy said.

"Got you coffee with oat milk, an apple fritter, and some news." He set the goodies on the table, snagged a mug for himself and plopped down in his chair. He leaned back, lifted his legs, his feet landing on his desk with a loud thud and he crossed his ankles, all while smiling.

Sometimes Buddy wanted to strangle the man.

"Start talking before I send you to Mallor's Landing to help Trent while he's laid up, just because I can."

"That's rude," Sterling said. "Even for you." He lowered his feet and stood. "Okay," Sterling leaned over the table and tapped a page listing shipping records from three different ports. "So—the compound under

Tannette Runon's fingernails? We finally found a match."

Buddy lifted his head. "I'm listening."

Sterling grinned without humor. "There's a legit marine-manufacturing company in Fort Lauderdale that produces a custom epoxy-silica mix used for sealing compartmental bulkheads in mid-size commercial boats. Exactly the kind used in smuggling operations. They keep meticulous records so that I couldn't trace it to anything."

"So, how do you know it's our company?" Buddy asked.

"That's where it gets fun." Sterling lifted a pen and twisted it between his fingers. "Everything is above board. Inspections clean. Taxes filed. Employees real. You've even looked into this company before. Bluewater Restoration."

"I remember them." Buddy shuffled a few pages until he found the one he was looking for. Something else with fucking Blue. It never ended. "We never did speak with the owner—actually, no owner listed, but the VP of operations was a paranoid sort. They had so many freaking checks and balances because they once had a break-in, and their compound was used in a gun run."

"Well, that's because Bluewater Restoration is owned by a clusterfuck of LLCs stacked like nesting dolls. Took me three hours just to untangle the shell trail."

Dove snorted. "Took me five seconds to bet money it's dirty."

Sterling nodded. "One of those LLCs? EJV Industries. Same LLC that's also listed as a part-owner of the Blue Heron Touring company out of Lauderdale. The one tied to the partial plate that appeared to be following —or at least looking at—Fallon."

Buddy's heart lurched once—hard. "You sure?"

"Got Mia running the full corporate pull now— owners, investors, subsidiary links, banking patterns. So far, she believes the company itself is clean. But the LLCs it's linked to, they tell a different story."

Buddy exhaled slowly. "When I arrested Simon and all the others, they were so fucking smug. Like it didn't matter. Like their world would still fucking turn. They kept telling me, I'd never save them all."

Dove looked up, forehead scrunched. "Has Flagler been able to get Simon to talk?"

"Doesn't matter if he did," Buddy said. "This is either someone he trained or someone he worked for—someone who learned the system—someone who hates me enough to take the long route—someone who's fucking patient enough to watch me sweat before destroying what he thinks I love. What I hold dear."

A soft knock sounded in the open doorway.

Decker stuck his head inside, blond hair sticking up like he'd run here. Which he probably had.

"Sorry to interrupt," Decker said, breathless. "And sorry for eavesdropping. I've been pacing outside for the last few minutes, and I can't let this slide."

"No worries. What's up?" Buddy had learned to trust Decker. It hadn't been easy. He'd come to Calusa Cove to hurt people. To hurt Buddy's friends. But when fire erupted, Decker did the right thing.

"Did you say EJV Industries?"

Buddy straightened. "Yeah. Why?"

Decker stepped in, shutting the door behind him. "When I was a kid in Miami—in my old neighborhood, when the cartels were moving in—there was a dude by the name of EJ. No one said his name out loud. And no one ever saw him. My uncle used to skim cash for one of his LLCs through fake tile imports. Laundry front. It's where it all started." He rubbed his jaw. "It was just one of many fronts, and I believe the Barbaros struck a deal with him, but there's always a play going on for small businesses near the ports."

"The Barbaros? As in Ken's in-laws?" Buddy rubbed the back of his neck.

"Who's Ken?" Sterling asked.

"Baily's brother. Also a decorated SEAL who was on the same team as Dawson, Keaton, and Hayes. But more importantly, he was married to Julie Barbaro, the daughter of a big crime family that run drugs, guns, and people," Decker said. "They owned my family. I thought I got away, but they fucked with my business and nearly destroyed me."

"All in the past." Buddy held Decker's gaze for a moment. "But I don't like how it's tied to EJV Industries."

"Your uncle worked for the Barbaros and this EJ guy?"

"I don't know how long my uncle did work for EJ, but I remember he once mentioned EJV Industries and that if I ever came in contact with that company, to run. But the Barbaros were the ones my uncle answered to. Unfortunately, he died in prison last year." Decker's gaze hardened. "His son—my cousin—he's still inside—same penitentiary. Low-level, but he remembers shit. Might talk."

"Might?" Sterling asked.

Decker shrugged. "Fear keeps people quiet, and some of them see me as the enemy. I turned on the Barbaros and some blame me for the collapse of their empire. They were promised shit when they got out. Now that might not happen, so they might not be willing to speak with me. But I'll try."

Buddy rolled his shoulders. "I don't want you to do anything that's going to upset anyone. You're getting married soon, and you don't need to poke that bear again."

Decker dipped his chin. "I can't sit back and do nothing. I did that once, and I ended up hating myself."

"Thanks, we appreciate it." Buddy stretched out his hand and Decker gave it a good shake before strolling out the door.

Buddy shoved aside another stack of photocopied reports and stared at them, but his vision wouldn't focus. His muscles twitched and tightened from too many hours leaning over that damn table. He needed to move, needed his blood circulating, because sitting still with this many files felt like drowning in paper. He paced to the wall, turned, paced back. Three steps one way, three steps back. His boots scuffed against the floor. The repetition didn't help. The tension still crawled under his skin.

He found himself at the window again. Blinds half-drawn, Florida sun cutting harsh lines across the floor. He'd been doing this for the last ten minutes—table to window, window to table—burning off energy that had nowhere else to go.

He nudged a slat with his knuckle.

A black Dodge Charger sat across the street. Parked. Engine running. Tinted so dark the glass looked like obsidian. Not just illegal-dark. Intentional-dark.

Sterling looked up from the paperwork he was sorting. "What?"

Buddy didn't shift his gaze. "Charger. Across the street. It fits the description of the one Fallon saw."

Dove pushed off the table and joined him, leaning sideways to get a look. "Are you sure?"

"Same model. Same tint. Same attitude," Buddy said. "Can't see the plate."

"Shit," Sterling muttered, already standing. "You want to call Dawson?"

Buddy shook his head. "Not yet. Let's see if it's watching or just passing time."

He grabbed his holster and snapped it in place. "We're heading out."

Dove smirked. "Finally, a little fun."

Buddy stepped into the humid slap of Florida air first, Sterling and Dove flanking him, all three scanning without drawing attention to themselves.

The Charger was exactly where it had been when he

saw it through the blinds—backed into the convenience store slot across the street, angled like it was waiting for permission to pounce.

Buddy didn't break stride. "Eyes open."

Dove stuffed her cell in her pocket. "Let's see if our friend wants to play."

They piled into Buddy's truck—Sterling taking shotgun, Dove behind him. Doors shut solidly, three clicks of readiness. Buddy started the engine and eased into traffic like it was any other Friday morning.

The Charger pulled out two cars behind them. Not aggressive. Not shy.

Just there.

Sterling watched the side mirror. "He's not really hiding it, but he's not making an announcement either."

"That's a statement all by itself," Buddy said. His knuckles tightened around the wheel. "The only question is whether or not he's gonna make a move or just watch."

Dove clicked her seat belt. "Nobody makes themselves known unless they plan on doing something. Not unless they're dumb fucks."

They made the turn onto Main Street, then a quick right onto Union Route, before taking the second right onto old Calusa Cove Drive. It ran parallel to Main and looped back onto Cypress Street before merging into Union Route, a couple of miles outside of town, where there was nothing but road.

"If I didn't know you better, I'd say you're leading us to our deaths," Dove whispered. "This street is creepy."

"That's the old theatre that Decker's going to eventually restore. He's also filed a proposal with the town to turn that old warehouse into a combo museum honoring local heritage, along with a wildlife learning center for locals, scouts, and tourists. Trent's all over that, and he'd be a great teacher."

"Of children?" Dove asked. "That man is a lot of things, but not sure he should be allowed near kids."

Buddy glanced at the review. The Charger followed.

Adrenaline unfurled in his veins, dark and cold and welcome. He took another right, deeper into the warehouse grid.

"Trent might surprise you," he managed as he pressed his foot on the gas.

The Charger closed the distance.

"You seeing this?" Sterling asked.

"Oh yeah," Buddy said.

The road narrowed after the theatre and the warehouse—nothing but empty space and echo.

The Charger surged forward.

"Here we go," Buddy said. "Be ready for anything, and someone can text Dawson now."

"Already did." Dove waved her cell. "I'm not too stupid to live. This road is clearly where clowns come to die. And in the horror movie world, clowns don't fucking die."

The Charger slipped into their blind spot on the left, pacing them, matching their speed within inches.

"What the fuck are these assholes doing," Sterling muttered.

The passenger window rolled down two inches.

Enough to fit a hand.

A silver canister flew out, bouncing twice before spinning under their front bumper—

"Fuck," Buddy yelled as he swerved, hitting the gas, hoping he didn't run the fucking thing over, and praying he got far enough away. "Tell me when you see that thing—"

"That canister's not the problem." Sterling pointed. "They're coming back."

The Charger raced toward them from the opposite direction.

"Looks like they want to play chicken." Buddy gripped the steering wheel, foot easy on the gas, not accelerating—not losing speed either.

The Dodge jerked to the right, and another canister came hurling at the hood of the truck before the Charger fishtailed and took off.

Buddy slammed on the brakes.

The canister detonated at the nose.

KSSSHFFFF—POOF

A geyser of blue, pink, gold, yellow, and green glitter erupted like a damn Mardi Gras parade.

"What the hell was that?" Dove asked.

Buddy rammed the gearshift into park and opened the door. He slid from the driver's seat and stared at the glitter that decorated his truck. A breeze kicked up, and the glitter floated through the air like fucking Tinkerbell.

Sterling stood beside him, slapping glitter off his face.

"Are you kidding me? Glitter? Why would someone stalk us and then hurl sparkly shit at us?"

Glitter bomb. But Buddy's instincts had screamed grenade, and that gap—between harmless and deadly—that was the message.

His pulse didn't spike—it condensed into something lethal.

He glanced over his shoulder, the Dodge Charger long gone. The only evidence it had ever been there was the faint sound of its engine revving in the distance and the glitter drifting down the windshield of Buddy's truck like toxic confetti.

Dove rolled her window down and held up her hand, wiggling her fingers, as the colorful stuff floated through the vehicle. "Obviously, they didn't want to hurt us, but they did want to send a message. Any idea what that is?"

Buddy's blood ran cold as understanding dawned.

Not because of the glitter — but because of the colors.

Blue. Pink. Gold. Yellow. Green.

Fallon's fundraiser colors.

The Tessa Project.

His gut twisted into an ugly, instinctive knot. "This isn't for us," he said, barely above a breath.

Sterling dusted glitter off his sleeves again. "No shit, it isn't for us. It looks like a unicorn sneezed."

"No," Buddy growled, jaw locking. "It's not random. These are Fallon's colors. These are tomorrow's colors."

Dove's amusement vanished. "What are you saying?"

Buddy knelt, swiped his fingers through the glitter on

the pavement. The cheap sparkle stuck to his skin like it meant to stain.

"A fundraiser for missing girls," he said softly. "A tribute to Tessa." He lifted his hand, watching the glitter shimmer. "And the biggest crowd of young girls this town sees all year."

Sterling's face paled. "Shit."

Dove's boot scraped gravel. "You think the message is: 'See you tomorrow'?"

Buddy didn't answer.

He didn't need to.

He stood quickly, pulling his phone from his pocket and bringing up Fallon's contact info. His fingers shook— not from fear, but from fury. He tapped the call button. It didn't even ring. It went straight to voicemail. "Shit. Fallon's not answering."

Sterling frowned. "She's at work, right? She said she was heading into the Glades."

"With Cullen," Buddy clipped out. "Which means she's on patrol. Which means she's exposed."

Dove stepped closer. "She's armed. Trained. Smart."

"And being hunted," Buddy said, stabbing at his contacts. "And I'm done giving these bastards a head start."

He tapped the call button a second time.

Straight to voicemail—again.

"Fuck." His pulse slammed hard enough that he felt it in his teeth. "Sterling, call Cullen's phone."

Sterling tried — same result.

Dove's expression shifted, sharp and grim. "Service is

spotty out where she patrols. Doesn't mean anything's wrong."

Buddy holstered that reassurance but stayed ready to draw. "You two wait here for Dawson. He's already on the way. Bring him up to speed. Tell Chloe and Flagler to mobilize. And text Fletcher, Keaton, and Hayes to get prepped."

"For what?" Sterling asked.

Buddy's stare darkened. "For whatever the hell is coming."

Dove nodded once, already typing. "We'll lock this area down. Dawson will be here in minutes."

Buddy didn't waste another second.

He jogged around the truck, slid behind the wheel, and slammed the door.

Sterling stepped close. "Buddy—what if they're baiting you? What if they want you to chase Fallon so they can—"

"They already have her in the crosshairs," Buddy said, voice breaking into something darker than anger. "And I'm not losing her. Not her."

That sentence tasted like poison.

Sterling swallowed hard. "Where do we meet you once Dawson gets here?"

Buddy started the engine, gravel spitting under the tires. "My place. As soon as you're all assembled. I want everyone armed and ready."

Buddy put the truck in gear. "Text me a report after you're done with Dawson."

"Will do," Dove said.

Buddy pressed his foot to the floor, the truck tearing down the glitter-stained road toward the Glades, toward the woman he refused to lose, toward the danger he could finally see—and toward the plan already unfolding for tomorrow.

The fundraiser.

The crowd.

The girls.

Fallon was at the center of it all.

Not a victim.

A target.

And the bastard behind this wanted Buddy to know it.

Chapter Seventeen

Fallon opened the front door of Buddy's rental before Keaton could knock a second time. He stood on the porch in his FWC greens, shoulders tight, gaze sweeping her face with that quiet, assessing steadiness she'd come to rely on.

"How ya doing?" he asked.

"Better than Buddy," she said. "He's obsessing. Combing through paperwork. Pacing. Mumbling. Everyone else is outside while he's in his office making himself crazy."

Keaton ran his fingers through his wavy hair. "He came in hot this afternoon, not only demanding I tell him exactly where you were in the Glades, but that I give you the rest of the day off."

"You humored him." She pursed his lips.

"Flying glitter caught everyone's attention."

"That was weird—and concerning," she admitted,

leading Keaton through the narrow living room. "There's beer, soda, and snacks outside. Just waiting on a few stragglers." The house seemed smaller with each step. She slid open the back door, letting the damp night air spill around them.

"You okay?" Keaton curled his fingers around her forearm.

"Define, okay?" She winced. Keaton was her boss. He might appreciate her sarcasm on occasion, but now was not the time. "It's been a long few days."

"Want to talk about it?" He leaned against the wall near the sliding glass doors that led to the patio.

She'd never been one to dump her problems on other people. She certainly didn't ramble about her relationships with her boss. However, everything about this situation was different. "Buddy's completely on edge. Like unraveling-on-edge, and I don't know how to talk him off the ledge."

"Same way you talked Trent down when some idiot tried to block off Mallor's landing." Keaton smiled. "A lot has happened. Buddy's past case and what happened to your friend have collided in ways we don't fully understand yet. And with you at the middle of it, well, Buddy's just doing what any normal human does when someone they care about is being threatened."

"I don't know how to help him." She glanced over her shoulder. Out of the corner of her eye, she saw Buddy step into the doorway of his office, then disappear just as quickly as he continued to pace. "Ever since he picked me up at the docks, he's had this fire in his eyes. I've never seen him like this before. Not even when he was working the Ring Finger case." She caught a glimpse of Buddy, standing in his office, holding a file, rubbing his temple. "It's killing me to watch him torture himself."

"He's been carrying guilt and grief a long time, just like you." Keaton lowered his chin. "You want to help him? Start by showing him how to let go of the past by doing it yourself."

The words landed on her ears like a slap.

"You've done incredible work. Raised awareness and money. But those weeks leading up to it? The days after? You bury yourself in it, and it's hard for anyone to really reach you." He tilted his head. "The rest of the year? I don't believe you need me telling you that you lock up that piece, keeping it close, as if it will protect you from ever feeling that rawness again. Only—"

"It lives there all the time," she finished his statement. This wasn't the first time she'd heard this. And he was right. God, she hated that he was right. "I use it like Trent uses his alligators and snakes. It keeps people from getting to close and seeing all of me."

"I was going to say it a little differently, but yeah, that's about it." Keaton rubbed his chest—that gesture he did when thinking about his late fiancée. "Grief ran my life for years. I didn't know that's what I was doing until I nearly lost the best thing that ever happened to me." He shifted his gaze down the hallway. "I can see how much you care about Buddy, and I know he's got it bad for you.

But he's stuck somewhere between what he wants and what he believes he can have." Keaton turned. "So are you. Now, what are you going to do about it?"

Fallon sucked in a deep breath and let it out slowly. This was something she'd normally respond to by handing out a laundry list of reasons why she was so happy with her life. That she was living it exactly the way she wanted. Silas once told her that if she had to explain it, she was not only lying to the world, but to herself.

"You're not arguing with me." Keaton smiled. Not a big one. More like a knowing twitch of the corners of his mouth. But she caught it.

"Since when did you get so wise?"

"I let go of the past, and my future walked in."

She laughed. Not hard. But the vibration of it in her throat settled her emotions. "That had to be the corniest thing I've ever heard."

"Maybe. But it's truth." He reached for the handle on the sliding glass door. "He needs to get through the case. We all do. Catch this asshole and put this part behind us. Then, both of you can release all the things that have prevented you from moving forward. Sometimes, all it takes is the right person." He pulled open the door.

The warm Florida breeze collided with the air conditioning like a wrecking ball crashing into a building. Hard, powerful, and full of destruction.

Keaton stepped out to the back patio and joined Hayes, Chloe, and the weight of a storm none of them could name yet. Hayes leaned against the railing, arms folded, eyes trained on the dark backyard as if he expected trouble to materialize between the palmettos. Keaton strolled across the patio, stood next to Hayes, and stared out toward the Glades. Both men radiated protective energy—restless, focused, keyed to danger.

Chloe sat straighter than usual, tapping a pen against her thigh, scanning the pages of a notebook like vigilance was wired into her.

Fallon hovered at the sliding glass door, silently watching them , but her gaze kept drifting inside... to Buddy.

She heard his footsteps creaking on old floorboards.

He couldn't go on like this much longer. She snagged a paper plate and a premade sandwich from the counter and made her way back to his office.

The space hadn't been properly set up with a large wooden desk shoved inside—looking like the room was about to split at the seams. Stacks of files, crime scene photos, scribbled notes, old case printouts, Tessa's file, Simon's case summaries, maps, shipping receipts—everything he had jammed together in one suffocating room.

He'd stop. Lean over a file. Dig through pages. Flip a photo over. Mumble to himself. Then push off the desk and start pacing again, hands on his hips, jaw clenched hard enough to crack.

She didn't knock.

He didn't notice her presence until she stepped fully inside and set a plate on the desk.

Buddy jerked his head up—eyes sharp, shadowed, burning. "What are you doing?"

"Making sure you don't pass out." Fallon nudged the plate closer. "Eat."

"I can't." He dragged a hand through his hair, pacing again. "I can't sit. I can't eat. I can barely fucking breathe."

She blinked. Hearing a grown man swear wasn't a big deal. She heard it every day. Hell, she used the word herself on a regular basis. But Buddy didn't have much of a foul mouth. It was like he saved those words for specific occasions and certain people.

"Don't make me tackle you, sit on you, and force it down your throat, because I will." She smiled, hoping that might ease the tension.

But it didn't. If anything, the air grew thicker, as if the oxygen were slowly depleting, and soon, they'd both be gasping and fighting over the last bit.

He glanced between the sandwich, her, and the papers in his hands. The papers won. "Thanks to Decker, we know that EJV Industries, LLC, which is part of Blue-water Restoration and Blue Heron Boat Tours is owned by EJ Vance. But that means nothing to me except that both Decker and his cousin say this EJ guy had a reputation years ago in Miami as an up-and-coming gangster. Decker's cousin wouldn't say who he worked for, but that EJ had big plans. However, I can't seem to connect him to Simon, and Simon won't talk to Flagler, me, or anyone else for that matter. No one from his ring will have any contact with law enforcement. Not even for a reduced sentence." Buddy leaned against the corner of the desk. "I had Mia start a check on this Vance guy. So far, he's clean. Too clean. Weirder still, she can't find a single image of him on the internet, or any company directory anywhere. It's like he's a fucking ghost."

"Why don't you take a breath. Eat some food. And come outside," she said softly. "Keaton just arrived. We can talk through this—"

"Something's going to happen tomorrow." His voice cracked low, gutted, raw. "Everything points to a major event tomorrow."

Tears burned the corners of Fallon's eyes. "We don't know that."

"Yes," he snapped, turning on her. "We do." He straightened and moved across the floor in a swift, military-like precision. His eyes were a storm—anger, fear, determination, guilt, churning together in a chaotic mix she'd never seen before. He braced both hands on the back of his chair and bent his head. "If I don't figure this out before tomorrow, someone is going to die," he whispered. "Either you... or some random young girl who shows up to honor Tessa."

Her heart punched her chest.

"And it'll be my fault."

"I understand why you'd feel that way and sure, we need to be prepared. That's why all our friends are here. Why Dawson is assigning as much manpower as he has and even calling in a few favors. But we don't know what's coming or when."

Buddy lifted his gaze. Darkness lurked behind his intense dark eyes. "I know exactly what's coming, and I know what he wants." He raised a single brow. "You want the truth?" The force of his stare nearly knocked her backward. "I can't choose. It's a lose-lose situation."

Her breath stopped. "Choose what?"

"Between love and duty." His voice rose, broke, then steadied into something terrifyingly honest. "Between saving the woman I'm falling in love with... and saving the next innocent girl who gets caught in the crossfire of someone else's sick game."

Falling in love with.

The words landed on her chest like a brick. Hard. Heavey. And real. He'd said it. Actually said it. And he wasn't taking it back, wasn't softening it with maybes or eventuallys. Just standing there, raw and exposed, like he'd ripped himself open and didn't care who saw.

Her pulse thundered in her ears. She wanted to say something—anything—but her throat locked up.

"It's why my marriage ended," he said, pacing again, hands flexing open and closed. "But I made her choose because I couldn't be the man she wanted at home and the agent I needed to be in the field." He pointed toward the spread of files. "Simon tried to force me into the same goddamn corner. He taunted me with the idea that I had to choose between saving the victims or catching him. And in the end, two girls who were within reach died because I chose to slap the cuffs on him."

Chest heaving, he shoved aside a stack of papers.

"And now this asshole—this EJ Vance, if that's his fucking name—is trying to make me choose between you and some girl who hasn't even screamed yet."

She'd known this was eating him alive—everyone

knew. Had seen it in every rigid line of his body, every hour he refused to sleep, every time he stared at that list he carried in his pocket like it held answers it would never give. But watching him say it out loud—watching him break open and bleed all this fear and guilt onto the floor between them—that was different. That was him trusting her with the worst parts of himself. The parts that kept him up at night. The parts that haunted every case he'd ever worked.

Fallon's knees softened. She inched closer. "Buddy…"

"How the hell do I do that?" He slammed both palms on the desk. "Tell me, Fallon. How does anyone make that choice and then turn around and live with the consequences?"

She didn't answer. She couldn't. Not when she could see—finally, painfully—what she hadn't understood before. He wasn't angry at her. He wasn't angry at the situation. He was furious at himself. At the shadows he couldn't shake. At not being able to save them all. At the way the past had dug its claws into him and refused to let go. And for the first time—truly, the first time—Fallon saw the mirror. Saw exactly what Keaton had been implying earlier.

She saw herself and Buddy so clearly.

Two people defined by grief and guilt.

Two people who didn't know how to stop punishing themselves for tragedies they hadn't caused.

If Fallon stopped punishing herself, she'd have to accept that Tessa was truly gone. Memory wiped out. Her loss would be in vain.

It was easy to blame herself for surviving.

And Buddy? He blamed himself for not being God.

Her breath stuttered out. "Stop pacing and look at me."

He did. Slowly. Like he was afraid of what he might see.

Fallon stepped closer, her voice barely above a whisper. "You can't choose between me and some hypothetical victim. You can't choose between Tessa and anyone else. You can't choose between what you lost and what you want."

He shook his head hard. "But that's the—"

"No," she said softly. "You can't. And you never should've been asked to. Not by your ex-wife. Not by Simon. Not by anyone. But you don't have to play the game by their rules. You just don't."

He went completely still.

Fallon's throat tightened. She had no idea if she was right. But she knew deep down she was holding onto the guilt because she'd been so afraid that if she let it go, she'd no longer feel the sting of her friend's life. Buddy needed to separate the choice from the game. "You keep thinking you failed those girls—all of them. But you didn't. You did everything you could. Yes, people died. But so many more lived because you made the only choice you could have. You had to put that bastard away. Otherwise, so many more would have been sold into sex slavery. But you still carry those deaths like anchors tied around your waist."

Something flickered in his eyes—pain, recognition, shame.

"And I know," she whispered, "because that's exactly what I do with Tessa."

"That's very different."

"Is it? Because I made a choice. A selfish one, and Tessa vanished. I've always believed that if I changed that one decision, everything would be different."

"But you might not be here," Buddy said. "You might've been the one..." his words trailed off as he ran a hand over his stubbly face.

"I think..." Fallon swallowed hard as all her defenses crumbled like sandcastles at high-tide and pooled at her feet, "...we both live life as if being alone is what we deserve. You, because you feel like someone or something made you choose. And me because I made one single decision that destroyed my best friend's life."

Silence tightened around them—heavy, intimate, suffocating. She had no idea if she'd gotten through to him, but she had a lightness in her heart that hadn't ever been there before. A sense of freedom spread through her chest like precious oxygen filling her lungs. There was still a deep wound. A core hurt, and that would take some time to heal. She had to admit to herself she hadn't been honoring Tessa the way she should, and that changed now. She only hoped that Buddy would be able to step outside himself and see that he needed to release the ghosts he carried. Not just for him, but for them.

His eyes softened—just a shift, barely noticeable—but it still made her breath catch.

"I'm scared I'm going to lose you," he said quietly. "Either because I can't protect you, or because I can't give what you need and deserve when this is all over."

She didn't flinch, but her muscles trembled. Her skin prickled with heat. "I'm scared I'll lose myself if I pretend I don't want this—you. I keep telling myself I'm okay with this being temporary when I'm not."

The truth settled between them, comforting and sharp all at once. Outside, the others planned for tomorrow, but in this cramped office, the world had narrowed to just the two of them—closer, quieter, strangely steadying.

He rubbed the back of his neck, the movement weary. "I don't know how to do... any of this. I tried once, and I failed. I broke Callie's heart, and that's another thing I haven't been able to forgive myself for."

"I don't know how to do this, either." Fallon took a step closer, meeting him without hesitation this time. "I'm great at surviving. Terrible at letting anyone get near me. I've made a career out of being the last one standing in my own life. Kind of like you. But I don't want to do that anymore."

His gaze lifted. It wasn't hungry or wild or broken. It was honest. That frightened her more than anything— even more than the possibility of him walking away.

"I told myself caring about someone would get me killed—or worse—them," he said. "I spent so many years believing feelings were a liability. That walls were strength and part of what made me so good at what I did."

Fallon's chest tightened—not with fear, but recognition. "Maybe strength isn't shutting everyone out. Maybe it's letting the right person in."

He went still at that—like she'd touched something he kept hidden away.

She'd gotten through. Actually gotten through. And the look on his face—raw, exposed, like he was seeing her see him—that terrified her more than any threat lurking in the Everglades. Because this was real. This mattered. And if she screwed this up, if she ran now, she'd regret it for the rest of her life.

They were the same. Both punishing themselves. Both convinced they didn't deserve good things. Both so damn sure that caring about someone would destroy them.

But standing here, watching him break open in front of her, Fallon realized something else—maybe they could save each other. Or maybe they'd just crash and burn together. Either way, she was done running.

She raised her hand, giving him plenty of time to step away. He didn't. Her palm settled over his chest, the steady, heavy thrumming beneath her fingers.

"You don't have to choose between protecting people and letting someone care about you," she said. "You've been punishing yourself for so long, you don't know the difference anymore."

His breath hitched, warm and uneven.

He lifted his hand and brushed her jaw with his thumb—tentative, reverent, almost disbelieving. "I never meant to drag you into the parts of my life that still hurt."

"You didn't drag me anywhere," she said. "I walked in. Willingly. Maybe stupidly. Definitely stubbornly." She leaned into his strong body "More importantly, I'm not walking out."

A faint, cracked laugh escaped him, the first she'd heard all night. He leaned his forehead against hers. Somehow, the simplest touch was the most intimate thing they'd ever shared.

She breathed him in—warmth, tension, quiet devastation—and let her fingers curl lightly into his shirt.

His hand slid to the back of her neck, steady and warm. "I didn't expect you. I wasn't looking for anything like this."

"Neither was I," she said. "But maybe that's why it matters."

His eyes met hers again—clearer, softer, and for the first time, she saw acceptance in them. Not of her, but of himself. Of what was happening. Of what they were.

The room seemed to still around them. No grand declarations. No promises they couldn't keep. Just two people who'd spent years hiding finally stepping out of the shadows to find each other.

He exhaled, the sound low and raw. "I'd kiss you again if I knew I could control myself, but I can't, and we have a house full of guests."

She smiled. "They'll go home eventually."

When he leaned in and took her mouth in a tender kiss, it wasn't desperation.

It was choice. It was connection.

And for the first time in years, Fallon didn't run from it.

***

The heat in the house settled into everything, thick and permanent like it owned the place. Buddy stood near the kitchen island where Dove had left the hard copies of Mia's findings, the edges of the pages curling slightly in the humidity. He'd read them twice. Maybe three times. They still didn't feel like anything concrete—just fragments of someone else's life scattered across too many counties.

Dawson dropped into the stool next to Buddy, rubbing a thumb along the edge of his badge before tucking it away, a habit he'd gotten into when he wasn't on duty. Sterling remained standing, one shoulder against the wall.

Buddy pushed the top file forward. "Seven companies—all tied to the same fucking thing."

Dawson drummed his fingers on the counter. "All with the same naming pattern."

"Blue something. Blue whatever. Blue this, Blue that. Doesn't matter what the business does—shell company ties eventually point to the same guy who's associated with EJV Industries."

Buddy stared at the list.

Blue Heron Boat Tours

Bluewater Restoration

Blue Coast Realty Group

Blue Marlin Logistics
Blue Reef Holdings
Blue Atlantic Renovation
Blue Horizon Imports

All of them arranged like steppingstones up the eastern coast of Florida. Not illegal. Not even suspicious in isolation. But together... they made too much noise in his head to ignore.

Buddy leaned back, the stool creaking under his weight. "EJ Vance. I've looked through my files from Simon's case, and he doesn't come up once. I called a few contacts, the name doesn't ring a bell, but they're digging."

Sterling rolled his shoulders. "He's the only person whose connections don't add up the way they should. Mia's been digging. She's done everything short of hacking into the DMV. Everyone on our team has called in favors from every alphabet agency. Nothing's pinging yet."

"I've exhausted my resources and haven't found anything of interest," Dawson said. Not defeat—just truth. "Tomorrow's gonna be controlled chaos. The entire town, plus another hundred or so. That's about 500 people cruising through town. We need to walk in with something. Even a maybe."

Buddy rubbed a hand along his jaw. The stubble rasped against his fingertips, grounding him when the night had gone sideways three times already. "He's got to be our guy. Nothing else makes sense."

"Because we've got nothing else," Dawson countered, "and he's also smart enough not to leave breadcrumbs."

Sterling shifted against the wall. "Or he's not involved at all, and we're staring at the wrong thing. Looking at the wrong clue. I'm stuck on the audible call."

"You mean, this asshole could change the game—again?" Dawson asked.

"I absolutely believe I was meant to find that first victim, not Fallon. I was out on the water, in that location for a client that bailed before we could even give them the report," Buddy said. "Second one was all about watching my response, by using my girlfriend, knowing she was my girlfriend based on the fact that this prick's been watching. The audible's already been called. It's up to me how this plays out and what Fallon's role in it is." Buddy didn't mention the memory that flashed through his mind —the jacket folded inside the box, the note tucked beneath it, the weight of it in Fallon's hands. He nudged the stack of files again. "Even if we've got the wrong guy, and this EJ Vance has nothing to do with this, someone is watching me and Fallon. They have been for a while."

Dawson's expression tightened. "That's the part we can't ignore. It's also the part we've got to exploit."

Buddy knew that was coming. He didn't want to face it. He certainly didn't want to express it. But there was no hiding from it.

Silence settled in again, thicker this time, the kind that clung to the walls and made the quiet feel inhabited.

Sterling broke it. "You know what we've got to do."

Buddy's pulse flicked hard at that—old instinct, old dread. "What exactly do you mean?"

"You can't be glued to her," Sterling said. "If someone wants to manipulate you, they're going to pick the moment you step away. So, we plan for that moment."

Dawson nodded slowly, reluctantly, as if he hadn't wanted to suggest it, and was grateful someone else had. "We make it predictable—we can control predictable."

Buddy stiffened. "I'm not so sure we can."

"We've done this a million times." Sterling didn't soften it. "Let her be where he expects her. Alone enough to look vulnerable. Visible enough to draw him out."

Buddy's jaw locked. "No."

"It's not—"

"I said no," Buddy interrupted Sterling.

Dawson leaned forward, elbows on his knees, the same posture he used on his kids when he needed to negotiate bedtime rituals. "She'll be surrounded by volunteers. Hundreds of people. That jacket... It's a beacon. If it means something to him, it might draw him faster than anything else. He'll be watching you, Fallon, maybe me, Keaton, and your team. But he can't watch everyone. He can't keep an eye on Cullen. Or Silas. Or Decker. Not to mention Bingo's back in town. He's one badass young dude who would do anything to protect the people of Calusa Cove."

"Outside of Cullen and Bingo, those men aren't trained operatives." Buddy shoved off the stool, pacing once, stopping himself. "And she's not bait."

"Aren't you the one who said he's watching her?"

Sterling asked quietly. "Whether we acknowledge it or not, she already is."

The words lodged deep, deeper than Buddy wanted to admit.

"We track her phone, and we use the jacket. Put one of those tags in it. We can get Baily to sew it into the lining." Dawson's voice dropped lower. "We can control the scenario, or our perp can. That's the only choice we've got." He raised his hand before Buddy could argue. "And before you ask, yeah, I'd be fighting this if it were my wife, but I'd also do it because it's the only option."

Buddy stared at the floor, the grain of the wood going blurry for a breath. He pulled up a mental image of Fallon from earlier. One of her outside on the patio. She'd been speaking with Chloe. They were standing off to the side, leaning against the railing, immersed in an intense conversation. He'd seen a tear fall. But he also saw her resolve. Her stubbornness. The fire she carried even when her hands were shaking.

Buddy closed his eyes for a moment before blinking them open. "We do this, it's on my terms. She's never truly alone. Someone has to have eyes on her at all times, and we track her."

Sterling nodded. "Of course."

"And the instant anything feels wrong—"

"We pull her," Dawson finished.

Buddy went still for a moment, the weight of tomorrow already settling over him. "Fine. I'll present it to Fallon, but she gets to decide. I'm not letting her walk blind into something we don't understand."

"None of us want that," Dawson said. "She's part of this team. Whether she meant to be or not."

That truth hurt more than it helped.

Sterling stepped toward the door, grabbing his jacket. "We'll bring it to the others in the morning."

Buddy nodded, though the motion felt heavier than it should have. "In the morning."

Dawson pushed himself to his feet. "Get some sleep."

Buddy didn't answer.

Sleep had left the house hours ago.

Buddy exhaled slowly and rubbed a hand over his face, trying to clear the pressure that had settled behind his eyes. The files on the counter didn't move, but the weight of them had changed—now that there was a name attached, even if that name didn't mean a damn thing yet. The room felt tighter, the silence heavy with the understanding tomorrow might demand a price none of them had agreed to pay.

The sound of bare feet padded softly down the hall. Fallon appeared a moment later, framed by the shadows from the hallway light. She wore one of Buddy's T-shirts —too big on her, hem brushing mid-thigh—and her hair was pulled into a loose knot that had mostly given up. She didn't look fragile. She looked like someone who'd stopped pretending the night wasn't as heavy as it was.

Her gaze moved from Buddy to the files to the unnatural stillness that had fallen over everyone.

"You're talking strategy," she said softly. Not an accusation. Not a question. Just understanding.

Dawson cleared his throat. "We were wrapping up.

We'll go over everything first thing." He nudged Sterling toward the door, giving Buddy a look that was equal parts warning and apology. "Try to get a couple of hours if you can."

Sterling gave Fallon a slight nod on his way out. "See you in the morning," he said, and then the door shut behind them.

Fallon waited until their footsteps faded outside before stepping farther into the room. She moved toward the counter slowly, not cautious—just thoughtful.

"How much of that did you hear?"

"Enough," she said.

Buddy's hands curled into fists against the back of a chair. "It's not a good plan."

She stopped across from him, the breakfast bar between them, the pendant lights highlighting the quiet determination settling into her features. "It's the only plan that makes sense."

He shook his head. "It's too risky. We don't know who we're dealing with. We don't know what they want."

"We know they're watching," she said, her voice steady. "We know they picked me for a reason. And we know whatever they're planning, it's meant to pull you off balance. So, we take control of the one thing we can."

He hated how logical it sounded when she said it— hated even more that she didn't sound afraid.

"You shouldn't have to be the one out front."

"I already am," she said. "Talking about it just made it official."

Buddy's breath caught—not because she was wrong,

but because she was right in the one way that mattered. She wasn't a pawn. She wasn't a symbol. She wasn't fragile. She was a woman who'd lost enough to know when running wasn't an option anymore.

She stepped closer to the counter, fingers brushing the edge of one of the files. "This ends tomorrow, or it starts again. And I'm not willing to live like that. Not with everything we've already survived. Not with..." She hesitated, searching for the words. Not shying away from them. Just giving them the gravity they deserved. "...whatever this is between us."

Buddy swallowed against the knot forming in his throat. "Fallon—"

She didn't let him finish. "We deserve a chance at something real," she said quietly. "Not fear. Not ghosts. Not running in circles because someone else decided our pasts make us easy targets." She lifted her eyes to his, and the vulnerability there didn't weaken her—it sharpened her. "If this gives us a shot at taking our lives back, even for one breath, then it's worth the risk."

Buddy's heartbeat kicked hard, too loud in the too-quiet room. He wanted to reach for her. He didn't. The line between them was thin, but it held a thousand unspoken things they weren't ready to name. "Tomorrow could go sideways."

"It could," she agreed. "But so could doing nothing."

He closed his eyes for a brief moment. "I can't lose you."

She stepped around the table and stopped in front of him—close enough that he felt the warmth of her in the space where his guard usually lived. "You're not going to."

Her words weren't a promise. They were a vow.

A quiet, steady, terrifying vow.

And in the silence that followed, he realized she wasn't just committed to the plan.

She was committed to him.

Tomorrow would be hell.

But for the first time, the storm didn't feel like the only thing waiting on the other side.

Chapter Eighteen

The memorial always drew a crowd, but today it felt like the entire damn county had poured itself into the space between the marina and the Crab Shack. Buddy and Sterling moved through the thick press of bodies, the air shimmering with heat and grief and the twisted kind of hope people carried to events like this. Laughter rose above the picnic tables, bright and sharp, colliding with the steady hum of the water and the occasional croak of a frog.

It should've felt vibrant.

Instead, it felt like static.

Buddy's skin buzzed with it, that low, electric warning he hadn't been able to shake since dawn. Sterling must've felt it too—his shoulders too tight, his eyes too alert for a man trying to look casual.

"My first year with the CIA, I was a Protective Agent, and I hated it." Sterling continued to scan the crowd.

Buddy didn't look at him. "Why?"

"Because I had to protect high-level officials at functions not all that different than this overseas. Civilians were always involved. If something were to happen, casualties were always part of the risk."

"You're not helping." Buddy rubbed the back of his neck.

Children darted between legs, their clothes sun-bleached, arms sticky from melted popsicles. Teen volunteers ferried donation buckets. Someone shouted near the dunk tank, another person threw a beanbag toward the ring toss, and someone else cursed when they dropped their funnel cake.

This was good. Normal. Joyful in ways that almost didn't make sense considering the event's purpose.

Perfect camouflage for a monster.

Buddy's gaze snapped to Fallon, magnetic and unavoidable. She stood under the shade of the raffle tent, the light-weight spirit jacket on her shoulders—the one she'd been sent, the one that was a replica of the jacket Tessa had been wearing the night she went missing.

Fallon greeted people with that careful, kind smile she used when she didn't want anyone to see the crack in the foundation. But he noticed how her grin didn't quite reach her eyes. Her hair was pulled back in a loose braid that flowed over her left shoulder.

Cullen lingered in the crowd behind her, pretending to examine a display of silent auction items. Too far to draw attention. Close enough to intervene. The man blended like the trained marine he was, and that worried Buddy.

Cullen had come a long way from the days when he'd first returned.

But he still had triggers, and PTSD didn't disappear overnight. The things Cullen had been through didn't just go away because he had people who loved him and a damn good therapist.

Sterling paused at one of the vendor booths, stuffed his hand in his pocket, pulled out a wad of tickets, and placed a couple in the basket. "Can I ask you something without you telling me to mind my own business?"

Buddy scowled. Sterling wasn't the kind of man to ask before asking. He usually just opened his mouth and spewed whatever he needed to say, so this was strange. "Sounds like I'm gonna be annoyed."

"Probably." Sterling continued walking, scanning.

Buddy moved along with Sterling, keeping his focus on Fallon. She smiled at everyone who stepped up to the raffle table, but her posture was all wrong. Her shoulders too high, her gaze darting, and her smile not wide enough.

"In the few months I've known you, I've never seen you take a girl out. Not once. I've never even seen your head turn when a beautiful woman walked into the room. But Fallon, she's had your attention from the second we rolled into town. You've been watching her like you're waiting for someone to try to steal the sun."

Buddy glared. "Yeah, because someone's fucking with me, and they're using her to do it."

Sterling side-stepped a couple of young boys running through the crowd while their mother alternated between yelling at them and quietly apologizing to everyone she passed. "I'm not judging. I'm just saying you've got that look."

"What look?"

"The one a man gets when he finally realizes he's got something to lose."

Buddy ran a hand over his mouth as he paused thirty paces from the raffle table. A familiar, uncomfortable tightness settled in his chest. He'd experienced the same feeling when his FBI colleague, Gino, lost his wife and kids, and Buddy realized that his career put his wife in danger every time he walked out the door. If he had no one, he had nothing to lose and no chance of anyone getting killed—but him.

"We're all here because we want to protect her, this town, and anyone who might get caught in the crosshairs of whatever game this asshole is playing," Buddy said. "You'd be just as diligent about this situation even if I wasn't involved with her."

"Not the point." Sterling lowered his chin. "Back in Jacksonville, you used to get this funny smile when someone would text you. Or sometimes, you'd excuse yourself because you got a phone call. Afterward, you'd come back to the room, lighter." Sterling shifted his weight, gaze drifting between the band doing a sound check on stage and Fallon. "Dove and I used to talk about it. We thought maybe you had a secret girlfriend. Turns out, we were right because I caught a glimpse of the name on your screen. It was Fallon's."

"We've been friends a long time."

"I'm not blind. I know what love looks like. Hell, I even know what it feels like." Sterling leaned against the wooden fence that lined the walkway. "You're in love with her. I saw it the first day out in the Glades and it explained why coming to Calusa Cove was so important to you when other towns or cities might have made more sense."

Buddy's breath caught in his throat. Falling in love with Fallon had probably happened while he'd been working the Ring Finger case. He'd done everything he could to make sure nothing could happen, including taking a job transfer, moving him further away from Calusa Cove. But after he put Simon behind bars, his heart kept guiding him back to Florida.

Back to Calusa Cove.

Back to Fallon.

"Let's get through this, make sure nothing happens to Fallon, or anyone else, and then you and Dove can pick on me all you want about my love life."

Sterling chuckled. "I'd *never*. Love's too important. But Dove, she's gonna enjoy razzing you, and not just because she can. I'm pretty sure love is the only thing that scares that woman."

"Dove frightens me sometimes." Buddy turned toward the remembrance board—bigger this year, covered in a mosaic of faces. Some laminated, some warped from past storms, some pinned by trembling hands only an hour ago.

Tessa's photo sat near the center—Fallon had placed it herself earlier, fingers lingering on the edges. Buddy touched the bottom. The warmth from the sun still trapped in the corners.

Sterling shifted beside him. "How long has this board been part of the fundraiser?"

"Fallon's always had a memory board with pictures of Tessa. I believe the first year, she asked friends to bring their own images or write a note or dedication to Tessa. It was smaller back then. Just local families raising money for a local women's shelter. Then, some mom came asking if she could put something about her daughter on there. Then a sister. Then it just became a thing. Now, Fallon not only raises a ton of money, but she helps raise awareness across all of Florida." Buddy's eyes burned. The images shared on that board were a silent testament to the suffocating weight of loss--reflected in the smiles that would never be seen again. He ran his fingers across the edges of what appeared to be newer images and his heart broke. "I remember when I first transferred to human trafficking. I hadn't even been assigned a case yet, and I came to this event. I stared at this board for hours trying to find reasons why. Or patterns."

"Find any?"

Buddy drew in a slow breath. "Nothing that ties all of them together in a meaningful way outside of the fact that they're all missing." He moved along the board, eyes sliding over each face.

Girls with braces.

Boys with dimples.

Mothers, fathers, young adults, teenagers.

People who were loved.

People someone still prayed for.

Simon's voice echoed in his head, throbbing like a bruise pressed too hard.

You can't save them all.

Buddy's stomach tightened. He pressed his thumb against the edge of the board to ground himself, but his pulse didn't ease.

Movement caught his eye—a sliver of glossy paper peeking out from behind another photo. Wrong. Out of place. Fallon kept this board meticulous, constantly checking it throughout the day. She curated every inch, made sure no one's child was hidden. If the board got too crowded, she pulled out the backup board from the marina's storage room—and there were two full boards already.

But this picture had been tucked behind another, as if the placement was deliberate.

A tremor ran through him as he reached out, his fingertip unsteady as he nudged the top photo aside.

One picture slid forward.

Then another.

And his world narrowed to a pinpoint.

Two girls smiled back at him—dark hair, bright eyes, joy frozen in a moment of a life they never got to finish.

Maya. Sophie.

The ones he couldn't save. The ones he lost.

The ones who still crawled into his chest at night and hollowed out the space beneath his ribs.

Sterling stilled beside him, sensing the shift. "Shit."

Buddy's throat tightened. "This jerk knew Fallon would check the boards. That she would make sure each victim was seen—that I'd care enough to look."

"That's a crazy game. A lot of things would have to align for you to see them."

Buddy swallowed hard, every instinct in him lighting up like a flare. He scanned the crowd—the families at the raffle table, the teens laughing by the water, the older volunteers chatting near the stage.

Any of them.

All of them.

None of them.

"Not really. Our guy put them here," Buddy said, voice rough. "He wanted me to see them. He wants me off balance. He wants me to know that while he's not Simon, he's bigger than Simon. Knows more." Buddy scanned the crowd, his old instincts kicking in. "I thought Simon and this guy, EJ, knew each other peripherally. But now? I get the feeling that I didn't shut down anything when I arrested Simon. I merely put a dent in a bigger operation."

Sterling's posture sharpened. "Jesus. You know what I'm thinking?"

"Besides, this bastard is already here?" Buddy stepped back from the board, eyes sweeping the marina. He focused on the males. Clocked what they were wearing. Who they were with. What they were doing. If they appeared suspicious or blended in seamlessly.

It was the latter that made him nervous.

His gaze stayed locked on Fallon across the walkway, her braid slipping over her shoulder as she laughed at something a volunteer said.

So damn alive.

So damn exposed.

And wearing a target with a bullseye on the back.

"I've been bothered by the whole Bluewater Restoration and how clean that fucking operation is," Sterling said. "You checked them when you were looking for that compound before Simon's arrest. Their books were solid. I've gone through all your older files on them and doing additional research. It's a legit business. Outside of the LLC burying who really owns it, there's nothing to look at."

"Could still be laundering money."

"True. However, the more I think about all those companies, the more I don't believe this one was doing that. I keep asking myself—How do all of them run legit? But all of them have an LLC or two in common and those all start with blue, something. That's a pattern."

"We've talked about that," Buddy said. "Get to the point." He continued to focus on the area near Fallon, looking for anything that might be out of place. Anything that might be a sign the clock for this game had started ticking down.

"Take the compound. It's not common. It's easy to trace back to specific companies that maintain meticulous records. But if Simon were working for this EJ Vance, who owns all these fucking companies, it would be easy for them to cover this up as long as EJ stayed clean and EJV Industries wasn't listed as an owner of any of those companies starting with blue."

Every muscle in Buddy's body tensed. "If that's the case, this is one massive organization. At least double the size of Simon's if he was a cell under Vance."

"Have you or Dawson tried looping in Flagler with regard to what's been happening to Fallon?" Sterling asked.

Buddy nodded, keeping a close eye on anyone who came close to Fallon. "Right now, this is a local issue—a harassment case at best. We've all been trying to find that connection, but nothing that Flagler's boss will take seriously, even though Flagler is. A team is close by. Flagler gave them EJ Vance's name—actually, anything we have, they have. But they have nothing to tie missing girls to EJ, or what's happening to Fallon."

"Guess we'll have to find them something," Sterling said.

Cullen inched into Buddy's vision and Fallon didn't flinch when Cullen drifted a little closer to her in the crowd. Two deputies stood near the raffle line. Dawson and Chloe were near the docks. If she noticed the invisible grid tightening around her, it didn't seem to bother her... too much.

She just continued on the same way she always did—the way she did when she wanted the world to believe she was fine.

God, he loved her.

The admission hit him so hard he reached for the edge of the remembrance board to steady himself. His palm landed inches from Maya and Sophie's faces. Innocent. Young. Gone.

You can't save them all.

Simon's voice.

The new bastard's echo.

Two threats layered over the only truth that mattered:

If he failed today, Fallon would join the rest of the victims.

His stomach dropped so fast he thought he might be sick. Sterling said something—Buddy caught the rumble of his voice but not the words. The noise of the crowd muffled to a dull roar, every sound swallowed by the thudding pulse in his ears.

He stared at Fallon.

He couldn't stop.

He didn't try.

He imagined reaching her too late.

He imagined losing her like he'd lost those girls.

He imagined his world cracking open in the same violent, irreversible way it had years ago.

And the thought nearly took him to his knees.

"Hey." Sterling's voice cut through the fog—quiet but sharp. "You with me?"

Buddy blinked slowly. "No."

Sterling didn't look away. "What do you need?"

Buddy swallowed, the motion painful. "I need her to

survive this."

Sterling exhaled, long and low. "Then you make sure she does."

Buddy nodded, but it wasn't agreement. It was surrender to the truth he'd been fighting since this whole damn mess began.

He wasn't choosing between Fallon and some hypothetical victim. He wasn't choosing between love and duty. He wasn't even choosing between past and present.

He was choosing how much of himself he was willing to lose to keep her whole.

And the cost didn't matter.

Not anymore.

Not with her in that jacket.

Not with Maya and Sophie staring back at him.

His hand closed over the edge of the board until the wood creaked.

"Whoever he is," Buddy whispered, "he picked the wrong woman. Because he doesn't get to take her."

Sterling nodded, grim. "So, what now?"

Buddy straightened slowly, eyes locked on Fallon like he was counting every second before the room burned down around them.

"Now?" he said, voice low and steady. "We hunt."

The raffle table had been busy all morning, and Fallon had barely had a second to breathe—exactly what she'd hoped for—noise, distraction, people. Anything to keep her mind occupied so she didn't hyperfocus on the jacket that reminded her of that night or the quiet storm humming below the surface of the crowd.

She was halfway through straightening a stack of raffle tickets, while the other volunteer at the table stood off to the side, yelling, "raffle tickets for sale", when she heard her name.

"Fallon, you outdid yourself this year."

She looked up—and broke into a smile.

Favoring his left side, Trent carefully made his way toward her, wrapped in a loose button-down someone had probably insisted he wear so people wouldn't see the bandages underneath. His mother, Linda, walked beside him, one hand lightly touching his arm, as if to steady him but without hovering.

They both looked thinner. Paler. Like the bullet and diagnosis had stolen more than blood and health—they'd taken peace, security, the belief that tomorrow was guaranteed.

But they were here.

Fallon stepped out from behind the table. "What are you doing here? You should be home resting and recovering."

Trent grinned, though it didn't quite reach his eyes. "I couldn't stand sitting still a second longer."

Linda rolled her eyes affectionately. "He keeps trying to help me with stuff around my house. I thought coming here was the lesser of two evils."

"I'm healing nicely," Trent said, though he seemed winded from the walk. "We weren't missing this."

Fallon swallowed the unexpected emotion rising in her throat. "I'm glad you're here. Really."

Linda reached out and squeezed Fallon's hand. "You've done something beautiful. We all need to remember those we've lost, those who have fallen, and those who are missing."

Fallon squeezed back. Linda's hand felt too light, her bones too sharp. The cancer was hitting fast. Hard. But she still stood straight, chin lifted, revealing the same quiet strength visible in Trent.

Just like Fallon had promised him, she didn't look at Linda with pity. She talked to her the same way she always had—warm, direct, unafraid. And Linda's shoulders began to ease, gratitude flickering in her eyes.

Falcon took a steadying breath. "At least, promise me you're not planning to run laps or volunteer as tribute for the cake walk."

Trent snorted. "Mom already threatened to sit on me if I push it."

"I meant it," Linda said primly.

Fallon laughed. "Good. Both of you take it slow. And drink water. It's healing."

"We won't stay long," Linda said. "Just wanted to be here. For Tessa. And for you."

Fallon nodded, unable to speak around the sudden tightness in her throat. The moment shimmered—fragile, real—and then the next group stepped up to buy raffle tickets, pulling her back into motion.

Trent and Linda drifted toward a quiet table in the

shade, Trent waved. She lifted her hand in return as a man stepped into her line of sight.

Button-down shirt worn under a sport coat. Khaki slacks. Sunglasses. Average height, average build, average everything. The sort of man she'd forget two minutes after passing him in Publix.

Still—something tugged at her memory.

He smiled. "Afternoon."

"Hi there," Fallon said, offering him a roll of tickets. "How many?"

"Let's do a hundred dollars' worth."

"That's very generous–thank you." She tore the strip, handed it over, and dropped his cash in the jar. He lingered—staring just long enough to be intrusive.

"Fallon Reeves, right?"

She stilled, suddenly aware she was on display. "Yes?"

He laughed lightly. "Ah. Thought so. You probably don't remember me."

"I'm sorry," she said, her cheeks heated. "I meet a lot of people at this event."

"We met long before the fundraiser started," he said gently. "I was a business acquaintance of your dad's. Quincy Bellows."

Her breath hitched—not fear, but surprise. "You... knew my dad?"

"Oh, yes." His smile softened. "We worked at the same company. Different jobs and different offices, for that matter. I travel for the corporate team, and one year I ended up down here, and he and I had dinner. You were still in high school, I think. I met you briefly—just a hello in the hallway."

A faint memory flickered—her father ushering a man through the living room. She couldn't recall the details. Just a blip of a fellow looking similar to this man having a quick drink in the living room before going out to dinner to discuss... she had no idea. All she remembered was waving from the kitchen before heading out to meet Tessa.

Her stomach twisted. "I think I remember. I, at least, remember your face."

He tapped his chest and smiled as if that meant the world to him. "My wife came across the flyer for the fundraiser online. She recognized your name. I put the pieces together and... well, I wanted to come pay my respects. Your father was a good man. I liked him."

Emotion pinched her throat. "Thank you."

"Would you have time," he asked, "for a drink? I only have maybe an hour to spare before I need to head over to Sarasota. I'd love to chat about this project and exchange a few stories about your father."

It was innocent. Perfectly reasonable. And Fallon wanted it—wanted to hear stories about her dad from someone who'd known him ways she hadn't. Her chest ached with it. The chance to learn something new, something unexpected. A memory that wasn't hers but could become hers. Like maybe, just for a moment, her father could reach through all that grief and loss and give her something lighter. Something that made him feel alive again instead of just gone.

"Sure," she said. "There's a table over there. We can grab some sweet tea—"

"Maybe someplace that isn't so loud," Quincy said. "I saw some tables on the side of the Crab Shack? They had reserved signs on them. I assume they're for volunteers."

"Sure. We can go there." She snagged her cell off the table. "I just need to get that girl over there to cover for me. Give me one second." She turned and scurried off toward one of the volunteers. She really didn't need the help since there were always two people at the raffle table, but she wanted the opportunity to text Buddy. Just to be safe.

"Hey, Val. Mind hanging out at the raffle table for a bit?" Fallon asked.

"Nope."

"Great. But give me a second," Fallon said. "Stand here with me while I send a couple of texts. Just chat away about anything."

"I can do that. My dad says I'm a chatterbox, and…"

Val continued to talk about boys, and school, and, well, Fallon didn't pay attention.

Fallon: *Having a drink with an old friend of my dad's. Name is Quincy Bellows. I'll be over at the Crab Shack tables.*

The reply arrived almost immediately.

Buddy: *Do you know him? Recognize him?*

Fallon: *Familiar looking. But no, I don't know him.*

Buddy: *I need you to stay alert. Be hyper-aware of what he says, how he acts. Don't trust anything.*

Fallon: *I know. I'll be careful.*

Buddy: *Stay in sight lines. I'll be close by. Someone will always be watching.*

She smiled to herself—not annoyed. Warm. Seen. Protected in a way that didn't cage her.

"Thanks, Val. I'll be back shortly." She turned and strolled toward Quincy, tucking her cell in her back pocket.

He gestured toward the drink stand. "Shall we?"

She stepped forward—and the crowd surged around them, a sudden bottleneck of bodies squeezing through the walkway. People laughing, stumbling, shoulders brushing hers.

Quincy moved behind her slightly, hand pressing against the small of her back to guide her forward—

Too familiar.

Too intentional.

Too much pressure.

Fallon's breath hitched.

Then he leaned in, his lips almost brushing her ear.

"Nice jacket," he murmured. "Makes an interesting statement, don't you think?"

"Excuse me?"

He smiled. But it wasn't friendly. "Wasn't that the one your friend wore the night she disappeared? The one you lent her... because it should've been you?"

Fallon froze. Ice poured down her spine. Her knees nearly buckled. She didn't turn. Couldn't. Because she felt it. A hard shape beneath his sports coat. Pressed into her ribs. Cold. Concealed. Deadly.

"No sudden moves," Quincy whispered. "Smile, sweetheart. You're surrounded."

Her legs went numb.

"You try anything," he continued, voice soft enough to get lost in the noise around them, "and you won't be the only one who dies today."

Her vision blurred. "What... what do you want?"

He chuckled, breath hot against her ear.

"For now, I want your cooperation, and that means you're going to tell the military-looking man who's been lurking close by—the one with the shaggy hair—to use the bathroom. Or get lost in the crowd. I don't care. And then you're gonna tell that boyfriend of yours that we're going to walk to my car and he's going to let us get in it, and drive away." The gun pressed harder. "And sweetheart... if you even breathe wrong, Trent's mother, that sweet, lovely old woman, she'll be the first to die. Don't try me, because we've already got her, and I won't hesitate. And if you and Buddy still don't want to play by my rules, then I've got a dozen teenage girls I can drop at his doorstep—dead."

Fallon's heart stopped.

The crowd swallowed them whole.

And she knew—she was in the jaws of the trap. Quincy—or EJ Vance—or whatever his name was, might think he had the upper hand—and well, he did have a gun shoved in her side. However, she could call an audible just as easily as he could.

Time to change the play.

Hopefully, it wouldn't get her, or anyone else, killed.

Chapter Nineteen

Buddy stood with Sterling at the remembrance board, not seeing a single face on it. His eyes were locked on Fallon's back as she drifted farther from the raffle booth with the man she'd claimed knew her father. She moved like someone trying to look unbothered—steady steps, shoulders squared—but something in the rhythm was off. Too controlled. Too careful.

Then the text hit Buddy's phone like someone had pressed a gun to his spine.

Fallon: *Stand down. Let me leave with him. Parking lot. His car. If you don't, Trent's mom dies. More girls die. I die.*

The words weren't Fallon's, not even close, but they were written with enough intent that he could feel the barrel pushing into her ribs as she typed them. He didn't stop walking—he didn't dare—but the world tunneled into a narrow corridor of motion where only one thing mattered. Her silhouette weaved through the thinning edge of the crowd as the bastard at her side steered her toward the parking lot.

He angled his body just enough to keep her in sight between sun-bleached tents and the heavy knot of people queuing for fried shrimp. The heat pulsed in from every direction, thick and sticky, amplifying voices, twisting laughter into something warped, making the air itself feel as if it were vibrating with wrongness. Sterling shifted half a step closer, but neither of them drew attention— just two men skirting the periphery of a fundraiser that had suddenly become a hunting ground.

"I need all eyes on Fallon," Buddy said, barely moving his lips, "we're live. Fallon's under direct threat. Parking lot trajectory."

Sterling nodded, jaw tight, eyes scanning for secondaries.

Buddy's phone buzzed again—not Fallon this time.

"Buddy! Buddy!" Trent's voice cracked through the noise before he collided into Buddy's shoulder, breath ragged, color wrong, the hospital pallor still clinging to him like frost. He grabbed Buddy's arm with shaking fingers, the bandage on his side pulling as he bent forward.

"I can't find my mom," Trent choked out. "I left her right there—right there by the picnic tables. I went to the bathroom, came back, and she was gone. She's not picking up. Her phone's off. I tried to call. Text. Track. She's just gone and that's not like my mother."

Buddy caught him by the elbows, steadying him before he tore something open. "Slow down." He waited until Trent's eyes locked on his. "You can't run around like this. You're injured."

"I don't care," Trent snapped, voice climbing. "She's all I have, and she's dying. What if…"

Buddy exhaled sharply and lowered his voice. "Listen to me." He held up his phone just long enough for Trent to see Fallon's text. "This is connected."

Trent's breath hitched. "Motherfucker. I'm gonna—"

"You can't do shit if you pull open those stitches. You need to rest, and I need to get back to making sure nothing happens to Fallon or your mom," Buddy said. "I promise to keep you in the loop."

"I'm not going to sit back and do nothing. That's my mother," Trent bit out, panic and anger wrestling in every syllable.

"You want your mom safe? Then you listen to me."

It landed. Not gracefully, not easily—but it landed. Trent swallowed and stepped back, chest heaving, fury and fear vibrating off him in waves. He wasn't okay with this. He never would be. But he stayed put.

Buddy hit comms. "Dawson, we've got a problem—Trent's mom is compromised. Fallon is being forced into compliance. She's being walked to the parking lot. I've still got a visual, but I'm gonna lose that soon."

Dawson's voice came through tight. "Copy. Chloe—redirect the crowd near the boardwalk to keep them from bottlenecking. Jasper and Grayson start looking for Mrs. Mallor."

Buddy kept moving, weaving between families and clusters of volunteers with the deliberate calm of a man on the verge of losing his mind. Fallon's pace hadn't changed, but her posture had—her shoulders were drawn slightly inward, her head angled just off the natural line of conversation. Anyone else would miss it.

Not him.

His phone buzzed again.

Fallon: *Stop moving closer. Stop following. If you don't, Trent's mom dies.*

Buddy didn't let the flinch show, but his ironclad resilience cracked like old bones. This was Simon's playbook all over again—the pressure points, the split focus, the rules designed to force him into choosing the order of who lived and who died.

Not again. Not this time.

"I'm climbing down." Dove's voice cut in, tight and breathless. "I've got limited visual on the exit road, but I'll be mobile in sixty seconds. Keaton and Hayes are repositioning from the water's edge."

Good. Good. Not enough. Never enough.

"Buddy—Bingo just arrived," Dawson said. "He came in a few minutes ago. He's heading your direction."

Relief hit Buddy's bloodstream fast and sharp, like a shot of oxygen. Bingo was a variable the bastard couldn't have predicted. Fallon didn't even know he was home.

"We can use him," Dawson continued. "He can create a diversion at the parking lot entrance. Natural. Casual. No tells."

Buddy angled left, slipping behind a food stall so Fallon wouldn't accidentally catch sight of him. "Someone needs to brief him like now. Get him comms.

He needs to identify the vehicle, the man, and any secondary weapons. And if they ditch her phone—"

"The jacket tracker has redundancy," Dove said. "We'll keep the signal even if the phone is tossed."

Buddy swallowed hard. "Good. Position Keaton, Hayes, and Dove on the only exit route. They shadow from a distance. No lights. No heroics. If she's moved, we follow."

Fallon and her captor crossed into the outer ring of the crowd, the noise thinning, the light shifting, the boards beneath their feet giving way to gravel as they reached the fringe of the parking lot.

Buddy's pulse slammed against his ribs. She was walking toward a car she might never walk away from.

He forced himself forward—slowly—threading through families unloading strollers and coolers, blending in as best he could while his insides twisted into something raw and electric. Sterling matched his pace, giving low updates—no alarms, no overt watchers, no weapons flashed—but that meant nothing.

Buddy saw Fallon's hand brush her thigh, the barest tremor in her fingers. She wasn't signaling him. She wasn't signaling anyone. That was fear bleeding through a crack she couldn't seal fast enough.

His throat tightened.

He loved her. God help him, he loved her. And he was being forced to follow slowly while the woman he loved was marched toward a killer's car.

Dawson's voice broke through the radio static. "Bingo's thirty feet out. Approaching from the west. He'll intersect naturally at the lane."

Buddy closed the distance just enough to see Bingo—relaxed stride, ball cap low, a beer in hand like he'd stepped out of a summer postcard instead of a tactical diversion.

Fallon didn't see him yet.

The man beside her did.

Buddy watched the shift—subtle, predatory, the way the guy's hand tightened fractionally at Fallon's back, angling her toward a darker corridor between parked cars. A place where visibility dropped. A place where extraction got harder.

Buddy's heart tanked to his stomach like a brick.

"Dawson," he said quietly, "he made Bingo. He knows someone unexpected just entered the field."

"Keep eyes on them," Dawson replied. "We're with you."

Buddy stepped behind a truck to get closer without being spotted. From here, he could see everything—the way Fallon's chin lifted as if trying not to tremble, the way Bingo's friendly smile faltered the moment he realized she wasn't just surprised, she was terrified, and the way the man beside her shifted his body to block any approach.

They were three steps from the shadow line.

Three steps from a car door.

Three steps from disappearing.

"Sterling," Buddy whispered, voice steady in a way

his body wasn't, "start your angle. If he draws, you take the shot."

Sterling moved like smoke.

Buddy kept moving too, blood roaring in his ears, every instinct screaming to run to her, pull her free, end this now—but he couldn't. Not yet. Not at the cost of Trent's mom. Not at the expense of more girls.

He fucking hated this.

Fallon flicked her gaze once—one narrow sliver of hope searching the edges of the parking lot.

She didn't see him.

But he saw her.

He always did.

She crossed the shadow line. And Buddy felt the world narrow into a single impossible truth. He was seconds away from losing her. He dropped his voice to a low, lethal whisper, words meant for no one but himself.

"I'm coming, sweetheart. Just hold on."

Heat rolled off the pavement in thick, shimmering waves, warping the laughter and music into something distant and wrong. Fallon's breath caught as the people ahead of her parted just enough to reveal a man cutting toward them with an easy stride and a beer in his hand. Bingo. Of all times—of all moments—he'd picked this one to find her.

"Fallon Reeves," Bingo said, grinning. "I've been

looking forward to surprising you all day." He stretched his arms out wide as he came close.

Quincy—or EJ—as she suspected his real name was, released his grip, but not before jabbing her quickly with the gun and then just as quickly, it disappeared into his coat.

"What? No hug?" Bingo asked.

"Of course, I am."

Bingo pulled her into a hug, one arm wrapping tight, the other casually keeping his beer upright. "Tell me that face means you're happy to see me, and that no one ruined my surprise."

Her breath stuttered against his shoulder.

"I'm speechless." She pulled back with a smile that felt stapled onto her face. "I had no idea you were coming home."

"Got in late last night. Had some family things I needed to do, but I didn't want to miss this. I know how much it means to you—and to Calusa Cove."

"I appreciate you making the effort."

He tipped his head toward EJ. "Who's your friend? I don't believe we've ever met."

EJ didn't offer a hand. Didn't offer anything except a polite-enough nod that didn't come close to touching his eyes.

Fallon's pulse skittered. "Someone who worked with my dad," she said quickly, hoping Bingo wouldn't ask the next question. "He, um—"

"Wow, your dad, huh?" Bingo tugged at his cap, lowering it over his darkened sunglasses. "I miss that man and his amazing stories. He was always so good to me."

"He liked you. Thought you were going places," she whispered, and she meant it. God, she meant it. But fear clamped cold fingers around her lungs. She needed him gone. Needed him safe. Needed Trent's mom alive.

And the girls. Always the girls.

Bingo glanced between them, still smiling, but Fallon knew him well enough that behind those shades—subtle, trained eyes were cataloging... everything.

EJ stepped forward lightly, like he'd been waiting for this moment. "We really do need to be going," he said, placing a hand on Fallon's elbow.

Bingo's head snapped up. "Going where? She never leaves the fundraiser early. Ever. You must be new."

Fallon's stomach dropped.

EJ's smile didn't change. "We've been working on something special. For the fundraiser. A surprise. I'd hate to ruin it."

The lie slid out of him like silk.

"Interesting," he said lightly, taking a sip of his beer, "I thought I knew most of the folks helping her. And here I thought I was the only surprise in the works this year."

EJ didn't blink. Didn't flinch. "We'd better go if we want this to work."

Fallon's hand trembled at her side. "I didn't tell anyone about this," she said. "I'll be right back."

She hadn't lied since she told her parents that she was working that shift at the Crab Shack the night Tessa disappeared. Now, that was irony at its best.

Bingo's jaw tightened almost imperceptibly. "Okay. But let me walk you—"

A second man appeared at EJ's shoulder, cutting off the offer with a quiet, "We need to move. Now."

He wasn't aggressive. Just... decisive. Confident he would be obeyed.

EJ touched Fallon's arm—not roughly, but firmly enough to inspire dread. "Come on."

"I'll see you shortly." Unable to meet Bingo's gaze, Fallon forced her feet to follow. Forced herself not to look back. Forced herself to believe Bingo would know that this wasn't normal, and he'd catch the license plate number. Or something. Anything he could give to Buddy that might save Linda, the girls, and herself.

Buddy wouldn't be able to live with himself if he couldn't save them.

The SUV waited at the far end of the lot—one of three lined up like they'd been positioned hours ago. Dark. Tinted. Ominous in a way that made her bones feel hollow.

"Get in the back," EJ murmured.

She expected empty seats. Maybe duct tape. Maybe rope.

Not Linda Mallor.

The older woman was slumped against the leather, wrists cuffed, gag pulled too tight across her mouth. Her eyes were red, panicked, pleading.

Fallon's own breath caught like barbed wire. "Please," she whispered to EJ's accomplice. "Take the gag off her. She can't breathe like that."

"No," the man said simply, already pulling out restraints. "Hands."

Fallon's pulse thundered. "Please—just the gag. She's terrified."

"Hands," the man repeated.

She didn't have a choice. She put her wrists forward, and the plastic ties cinched tight—too tight—burning into skin that had been unblemished only minutes ago.

The SUV lurched forward, following another just ahead of them. Fallon's stomach twisted as the marina blurred behind them.

Then—they stopped. Not gradually. Abruptly.

The entrance was blocked by an ambulance, parked sideways, lights off but hazard blinkers on like it had broken down in the wrong damn place.

The driver leaned out. "Gonna be a few minutes," he shouted. "Emergency call. We've got to unload."

Her heart hammered. Too loud. Too hopeful. Too dangerous.

The back doors of the ambulance swung open.

Two EMTs jumped out, rolling a gurney—white sheets, metal frame, equipment clipped to the sides.

One of them was Hayes. Only, Hayes wasn't an EMT, at least not for the Calusa Cove Fire Department. Sure, he was a firefighter, but he'd given up his role as medic when he'd left the military.

He didn't look at her.

He didn't even flick his eyes toward the SUV. Of course, he couldn't see through the tinted windows.

He just moved with the calm, practiced urgency of a man doing his job.

But Fallon felt it. Hope tightened like a fist in her throat. Help wasn't here. Not yet.

But it was close. So close, she could sense it. Even as the SUV idled. Even as EJ's hand settled lightly on the seat beside her. Even as Linda's muffled sob shook the dark.

Fallon lifted her chin, heart pounding, wrists burning against the ties. She was out. But she wasn't lost.

Not yet.

Chapter Twenty

The ambulance blocked the only exit exactly as planned—angled across the asphalt, hazards pulsing, the back doors open while Hayes played the part so well, Buddy almost believed it. Engines rumbled behind them. Three black SUVs. One holding Fallon. And one holding the men who thought forcing the choice would break him.

Dawson stood at his side at the parking lot edge, posture so tight it could snap. Somewhere behind them, Trent paced in sharp, uneven lines, one hand pressed to his side, the other shaking with fury he couldn't burn off. His voice cut through the air once—raw, terrified—but Buddy didn't turn. He couldn't. Not without losing focus.

Fallon's last message burned in his head, anyway.

It dug under his ribs like wire.

He keyed into comms. "Status."

Dove answered first. "Keaton and I are staged down

the bend. No interference. Hayes can hold another thirty seconds."

"Sterling?"

"Eyes on SUV Two."

"Fletcher?" Buddy asked.

"With Bingo. Ready to roll."

Buddy nodded once, breath clipped, controlled. Fallon was out of sight but not gone. Not yet.

Dawson touched his arm. "When they split, we won't be tailing Fallon's vehicle. We'll let Fletcher take that one."

Buddy exhaled through his nose—a sound that wasn't a laugh and wasn't agreement. "Try to keep me off it."

"I mean it," Dawson said. "You love her. You're not capable of being objective."

Buddy turned just enough to meet his eyes. "If it were Audra in that SUV, you'd already be behind the wheel."

Dawson didn't deny it. "Fine," he muttered. "But keep your head clear. and I'm driving."

"That's fair."

"Hayes is ready to move the ambulance," Fletcher said.

"Let's go." Dawson jogged toward his personal vehicle and jumped behind the steering wheel. "We follow Dove and Keaton, and we stay a safe distance behind them."

Buddy wasn't about to argue.

The ambulance began rolling back, clearing the lane. Hayes made a hand gesture, a subtle signal—move—and the three SUVs pulled forward in a slow, synchronized glide before gaining speed.

Each team followed their respective SUVs. Buddy couldn't see shit inside.

"Vehicle two northbound," Sterling said. "Going the speed limit. Nothing out of the ordinary."

"Vehicle three also heading north," Cullen added.

"Vehicle one heading east," Dove confirmed.

Dawson clapped his shoulder. Quick. Hard.

Buddy's pulse hammered as Dawson pulled out into traffic, far enough behind to look harmless, close enough to pounce the second he had an opening.

This wasn't surveillance.

This was war.

And Buddy Ballard wasn't losing a single one of them —not Fallon, not Linda, not the girls whose names he didn't even know yet.

Not today.

The road thinned as they left the town limits, the noise of the fundraiser falling away behind him. Live music faded into engine rumble. Laughter into wind. The shift in sound sharpened the world around him—like someone had twisted a dial and stripped everything down to threat and motion.

Dawson's SUV hummed under them as he guided it six car lengths behind the vehicle Fallon had been forced into. Any closer, and they'd tip their hand. Too far, and Buddy would lose sight of her. Neither option sat well. Nothing about this night sat well.

Buddy kept one hand braced against the dash, the

other curled tight in his lap. Fallon's SUV drifted through the last stretch of marina traffic. Every time its brake lights flared, Buddy's chest locked.

His phone vibrated.

Unknown number. But he knew who it was, and in that instant, the world narrowed to the screen.

Buddy answered. "Hello?"

A low chuckle slid through the speaker—soft, pleased, dangerous.

Like EJ had been waiting for the moment Buddy picked up.

"There he is," EJ said, his voice a lazy coil of satisfaction. "I was starting to think you'd let someone else answer your calls."

Buddy's molars ground together. He kept his gaze locked on the SUV ahead—the one that held the woman he loved—while the monster behind the voice dripped poison into his ear.

"What do you want?" Buddy asked. Not polite. Not patient. A barely leashed snarl.

"Oh, don't rush this," EJ said. "I want you to understand where we stand." A pause. A breath. Like he was savoring the moment. "You really think you can follow me without consequences?"

Buddy's fingers dug into his knee. He didn't look at Dawson. Didn't blink. "Where are they?"

"Who? The girls? Your girlfriend? Or Linda?"

"All of them."

"Well, Linda," EJ said lightly, like they were discussing

the weather. "She's right here with me. Terrified little thing. She begged for her son, you know. Thought he, or you, or some guy by the name of Dawson might come and save her."

The air left Buddy's lungs in splinters of terror. He forced it back in.

"And Fallon, well, you know she's here, too," EJ said. "And she's exactly what I hoped—what I remember— brave, stubborn, still trying to keep her chin up. I'm almost disappointed I have to break her... but rules are rules."

A white-hot flash detonated behind Buddy's ribs. His voice came out low, lethal. "If you so much as touch her—"

"Oh, I'll do far more than touch her," EJ said. "But we're getting ahead of ourselves."

Buddy's heartbeat slammed against sternum, tight, pounding, a war drum in his own chest.

EJ rustled something on the line—paper, maybe. Buddy's gut clenched.

"Linda and Fallon are lovely bargaining chips. But I'm feeling generous tonight. So, here's my offer."

Buddy's jaw locked. "Say it."

"I have thirty girls," EJ said, soft a penitent looking for absolution. "Thirty. Lost. Forgotten. Easy to move. Easy to keep. They cry like ghosts when the lights go out."

Buddy's stomach turned to ice.

"This is your choice. It's always been your choice." EJ's voice warmed, almost affectionate. "I'll let the girls go... but then I keep these two. Or, I kill the girls and let these two go. Simple."

Buddy's pulse stuttered, then roared back harder, as if bursting through a dam. "Where are the girls?"

"You care more about them than your lover? Your friend's dying mother? Interesting." EJ laughed. "That's a twist I didn't expect."

Buddy's vision whitened at the edges. Blood raced in his ears. Fury climbed his spine like fire.

"I didn't say that."

"What are you saying?" EJ asked, but it was more of a taunt than anything else. "Simon tried to teach you how this works. Shame he didn't get far. You locked up the errand boy, not the man he worked for."

Buddy's breath hitched—once—before he forced it steady. "What do you really want?"

"For you to make your choice." The words sliced like a knife. "Tell all your teams to back off. Stop trailing us. Call everyone off. You do that, and I pull over and let Fallon and Linda walk away. Alive. I swear it."

"And if we don't?" Buddy asked, even though he already knew.

"Oh, then they die first," EJ said. "And the girls go next."

Buddy's throat closed. Rage and terror fused until he couldn't tell one from the other. "You expect me to choose between—"

"No." EJ cut him off, tone turning almost tender. "I expect you to lose. You've always been good at that."

Buddy's fingers curled into a fist so tight his nails bit into his skin.

"Choose who dies. Or everyone does," EJ said. "You've got ten minutes."

The line went dead.

Buddy's world detonated. "Fuck." He slammed the dashboard hard enough that Dawson flinched. The second hit was worse—fist connecting with plastic and metal until pain streaked up his arm. "Son of a—fuck!"

He couldn't breathe. Couldn't see anything except Fallon trapped behind that blacked-out glass. Linda beside her. Thirty girls whose names he didn't even know.

Dawson grabbed Buddy's forearm, yanking him back before he put a hole through the dash. "Look at me."

Buddy didn't. Couldn't. His rage was a living thing—clawing, burning, ripping its way up his throat.

"That sick bastard—" Buddy gunned the heel of his hand into the glove box this time, harder, breath breaking. "He has Fallon. Linda. Thirty fucking—Jesus Christ—thirty girls—"

"Buddy." Dawson's voice sharpened into command. "Reign it in. Focus."

Buddy's chest seized. He sucked in air, but it didn't feel like enough. Didn't feel like anything.

"He wants me to choose." Buddy's voice cracked. Then it hardened into something carved from bone. "He actually—he thinks I'm going to choose."

"He's trying to break you," Dawson said. "So, don't break."

Buddy dragged both hands over his face, shaking. "I can't lose her. I can't lose any of them."

"You're not losing anyone," Dawson said, steadier now, the kind of calm that came from years of dragging men back from cliffs. "Use your head. Not your fear."

Fear. No—worse. Memory. Simon's case. Georgia. The pipeline.

Those hidden bulkheads sealed with marine epoxy.

The blue-gray silica dust under that girl's nails.

The trail that had never quite added up.

Blue Heron.

Bluewater Restoration.

Blue Coast.

Blue Reef.

Blue Horizon.

Shells stacked head to tail up the coast like bread-crumbs meant to mislead.

And then Decker—quiet, broken Decker—murmuring about Miami, about his childhood tied to the Barbaros, about the shipping yards and the way boats came in heavy and left light.

Containers.

Ports.

Buddy's breath caught.

A click—small, sharp—sounded in his head.

He reached for his phone with hands that still shook. "Mia," he whispered as he pulled up her contact information.

She answered before the first ring finished. "Hey,

Buddy. Hayes called a bit ago, and I'm already in the system—"

"Pull the last set of invoices from Bluewater Restoration," he said. "Look for transfers connected to port facilities. Cross-reference Quincy Bellows with shipping manifests in Miami. Check for spelling variations. Anything close."

"On it."

Every second she typed, Buddy's pulse hammered harder.

"Nothing for Quincy," Mia said.

Buddy's gut dropped—

"—but—hold on—Quinn Porter Bellows—but it looks like it might be just Quinn Porter now."

Buddy's spine went rigid. "Say it again."

"Quinn Porter. Female. Previously, Quinn Bellows, and she was married to EJ Vance. She owns a shipping company operating out of the Miami port. High-volume containers. Restricted processing yards."

Buddy's throat went dry. Dawson swore under his breath.

"Buddy," Mia said, voice tightening, "this looks bad."

"Yeah," he rasped. "It should, because it's fucking human trafficking at its finest."

"We have two team members in Miami. Nick Sarich, who you know, and a new guy named Parker Udell. They can be at the port in ten minutes."

"I need to call Flagler with the FBI. We need to make the trafficking charge stick."

"That's gonna take some work, but I can send him

what I have," Mia said. "I'll also work some magic and get him more. Methods might be questionable, but I'll make them as legal as possible."

"Do what you need to."

"Nick has contacts with the Miami PD. He also knows the local fed there. He'll loop them in," Mia said. "Let me go. This will take time. Do your best to stall."

"Got it." Buddy ended the call and pinched the bridge of his nose.

Dawson leaned in toward the comm. "You think that's where the girls are?"

"I think," Buddy said, "they're already packed and waiting to disappear. I believe the second I choose, they're either dead, or they'll be moved."

He didn't let himself feel it. Not yet. Not the terror. Not the grief. Not the fury threatening to tear him apart.

"Or he could be playing you and he's just gonna move the girls anyway," Dawson said. "To stick with the football analogy, the audible's been called, and the taunt, *you can't save them all*, might not mean death."

"I know," Buddy said. "Simon once told me he'd rather not kill product." He swallowed thick bile that felt more like tar lodged in his throat. He hit Flagler's contact information.

"Ballard," Flagler answered on the second ring. "Tell me you've got something."

"I've got a location," Buddy said. "Miami port. Shipping containers under Quinn Bellows. EJ's ex-wife. High-volume lanes. Restricted access. And I'm following EJ right now. He's got Fallon and Linda Mallor. We've got him on kidnapping. All I need you to do is make it possible to get into that shipping yard, and make it fucking legal. Mia Sarich is sending you intel. We've got two Aegis Network operatives in the area. They're contacting local PD and local Fed."

Silence—sharp, heavy.

"Buddy," Flagler said slowly, "if you're wrong, I'm about to blow about ten million dollars' worth of political capital."

"I'm not wrong."

"You're guessing based on shell companies—"

"I'm not guessing, and Mia will send you everything she's got, but you need to move fast, or those girls will disappear before Dawson can slap the cuffs on EJ," Buddy snapped. "He's moving product. He always has been. Simon wasn't the mastermind—EJ was. And 'Bluewater Restoration' doesn't restore shit. It moves it."

Flagler exhaled. "Christ."

"Fallon and Linda stay alive," Buddy said, voice thickening with the weight of his decisions, "but those girls? They don't get that chance if we're late. They'll be sold to the highest bidder and disappear forever. Or die. I am not letting that happen."

Flagler muttered something Buddy didn't catch— something sharp, federal, furious. "Fine. I'll burn every favor I've got. I know people at Miami PD, too. I've also got Harbor Patrol, DHS, Coast Guard—I'll get them all. We'll converge on the port."

Buddy sagged back into the seat, breath shaking. "Thank you."

"Ballard," Flagler said, voice harder now, resolute instead of cautious, "if you're wrong, it's my career. If you're right, I'll owe you some serious shit."

The call ended.

Buddy stared ahead at the black SUV carrying Fallon into the dark. His heart hammered like a wild beast. He tapped the comms in his ear. "Dove, Sterling, you read?"

"What's up, boss?" Dove asked.

"Copy," Sterling said.

"Dump the SUVs and come to my location." Buddy glanced in Dawson's direction, who nodded, as if he knew exactly what he was thinking. "Dove, try to get around in front of us. You're gonna have to haul ass to do that."

"Won't be that hard," Dove said. "We're on the highway, headed northeast."

"Sterling, tuck in behind me until told otherwise."

"Consider it done," Sterling said.

"I'm not giving him what he wants." Buddy rubbed his neck. "I'm going to trust that Nick and Flagler can deal with the situation in Miami, and we're gonna turn the tables on this asshole."

"Sounds like a plan to me," Dawson said.

There was no way Buddy was going to actually choose between anyone.

He was choosing all of them.

Or he'd die trying.

Chapter Twenty-One

Darkness swallowed the SUV whole—thick, absolute, the kind that erased the world beyond the windows. No streetlights. No moon. No landmarks to indicate where they were taking her. Just an endless black void rushing past, punctuated by the occasional blur of trees that materialized then vanished like ghosts.

Inside, every vibration of the road jolted through Fallon's bones. The zip tie bit into her wrists with each bump, each turn into that suffocating nothingness.

The confinement sank into her bones, grinding against joints she couldn't shift.

Linda trembled beside her, frail and folded in on herself, her wrists purpling against her cuffs. Her staggered breaths whistled through the gag covering her mouth. Fallon nudged her shoulder gently, solidarity in the dark.

"It's okay," Fallon whispered, even though nothing about this was okay. "I'm here."

EJ's eyes flicked to her through the rearview—amused, curious, like she was a puzzle he already knew the ending to.

"You don't need to bother comforting her," he said. "She won't matter much longer."

Fallon swallowed the urge to scream. It wouldn't help or solve anything. "Where are you taking us?" Her pulse spiked with something icy and brutal, as she waited for a response she wasn't sure she wanted to hear.

"That depends," EJ said casually, as if discussing a scenic detour. "On whether your hero understands simple instructions."

Her jaw tightened. This was an impossible situation with no good outcome. "Why us? Why Buddy? Why this?" A million more questions rattled her brain, but she doubted EJ would even answer these.

The driver chuckled under his breath.

EJ didn't. He watched her instead, gaze sharpening with interest—like she'd finally stepped onto the exact mental square he wanted.

"Still thinking small," he murmured. "Still thinking this is about tonight." He shifted slightly, turning just enough that she caught the shadow of his smile.

"What do you mean, small?"

He tapped his temple. "Use your brain. I know you have one. I've been watching you for a while now, and you're smart. Maybe even smarter than that boyfriend of yours."

Her heart raced. Her mind rattled. "Watching? For how long?"

"Honestly? On and off for years." He licked his lips like she was a meal about to be devoured. "I never anticipated you and Buddy. That wasn't originally part of the plan. Hell, you weren't part of my plan to get back at Buddy for what he did, but you just landed there nice and neat."

"That doesn't make any sense if you've been watching for years. It doesn't explain why me? Why Linda?"

EJ waved his hand as if he were swatting a fly. "The old woman? She's collateral damage. An easy mark. Someone you care about. Someone the community cares about. Someone who would give me insurance on walking out of that fundraiser with you on my arm."

Linda moaned.

Fallon tried to scoot closer. "That's cruel."

"It's business," EJ said sharply. "Buddy destroyed a large portion of my pipeline, and he cost me millions. It's time for him to pay. You just made it even easier for me. And you gave me the chance to redeem myself for a mistake made years ago."

"What does that mean?"

"Here's a piece of truth you can choke on," EJ said.

Fallon straightened despite the restraints.

"Why you?" EJ repeated softly. "Because you were chosen."

Her blood iced.

"Years ago," EJ went on. "Pretty little thing living in a pretty little house. A father who traveled. A mother who left routines like breadcrumbs.

Predictable. Ideal. Your buyer called you a rare find. He was the kind of client who paid top dollar for a certain kind of girl, and I couldn't let just any thug come and get you."

"My buyer?"

"I came to Calusa Cove with one of my top people. We came just for you," EJ said.

"Who?" she asked with her heart in her throat.

"The who isn't important," EJ said. "All you need to know was that he was willing to pay a hefty sum for you. So, I introduced myself to your father. I told him I worked for a company he was dying to do business with. We had a drink. Walked the halls of your home." His eyes glittered in the mirror. "My client was right. You were a rare find. All fire and ice. The kind of girl that would be fun to break."

Fallon's heart stumbled—hard, painful, once. "No," she breathed.

"Yes," EJ said simply. "But fate pulled a fast one. You didn't work that next night at the Crab Shack."

Her stomach bottomed out. "Tessa took my place."

"At first, we thought she was you—same color hair. And you lent her that damn jacket," EJ replied. "We left it behind. I wanted to send a message. It's been fun watching you honor your friend when deep down, I suspect, you know it was always supposed to be you snatched in the night. Sadly, my client didn't want Tessa, but she still had value." He shrugged. "I sold her quick enough."

Fallon's vision blurred. Sold. Fucking sold. Somewhere Fallon couldn't reach. Somewhere Tessa could never be found.

"I wanted to come back for you," EJ said softly, as if he'd been robbed of something precious. "But the heat was everywhere, and by the time it really calmed down, it was too late—you'd made too much noise about finding Tessa. About starting the Tessa Project. I had to let it go—had to let you go. But I've watched you."

The words crawled over her skin like something living. *Watched.* He'd been *watching* her grieve, watching her search, watching her build the Tessa Project from nothing—and he'd done it from safety. From shadows.

"So, after Buddy fucked me over, and I learned you two were friends... then an item... damn. I nearly lost it."

A sound tore from Fallon's throat, part inhale, part sob, part disbelieving horror. "Where's Tessa? Where's my friend?"

"I'm not a keeper," EJ said with a shrug. "I move product, I don't track it. She could be alive. Or dead. Or wishing she were. But wherever she is, she's long gone."

The world swerved—not the SUV, her world—and for one horrifying beat, Fallon couldn't draw breath. It felt like hands were around her throat. Tessa's hands. Reaching. Pleading.

Linda whimpered beside her, muffled and high, and Fallon forced her body to move—leaning in, pressing her temple to the older woman's shoulder.

"I'm here," Fallon whispered, raw. "Please hang on. Please."

Linda's tears slid silently down her face.

EJ studied them like they were a fascinating wildlife documentary.

"You see," he said, conversational again, "you became a neat little loose end. And Buddy? Well, he's made a career of tripping over loose ends."

Fallon's heart crashed against her ribs. "Buddy didn't even know me then."

"No," EJ said, "but he knows you now. And that's even better. A hero with a weakness is far more entertaining than a missing teenager."

Fallon grinded her teeth. "You're using me to hurt him."

"Of course I am," EJ said brightly. "Simon failed me in that regard. I fully intend to correct that."

Her breath stuttered.

Simon.

The name hit harder now, like the last puzzle piece she didn't want to recognize. Buddy had nightmares carved into his bones because of that man—because of who he couldn't save.

And EJ...

EJ was the root that fed the whole damn thing.

Fallon's voice shook, but she didn't back down. "You don't get to break him. Or me."

EJ smiled. It was wide. Big. Happy, even. "I already have."

Her wrists throbbed. Her ribs hurt. Grief swelled so big inside her she almost couldn't speak.

"How many girls?" Fallon whispered.

"So many," EJ said with boredom. "And thirty more

waiting, right now. Neatly packaged. Ready to move. My ex-wife is moving them in an hour."

"Wait. You told Buddy—"

EJ laughed. Hard. "He can't save them. They're already locked up in a shipping container. He'll never find them. He thinks he has a choice. And my guess is, he'll choose you and the old lady. As for the girls? It won't matter."

"And if he chooses the girls?"

"That's the fun part of this game, because no matter who he chooses, everyone still dies." He turned away. "Sorry. But it's my playbook. My rules. And Buddy has to suffer the consequences of his actions." He lifted his phone. "So predictable." He sighed. "He's already called off his other drivers and they will, no doubt, be racing toward our direction. But my team will follow, and there are more along the way. They'll get cut off at the pass. Buddy can't win no matter what he does. This time, he won't be able to save anyone."

Fallon swallowed salt and fire. "You won't get away with this."

EJ chuckled. "Sweetheart, I already have."

Something shifted in the SUV—subtle as a breath, sharp as a blade slipping between ribs. Fallon couldn't name it, but she felt it, a wrongness coiling under the floorboards, vibrating up the zip ties cutting her skin. EJ straightened in the front seat, not alert, not tense—satisfied, like he'd just reached the chapter of a story he'd been dying to tell. The road grew quieter, narrower, darker, and c dread crawled up Fallon's spine with cold, certain fingers. Whatever was coming next wasn't negotiation. It wasn't posturing. It was the moment everything tilted—and every instinct she owned screamed that Buddy was about to walk straight into something designed to break him.

Flagler's number lit Buddy's phone like a flare in the dark.

He answered before the second ring. "Tell me you've got something."

Flagler didn't waste breath. "We've got confirmation. A tanker under Quinn Bellows' manifest is scheduled to leave Miami in an hour. Containers loaded. Coast Guard has been authorized to lock it down. If those girls are on that ship, they're not going anywhere."

Relief didn't come. Not even close. Too much could still go wrong.

"You won't be there in time," Buddy said.

"Forty-five minutes out," Flagler said. "Pisses me off, but the port's covered. Your two men are there. Miami PD. Feds. It's covered. Your job is not to die before the night is over."

Buddy almost laughed. It came out as breath—thin, strained. "Copy." He ended the call.

Dawson shot him a quick glance. "That sounded promising."

"It's something," Buddy said, which wasn't a lie, but

wasn't close to the whole truth. His pulse hammered hard enough to make his jaw ache.

The comm crackled.

Dove's voice—tight. Moving. "Buddy—we've got a situation."

Buddy tensed. "Report."

"When we broke off to go dark? They tailed us. They're following Keaton and me, now."

Sterling chimed in next. "Same here. The second we pulled out, they pulled in behind us. They're not subtle about it either. Riding my ass like they want to be lovers."

Dawson's fingers tightened on the wheel. "We're driving into a trap."

Buddy didn't deny it. Couldn't. His brain had already leapt ahead to the conclusion he'd been trying not to look at head-on:

EJ didn't need them split. He needed them funneled.

"How far out are you?" Buddy asked.

"Ten minutes," Dove answered. Breathless.

"Ten-ish here," Sterling added.

Ten minutes. Fuck.

They'd already been following longer than that.

Longer than the deadline EJ had given him to decide.

You can't save them all.

He'd known that. But hearing Sterling and Dove confirm it? Feeling the pull of the trap springing shut?

It scorched something inside him.

"Dove," Buddy said, voice like grit. "Lose your tail."

"What?"

"Now. Fast. Clean. Just fucking do it. And then get

close to me. Close enough that you can feel me breathe but not see me. You know what I mean?"

A beat. "Copy that."

"Sterling," Buddy said next. "Same order. Drop them hard. Go dark."

"Understood." Sterling's tone shifted—professional, razor-sharp.

Dawson shifted his grip on the wheel. "This is nuts, even for you."

"I know," Buddy said. He didn't. Not fully. But he knew enough.

The SUV in front of them changed speed slightly—subtle drift, not enough to draw attention, just enough to remind him whose game they were in.

"Vehicle One," Buddy said into comms, "peel off. Do it slowly. Natural."

Fletcher answered, "Roger that. Breaking."

The road stretched out ahead like a throat tightening with every mile. Darkness pressed in from all sides. No streetlights. No traffic. No witnesses. Exactly what EJ needed.

Buddy's phone was suddenly heavy in his hand.

Dawson saw it. Saw where Buddy's mind was going. Shook his head once. "This is insane."

"Yeah," Buddy murmured. "It is. But you know it's the only way out of this mess." He hit EJ's number.

The line clicked instantly, like EJ had been waiting with his finger over the button.

"Well," EJ said, "this is a pleasant surprise."

Buddy stared through the windshield at the black

SUV carting Fallon deeper into darkness. His heartbeat was a fist trying to punch his ribs open. "It's been more than ten minutes," Buddy said. "I thought I would've heard from you by now."

"I wanted to be generous," EJ said. "It's a difficult decision. I thought you deserved a little extra time to contemplate—"

"I've decided," Buddy cut in.

"Oh, really?"

"Fallon and Linda," Buddy said as his pulse hit his throat like a bomb.

"I'm not shocked, but I am a little surprised that you said that with such conviction. Where's the horror over the ones you can't save?"

"I'm not a fed anymore. Those girls aren't my problem. I don't care what you do with them."

Dawson flinched. Hard.

Buddy remained stone-faced.

"Lovers over strangers. It's predictable, even for you. But the callousness of your decision is a fascinating development."

"What can I say? After a while, you stop noticing all the dead girls piling up around you."

"Fine. You made the choice. Not me."

"I want them alive and unharmed," Buddy said. "That's the deal."

"Oh, you'll get them," EJ said. "I'll text you a location—"

"No." Buddy's voice cracked like a gunshot. "You're not dictating terms."

Dawson hissed a warning under his breath but didn't speak.

"You're in no position to negotiate," EJ said with an amused tone.

"Bullshit," Buddy snapped. "My team is standing down. I'm coming alone. You pull over half a mile up the road. You hand Fallon and Linda over. I drive away. You drive away. And that's the end of it."

Silence crackled for what seemed like minutes, but in reality, was only seconds.

"And the cop?" EJ asked pleasantly. "The one driving your car?"

Buddy didn't blink. "Small-town cop. No jurisdiction. No credibility. He can't touch you." He stared straight ahead, refusing to chance glimpsing Dawson's expression. "He'll learn to live with the choice."

A soft, delighted exhale. "Ballard... I misjudged you."

Buddy's stomach rebelled at the praise, but he pushed through it. "So?" Buddy asked. "Do we have a deal?"

"We do," EJ said. "Half a mile. Don't be late."

The line went dead.

Buddy lowered the phone.

Dawson stared at him. "You think he's actually going to let them go?"

"No," Buddy said. "I think he's going to try to kill all three of us."

Dawson nodded once—grim, steady. "Good. Then we're on the same page."

Buddy's chest tightened, but not from fear. From certainty.

"Get everyone ready," Buddy said, his voice low, dangerous. "Because this ends tonight."

He looked straight ahead—into darkness, into what waited, into the trap EJ laid—and refused to flinch.

He wasn't walking in to sacrifice himself.

He was walking in to win.

Even if he had to burn the whole damn world down to do it.

The SUV rolled to a stop so smoothly Fallon almost didn't feel it—just the faint forward sway of her body and the soft, deliberate click of the transmission sliding into park.

"Radio." EJ's voice dropped to a near-whisper.

The driver handed it back without a word.

EJ pressed the button. "No one touches him. Not yet. I'll have a word or two before we begin." A beat. "And hold your fire until I say. I want the old lady dropped clean. I want to see his face when it happens."

Fallon's stomach turned to stone.

Linda whimpered beside her, a thin sound crushed beneath layers of gag and fear. Fallon leaned her shoulder in, as close as her zip-tied wrists allowed. "I've got you," she whispered. "I promise. I've got you." Her voice shook. She didn't care.

EJ clicked off the radio, pocketed it, and looked over

his shoulder. "Try not to faint," he told Fallon lightly. "I'd hate for you to miss the show."

The driver climbed out. Warm night air slipped inside—sticky, swamp-scented, and too quiet. No traffic. No witnesses. No chance in hell this ended well.

Fallon inched forward just enough to see through a sliver of the door.

Buddy stood outside Dawson's SUV.

Alive.

Walking.

Steady—though his shoulders held a tension she hadn't seen since the Ring Finger case. He scanned the tree line like he expected it to spit out demons.

Maybe it would.

EJ opened his door and stepped out.

Fallon couldn't see Buddy's expression, but she heard his voice—low, gravel dragged across steel. "Where are they?"

EJ laughed softly. "Tucked away safely in the backseat. Don't worry. You'll get your tearful reunion."

"Cut the shit," Buddy said.

Buddy's voice stabbed something sharp and hot into Fallon's ribs—love, fear, fury, all boiling together.

The conversation blurred for her—not the words, the intent. EJ was soaking up every second. Buddy wasn't giving him a damn thing.

Then the driver approached EJ, bent in, and whispered something too low for Fallon to catch.

EJ froze.

A strange flicker crossed his face—shock, confusion, maybe even fear.

Buddy's voice sharpened. "Is there a problem?"

EJ straightened. "There's been a change of plans." He drew his gun.

Everything turned to chaos.

Gunfire erupted from the trees—sharp cracks tearing through the night. Bullets spat into metal. Glass exploded behind Fallon's head. She dropped instantly, dragging Linda with her, curling her body over the older woman's as best she could. Linda shook. Fallon shook harder.

Someone screamed—maybe the driver—before a body slammed against the outside of the vehicle hard enough to rock the frame. More shots rained down, punching holes into the doors, the hood, everywhere.

Fallon kept her head down, breath ragged, ears ringing. The world shrank to Linda's trembling and the acrid sting of gunpowder seeping into the SUV.

More shots. A grunt. Something hit the pavement.

She risked a glance—just a split second.

A shattered window. Tree line lit by muzzle flashes. Shadows moving. Someone in dark clothes falling. Someone else shouting orders she couldn't make out.

Then pain ripped across her forearm—fast and white-hot.

She gasped and dropped down again. Warmth spread across her arm. Not deep. Not deadly. But blood was blood.

"Fallon," Linda's voice was muffled, terrified, barely a sound under the gag.

"I'm okay," Fallon whispered, even though her pulse was slamming at her throat.

Then... Silence. Not peace. But the kind of quiet that vibrated with leftover violence.

A crunch of gravel approached the SUV.

Fallon braced—every muscle tight, breath trapped.

The door yanked open, and she gasped.

Buddy.

Bloody lip. Blackened eye. Sweat streaked down his cheek. A gunshot wound punched through his thigh, staining denim dark. And yet—he stood solid in the door-way, chest heaving, jaw set like he'd kill the entire world before he'd let anyone hurt her.

Fallon's breath broke. "Buddy—"

He moved in immediately, pocketknife out, cutting her restraints with a sharp, angry swipe that felt like a vow.

"Are you hurt?" His voice was rough, panicked under the gravel.

"Just—my arm," she whispered.

His gaze flicked down. Fury lit his eyes—bright and lethal. "I've got you," he said, and this time it wasn't a promise. It was a damn oath.

He cut Linda free next. The older woman collapsed into Fallon's arms, sobbing. Buddy supported them both, steady despite the blood soaking through his jeans.

Dove and Keaton appeared behind him. Sterling and Cullen came from the other side. Shadows moved every-where—team members barking orders, dragging bodies clear, checking for threats.

Fallon didn't look at any of it.

Just him. He was alive. He was standing. He'd come for her.

Buddy cupped her face with a shaking hand. "Fallon..." His forehead dropped to hers, breath ragged with adrenaline and something rawer.

She lifted her good arm around his waist, fingers gripping the back of his shirt. "I thought—you—"

"No." His voice cracked. He pulled her closer, one hand splayed across the back of her neck like he needed the contact to stay upright. "I'm here. I'm right here."

She mouthed his name. He kissed her—desperate, messy, tasting like blood and smoke and everything she'd prayed she wouldn't lose.

When he pulled back, his thumb brushed her cheek. His eyes were wrecked.

"I love you," he said—no hesitation, no fear, just truth spoken by a man who'd nearly died with it unsaid. "I've loved you for a long damn time."

Her breath left her in a trembling rush. "I love you, too."

Sirens screamed in the distance—loud, sharp, cutting through the night.

Dove jogged closer. "Ambulance is three minutes out. You both need to get checked out."

Buddy didn't let go of her.

Didn't even try.

Fallon leaned her forehead into his shoulder, letting herself finally shake, finally breathe, finally feel everything at once—terror, grief, love, relief—

Alive.

They were alive.

And EJ Vance would never again touch another girl.

Tears blurred the edges of everything—Buddy's face, the trees, the distant blue wash of emergency lights. "Tessa," Fallon whispered. "He told me he sold her. That it was supposed to be me, but because—"

Buddy pressed a gentle finger to her lips. "Don't do that to yourself."

His fingers threaded through the stray stands of hair fanning her face, slow, grounding, tender in a way that made her breath hitch. "If EJ was responsible for Tessa's disappearance, then we finally have a starting point. A real one. And I'll follow it until there's nothing left to chase." His voice settled into something fierce and protective. "I'll do whatever it takes to find out what happened to her. I swear it."

The ambulance rolled to a stop twenty feet away, its lights strobing across the asphalt. Sterling carried Linda toward the paramedics, calling for blankets, saline, and a stretcher.

Fallon held on to Buddy like he was the only solid thing left in a world that had tried to split open beneath her feet. His eyes—God, those eyes—were steady and warm and full of a love she could actually see now, not just feel.

In that moment, she knew—absolutely, undeniably— that this man would walk through hell for her. And ... she'd wrestle an angry python and a mother alligator at the same damn time for him.

Her chest swelled with something she hadn't dared imagine she'd ever get again.

A future.

A real one.

For the first time in her adult life, she saw it—sharp and whole, and not the least bit temporary. She saw the porch light and the picket fence. She saw the baby carriage. She saw them. Together.

Hopefully, the baby carriage part wouldn't scare him away.

Though, judging by the way he held her—bloody, battered, refusing to let go—she didn't think anything could.

Chapter Twenty-Two

The Aegis office didn't look any different than it had the week before—same tired paint, same humming window units, same stubborn patch of mildew near the back corner—but the air felt different. Lighter somehow. Or maybe that was just Buddy finally breathing again.

He eased into the old rolling chair behind the desk he'd brought from the Jacksonville office, because he liked stability, and he liked having roots, which was odd, considering he'd been single for a long time.

Not anymore.

He stretched his leg, and it protested the movement. A dull throb radiated up his thigh, but he ignored it. The stitches would hold. The doctor had warned him about "overexertion," which Buddy translated to "don't be an idiot," and then promptly went back to work, anyway.

He set aside a stack of reports—Flagler's preliminary statements, DHS logs, Miami PD confirmations—and was halfway through signing the last incident form when a shadow crossed the doorway.

Trent stood there.

Still too pale. Still too thin. Still moving like every stitch in his body had been pulled in the wrong direction. But upright, breathing, and wearing a lopsided grin.

"Got a minute?" Trent asked.

Buddy leaned back. "For you? Depends. You planning to pass out again? Because I'm not lifting you."

Trent snorted and stepped inside. "No promises." He lowered himself into one of the chairs with a wince he tried to hide. "I, uh... wanted to say thank you."

"For what? You're the one who got shot."

"So did you." Trent waved his hand toward Buddy's leg. "I wanted to thank you for saving my mom." Trent's voice cracked the tiniest bit—just enough to betray how close he'd come to losing her. "For saving Fallon. For—hell—everything. You didn't have to do any of it, but you did."

Buddy swallowed, looked away for half a beat. Accepting compliments wasn't his strong suit. "She's family," he said simply. "Both of you are. That's the job."

Trent huffed a laugh. "Funny. Thought it was your former job."

"Doesn't change anything."

A beat of silence stretched between them—comfortable, honest. Then Trent cleared his throat and sat forward, bracing his hands on his knees like a man about to deliver news no one asked for.

"One more thing," Trent said. "If you ever hurt

Fallon—emotionally, physically, accidentally, intentionally, spiritually, telepathically, in a dream or otherwise—I'll kick your ass."

Buddy blinked. "Telepathically?"

"Don't test me, man. I'm creative when I'm pissed."

A genuine laugh escaped Buddy—deep, unexpected, cutting through the last of the tension lodged under his ribs. "Duly noted."

Trent stood, nodded , then gripped the doorframe for balance before limping out into the hall. Buddy watched him go, a quiet swell of relief settling under his sternum. Linda was still recovering, but she was safe. Still dying of cancer, but safe. And she would have those last moments with her son—on her terms. No one else's. That was something.

Trent was mending, and even though he could be a pain in the ass, he was one hell of a good man—the best. Buddy would hire him in a nanosecond.

Fallon... God, Fallon had survived the kind of night that carved scars into bone.

And she was still smiling.

He'd take the stitches, the bruises, the nightmares—every last piece of it.

A knock tapped twice against the door.

Buddy sighed. "If this is someone else threatening bodily harm, take a number."

"It's worse," a familiar voice drawled. "It's the federal government."

Flagler stepped inside like the office owed him dinner

—suit jacket off, sleeves rolled, tie crooked, and an expression like he hadn't slept in ten years.

Buddy gestured toward a chair. "If you're here to write me up, get in line. Dawson already tried."

"I'm not here to write you up." Flagler dropped a thick folder on the desk. "I'm here to tell you what the last seven days of federal chaos looks like on paper."

"Right. Because I've never done that before."

Flagler flipped open the folder. "The tanker was locked down. Miami PD, DHS, Harbor Patrol, and two pissed-off Coast Guard captains converged on the port. We recovered all thirty girls. Alive." His voice softened for half a second. "Some are in rough shape, but alive."

Buddy exhaled, tension loosening from his muscles.

"We also raided three warehouses owned by Quinn Porter," Flagler continued. "Found evidence of long-term trafficking routes, international buyers, and encrypted manifests. The works. The entire pipeline collapsed in under two days." He leaned back. "Biggest takedown I've seen in a decade. Bigger than yours."

Buddy rubbed his jaw. "Good."

"Good?" Flagler repeated, incredulous. "Ballard, this should be the part where you ask about commendations or promotions or at least enjoy the fact you took down one of the largest trafficking networks on the eastern seaboard."

Buddy shrugged. "I'm not a fed anymore. And I didn't do it alone."

Flagler pointed at him with a pen. "See, that right

there? That's why they're recommending me for the damn commendation instead of you."

Buddy barked a laugh. "Figures."

"I also wanted you to know, and please tell Fallon, we're doing everything we can to find out what happened to Tessa," Flagler said. "I've spoken to her parents, and we've updated the files with all the new information. I'll keep an eye out, and if anything at all comes across my desk, you'll be the first to know."

"I really appreciate that."

Flagler slipped the file shut and stood. "Two more things. One. If you ever pull a stunt like that again, call me five minutes earlier. I had exactly zero prep time to brief Washington."

Buddy smirked. "Didn't have five minutes."

"Second thing," Flagler said, tone shifting one notch toward sincerity. "No more favors. I mean it. You've used up a decade's worth. And next time you need help, someone better be actively dying."

"That's a high bar," Buddy said.

Flagler patted his shoulder on the way out. "Good thing you're creative."

The door clicked shut behind him.

Buddy sat back, the room settling around him in a way that finally felt like an ending—not the kind that closed doors, but the kind that left the horizon open and waiting.

Fallon.

He needed to see her.

Not because she was fragile—hell no—but because

she was his. Because somewhere between the chaos and the sirens and the kiss that tasted like survival, he'd realized he didn't want a life that didn't have her in it.

He reached for the cane he hated to use and pushed himself to his feet.

He had somewhere to be.

Someone to be.

And she was waiting for him.

Fallon sat at the kitchen counter with an open scrapbook in front of her, pages warped at the edges from years of humidity and poor storage. Tessa's handwriting curled in bright blue ink across one of the captions—Spring Fling, 2009!!—so earnest and obnoxious she could almost hear her friend laughing while they glued down the pictures.

A half inch of whiskey glowed amber in Fallon's glass. It wasn't doing the job. Not numbing, not smoothing, not settling. Just sitting there like a companion she didn't ask for.

Her forearm ached with that familiar post-stitch throb. Her ribs felt too tight. And in the soft spill of the kitchen lights, Tessa's smile—alive and seventeen and untouched by monsters—was too much and not enough all at once.

The front door opened.

She didn't turn. Only one person walked into her house like he belonged there.

Buddy's steps were slow, measured, the soft tap of his

cane announcing each one. He wasn't supposed to ditch it yet—stubborn fool—but he was using it just enough to keep her from lecturing him into bed rest.

He stopped beside her, leaned down, and kissed her cheek—warm, familiar, grounding in a way nothing else in the last week had been.

"Hey," he murmured.

Fallon slid the whiskey bottle toward him. "Want some?"

"Yeah," he said, "but I'll get it."

He reached for a glass himself—slow, careful, refusing the help she offered even as he winced, sitting down beside her. He poured two fingers, took a quiet sip, then set the glass between them.

His hand drifted to the scrapbook. He flipped to the next page, thumb brushing over a photo of Fallon and Tessa splashing each other from a half-sunken rope swing.

"Found a couple of new leads this morning," he said softly. "Nothing solid yet. But I'm not stopping."

She swallowed hard. "I know. I love that you're trying. I do. But..." Her throat tightened. "I also know I might never get answers. Not the ones that matter. Not whether she's alive. Or if she suffered. Or if—" She pressed her lips together. "Some things just... stay missing."

Buddy's hand covered hers, warm and steady. "Maybe. But as long as I've got breath, I won't stop looking for her. Not for you. Not for her family. Not for what she deserves."

Fallon blinked against the sting in her eyes. "I know."

His thumb traced slow circles over her knuckles. "But that's not the only thing bothering you."

She tensed. "It's nothing."

"I know you better than that." His voice softened, deepened, that low rumble that always found the truth she tried to bury.

She looked down at their joined hands, at the way his larger fingers wrapped around hers like they belonged there. Permanently. "You moved here to be closer to me," she whispered.

"Yeah," he said, no hesitation. "Because this—" his thumb brushed her hand once more "—is permanent."

She believed him. She really did. But the words still lodged in her throat like a stone.

He tilted his head, brushing her temple with his nose. "Talk to me."

She inhaled, slow and shaky. "Kids."

Buddy blinked. "Kids?"

"Yeah." She forced herself to meet his eyes. "Do you want them?"

For a beat, he just stared at her—then a slow, warm smile appeared, softening every edge he'd spent years sharpening.

"I want everything with you."

Her breath trembled out.

"And speaking of everything," he added, clearing his throat like he was trying for casual and failing adorably, "we've been basically living here anyway. So, I talked to my landlord this morning. He's got someone who wants my place. And since most of my stuff is still in boxes, I was thinking... why don't I officially move in here? With you."

She blinked. "You're asking me to live together?"

"I'm asking that we stop paying rent on two houses when we only sleep in one." He smirked. "Also—this place is nicer."

She laughed—really laughed—for the first time all day. "It is nicer. And you're still an invalid."

He tapped the cane against the floor. "Temporary. Give it three weeks, and Trent and I will be wrangling gators behind the Crab Shack."

"God, don't even joke about that."

He leaned in. "Not joking. Just preparing you for the reality of being with me."

Her laughter faded into something softer when he cupped her cheek and brushed his lips over hers.

A slow kiss. Warm. Certain. Sealing something that had been growing for months.

When he pulled back, he rested his forehead gently against hers. "Fallon Reeves... I'm all in. Whatever future you see—kids, sooner rather than later, because this old man ain't getting any younger, chaos, maybe even that picket fence you pretend you don't want—I'm there."

Her eyes flooded.

She didn't look away this time.

She didn't have to.

Her heart cracked open—quietly, beautifully, fully.

And for the first time since Tessa vanished, since her

world collapsed at seventeen, since she learned monsters were real, Fallon Reeves felt hope that didn't hurt.

Thank you for taking the time to read *Hunted in Calusa Cove*. Please feel free to leave an honest review. Next up in the series is ***Shadows in Calusa Cove.***

I'm thrilled to share some exciting news with you! I'm collaborating with the talented Kris Norris on a brand new series called **Black Hollow**. This four-book military romantic suspense series is something we're both incredibly passionate about. Kris will be writing books 1 and 3, and I'll be writing books 2 and 4. We can't wait for you to meet these characters and dive into their dangerous, pulse-pounding stories.

The BLACK HOLLOW series.
Hollow Point (written by Kris Norris)
Hollow Code (written by Jen Talty

About Jen Talty

Jen Talty is the *USA Today* Bestselling Author of Contemporary Romance, Romantic Suspense, and Paranormal Romance. In the fall of 2020, her short story was selected and featured in a 1001 Dark Nights Anthology.

Regardless of the genre, her goal is to take you on a ride that will leave you floating under the sun with warmth in your heart. She writes stories about broken heroes and heroines who aren't necessarily looking for romance, but in the end, they find the kind of love books are written about :).

She first started writing while carting her kids to one hockey rink after the other, averaging 170 games per year between 3 kids in 2 countries and 5 states. Her first book, IN TWO WEEKS was originally published in 2007. In 2010 she helped form a publishing company (Cool Gus Publishing) with *NY Times* Bestselling Author Bob Mayer where she ran the technical side of the business through 2016.

Jen is currently enjoying the next phase of her life...the

empty nester! She and her husband reside in Jupiter, Florida.

Grab a glass of vino, kick back, relax, and let the romance roll in...

Sign up for my Newsletter (https://dl.bookfunnel. com/82gm8b9k4y). where I often give away free books before publication.

Join my private Facebook group (https://www.facebook. com/groups/191706547909047/) where I post exclusive excerpts and discuss all things murder and love!

Never miss a new release. Follow me on Amazon: amazon.com/author/jentalty

And on Bookbub: bookbub.com/authors/jen-talty

Also by Jen Talty

Brand New Series
Collaboration with Kris Norris!!!!!
The BLACK HOLLOW series.
Hollow Point (written by Kris Norris)
Hollow Code (written by Jen Talty

Brand New Series!
The Aegis Network: The Everglades Division
Hunted in Calusa Cove
Shadows in Calusa Cove

Welcome to…Everglades Overwatch!
Secrets in Calusa Cove
Pirates in Calusa Cove
Murder in Calusa Cove
Betrayal in Calusa Cove

THE AEGIS NETWORK

Also by Jen Talty

The Sarich Brothers
The Lighthouse
Her Last Hope
The Last Flight
The Return Home
The Matriarch

Aegis Network: Jacksonville Division
A SEAL's Honor
Talon's Honor
Arthur's Honor
Rex's Honor
Kent's Honor
Buddy's Honor
Duncan's Honor
Garth's Honor
Hawke's Honor

Aegis Network Short Stories
Max & Milian
A Christmas Miracle
Spinning Wheels
Holiday's Vacation

The Secrets of Stone Bridge
A Vintage of Regret
A Harvest of Lies

Safe Harbor Series
Mine To Keep